Held Captive

Grace A. Johnson

Updated and republished October 2019

ISBN: 9781091154575

Dedication

To Mom
If all mothers are as you are, then all the blessing a person needs is a mother.
I love you more than words can say.

"Though your sins are like scarlet, they shall be as white as snow;
though they are red as crimson,
they shall be like wool."
Isaiah 1: 18

You will again have compassion on us;
you will tread our sins underfoot and hurl all our iniquities into the depths of the sea.
Micah 7: 19

Acknowledgments

All of the gratitude in this world belongs to God. And it is Him I thank for gifting me with the passion and desire to write, and for being with me every step of the way. I thank you, Father, for holding me captive by Your Love and keeping me safe in Your strong arms. All of the glory and honor belongs to You alone.

Also, I have to thank my wonderful mother and earthly father. I couldn't have done this without your help and encouragement! I love you both so much!

And a special thanks to my siblings: Abby, Rayson, Joy, John, Joanna, and Jacob. Y'all have put up with me and my endless prattle for so long, and I greatly appreciate it! I love each and every one of you so very much!

Thanks to Hannah Wildes for proofreading my manuscript and picking out all my mistakes. You are a bigger help than you know!

And thanks to Rachel Sweatt for her encouragement and enthusiasm, and Dr. Proenza for his tips and assistance.

Super special thanks to Suzie Hemphill and Majestic Velvets for the beautiful cover photo!

Part one

Chapter 1

Atlantic Ocean
July 1683

The ship was slowly coming into view, and anticipation seemed to take over me. It was huge, one of the largest merchant ships I had ever had the pleasure of resting my gaze upon, and I could only imagine the cargo on board that ship. Silk and lace, tea and coffee, flour and sugar; the usual products my crew and I stole. But I was certain that there were plenty of ropes, coins, and vials of desperately needed medicine stored on that ship. And it was to be mine in only an hour or so. The regular merchandise would garner quite a bit of money as it always did, but it was the hope of finding a few golden coins and perhaps a couple bottles of laudanum that had me filled with expectation.

I was also short on crew members at the moment, so if I could find a few men worthy of hoisting my mainsail, I wouldn't complain. Not that an "honorable and respectable" stuffy little Englishman could ever be worthy of stepping onto my deck.

But after the last storm, when several of the cowards had been weeded out by jumping off my ship in hopes of saving themselves—though a few men had caught pneumonia and died during that time—I was short. With a man-o'-war ship as big as mine, I needed plenty of men to handle it, for I couldn't do it all on my own. Although if one wanted something done correctly, I would heartily recommend doing it oneself.

Honestly, I missed Father's crew. Old men, they had been, but experienced and trustworthy. If only all of them, save Charlie, hadn't died over the past decade. Now, all I had were silly young men, naught but little babes, the whole lot of them. Though Keaton Clarke, one of my late crew members' nephew, was quite the pirate. He was hardworking and reliable, intelligent as well, as he had been raised a gentleman on land. And, of course, there was Elliot Fulton, not only my first mate but the man like a brother to me. Of all the men on my ship, Elliot had to be my favorite, not that I had time for such foolishness as singling out one man to favor. But despite Elliot and his brotherly trust and devotion, I missed Julius, would miss the little scalawag till the very day I died. One day, I continually vowed to myself, I would find my younger brother and serve Timothy Wilde a large slice of revenge for taking Julius and killing our father.

I banished the thought, the dreaded memory, as soon as it appeared, drawing my attention back to the merchant ship drifting closer to mine. Adjusting the spyglass I held in my hand, I looked out the small hole, studying every inch of the ship ahead of me. A name had been carved into the side of the hull, and it took me a moment to realize I could not read the engraving. Blast—well, I wasn't quite sure what I was to blast, but blast something for my lack of knowledge of letters. Well, it was more like no knowledge rather than lack of. I had no idea how to read, not even my own name, as that ability was never needed in my profession. But it would help if I could read the name of the vessels I plundered, would it not?

"Charlie," I called over my shoulder, relieved when I heard the familiar slow but steady clomp of Charlie Acton's boots.

"Aye, Cap'n?" came Charlie's low, age-hardened voice from a few feet behind me. Barely reaching my collarbone, he was a rather short, stout man with broad shoulders and a burly chest. But despite his size, Charlie was quick; not just with his reflexes but with his mind. Sometimes, if one stared long and hard enough into his keen sapphire blue eyes, one could almost see his mind working.

His weathered, sun-bronzed skin contrasted with the graying blond hair that hung down his back in one long braid. Perhaps in his youth he had been quite the handsome man, what with his strong features and yellow mane, but now that he was older, I saw him only as a wise man that anyone would be honored to call their friend.

I turned, tossing him the spyglass. "Tell me the ship's name," I commanded with a frown as I leaned back against the balustrade, arms crossed over my chest. Sometimes it felt rather odd ordering around my father's oldest friend, the man who'd stepped into Father's place as mentor and guide after he had been murdered ten years past. But just as I had learned from Father, it was not wise to treat one man differently than the other, for jealousy was easily stricken between the men on board. One could never know when someone would turn against his fellow over something as simple as a breadcrumb. When one lived this sort of life, forever on the sea, agitation was easily borrowed.

Charlie held the spyglass up to his uncovered eye, taking only one glance out of the opening before replying. "*Paris*," was his answer.

I couldn't help but scoff. What a terrible name for such a glorious vessel. But to each his own, I supposed. Which *Rina* wasn't the most common name for a pirate ship, but it was what Father had named it, and it was to stay that way. Father's first ship had been named *Bella* – after whom, he had never told me. At times I wondered if perhaps that had been my mother's name. I knew next to nothing about my mother, for Father had never dared to speak of her. I had long ago reasoned that she must have died while birthing me, and Father's heart was too broken to ever think of her. He must have truly loved her, whomever she may have been. I could remember, though, the deep attraction between Father and Julius' mother Lavinia Shawe. Odd, I found it, how he had been so quick to love Julius' mother, and yet at the same time wouldn't speak of mine for all of the gold in Spain.

Charlie gave me a gap-tooth grin, handing me the spyglass. "*Paris,* as in the Greek god, Cap'n. 'Tisn't the worst o' names," he explained to me, though I still wondered why anyone would name a ship that. If perhaps the captain was from the French city, I might would understand.

I brushed off my petty distaste toward the name, focusing solely on all the treasure that was waiting for me on that ship. Ah, 'twas so sweet, I could taste it. And riches tasted rather good, not much different than those oranges I'd found last week.

At the thought of oranges, I began to wonder what kind of exotic fruit might be on the *Paris*. Perhaps some mangoes or coconuts. And some rubies, sapphires, emeralds, and diamonds. Not to mention strong, trustworthy men that I could use.

"Charlie, gather up the men, would you? We've got us a ship to raid," I said, tucking the spyglass into my belt and making my way to where Elliot stood commandeering the ship.

His rough hands gripping the helm, a smirk forming on his lips, was Elliot Fulton Sr, my best friend and first mate. He was not only the most experienced man on my ship, but he also the father to a beautiful son, Elliot Jr, whom I oft referred to as Ellie. Elliot Sr was the son of one of my father's original crew members—as were several of my men—and I found him to be the most recklessly courageous of them all. Perhaps 'twas because of the pirate blood so deep in his veins, or just his natural stupidity, that he was the most rash of all the seamen I had ever met, but for those very same things, I found Elliot to be the better of my men. Sometimes, I had to admit, he became slightly rowdy, and was regularly the beginner of most arguments and fights between the men.

He was the only person on board that met my abnormally tall height, and had the same muscular yet slender physique as I did. His long dark brown hair was pulled back in a queue, but a few strands were flying around his face, getting caught in his dark beard. His piercing murky green-brown eye, the one not covered by his eye-patch, softened at the sight of me, and his smile broadened.

Oftentimes I felt an odd sense of pity for my friend—not out of the nonexistent goodness of my heart, mind you—but because I knew the loss he dealt with. You see, a year past he lost his wife in childbirth. I had to admit that originally I hadn't approved of the union between Elliot and his bride, Mary Lynde, for I had believed that marriage was a waste of time – and I still thought so – but once Elliot's son had entered the world, I supposed that I forgave my friend for growing soft and taking a wife.

Mary herself had been strong mentally, I had to say, if not physically, as ever since stepping on board my ship, seasickness had plagued her. She had already been much too fragile to bear a child, and I was not shocked when the pain of birthing took her. I'd then taken her child under my wing, protecting him while on the ship, as I figured was my duty as captain. I still thought sending the child to England to live with a respectable family in assured safety would be ideal, but I had never to pressure my friend for the sake of breaking Elliot's heart completely in two, if it wasn't already.

"Awfully large ship there, wouldn't ye say, Cap'n?" he questioned with a mirthful chuckle.

I rolled my eye at his joviality, as it was always present at the most inappropriate moments. But even

I could not suppress a grin. And it was good to see him smiling again.

"Not large enough," I countered, erasing the inkling of a smile from my lips. "Money is dwindling, and I am unsure if that is the result of less cargo being sold or if one of the men has been stealing from my coffer. And you know how I feel about such." A sigh that bordered on a huff slipped through clenched teeth, as I remembered the last time I had reviewed my account book. At the least, ten pounds were missing, and it wouldn't be long before ten pounds became twenty, and so forth. I couldn't afford to lose my ill-gotten gains. And my crew couldn't afford to lose a man should one of them be stealing.

Elliot's eye went dim and he began to scratch his whiskered chin, a flicker of thought in his gaze. "Aye, that I do. Ought I do ye some investigatin'?"

I hitched a shoulder. "'Twouldn't hurt." In all honesty, looking into my crew was the furthest thing from my mind. All I could concentrate on was plundering that vessel.

I watched with delight as the boy squirmed beneath my blade, his bright blue eyes teeming with tears. I knew that I wasn't going to kill him; Elliot knew the same. But the child didn't, which in turn made my persuasion much easier. Yes, I was in need of men—strong, mature men—but one day my older crew would no longer be able to perform their duties as they did now, and I needed fresh, younger people to take their place. And so a child no more than ten and five years of age would make a great pupil to train. He was far from sea-hardened, probably had not set sail for his first time but just a fortnight ago, at the most, and I could only imagine his swordsmanship, but the younger I could break them in, the stronger they would be in the years to come.

"You are to cooperate with me, do you hear? And if you do not, it only takes one swipe of m cutlass to dispose of you," I growled to the fair-haired, bright-eyed boy, letting the edge of my cutlass gently graze his collarbone. "So then, what say you, hmm?"

The boy was trembling violently, and his voice shook with cold fear as he replied, "Y-y-yes! Pl-please don't kill me. I-I'll do whatever you ask of me, I swear."

I stepped back, slid my cutlass back into its sheath, and met the smirking gaze of my comrade. "Good. Now, stand up and dry your eyes. My crew is the best in the Seven Seas, and I shan't have that reputation tarnished by one man's childish actions. Elliot, I will let you handle him now," I said, tossing the words over my shoulder as I pivoted on my heel and walked away.

I, as always, was correct about the *Paris'* cargo, and had managed to find a crate of medicine stored away along with three barrels of rum in the cargo hold, not to mention crates of food and fabric. And, of course, I had raided the captain's money chest and filled mine.

And though the brigantine I had captured was small, the size of the crew on board was decent. Those who had accepted my offer to pirate and willingly signed my articles remained alive, while those who refused tasted death along with their captain. The ship, on the other hand, I had burned. I had, along with my *Rina*, an ex-navy frigate and a small brig at my disposal already. I had no need for more ships.

I marched into my cabin, a decent-sized room that almost resembled a noble's bedchamber in its finery. This was the only personal thing of mine that actually exuded my vast riches and fine taste, unless one desired to count the *Rina* herself. In this room I had once dreamt of a wealthy life on land, with both a father and mother, sisters and brothers, before Julius had been born when I was but a child.

Now I never bothered with such petty, infantile fantasies. My life was on the sea, and no other place could compare. No other place would ever have the same soft lady's breeze that ruffled one's hair, the same salty smell that flooded one's senses every time they stepped on deck. None other could dare to have the same cloudless sky some mornings, then burst into a living gale come evening. And no other place could ever be a home to me as the sea.

Shutting the wooden door behind me—did I mention the doorknob was pure gold?—I walked across the threshold as silently as possible, as not to awake young Ellie who slept soundly in the cradle alongside my bed, even if it would serve no purpose.

It often surprised me how that child could sleep so peacefully even as a tempest raged outside. I could find nothing to cast the blame upon, yet I did know that it was the pirate blood flowing so deep in his veins that allowed him to be so accustomed to the ocean, even if that meant he didn't dare to wake during a storm as a good sailor should. He rarely made a peep, and was far from afeared of a little blood or battle. I knew Elliot would have a very easy time raising this boy in the ways of his father and the one before him.

I made my way to where my small desk rested, nailed to the floor underneath a window that allowed me a rather nice view of the ocean that trailed behind us. I pulled out of the locked drawer a sheet of paper filled with numbers. To any other person than myself, the blurred ink numerals would make absolutely no sense, but I could easily make out my smudges.

Though I had no knowledge in the subjects of reading and writing, I was accomplished in arithmetic and could write the symbols, albeit sloppily. And this particular sheet was more than a little sloppy in appearance. I doubted anyone could tell, but I had a certain form of organization to not only my math, but to my entire ship. A rather odd form, I would say, but one nonetheless.

As I retrieved my feather quill from the depths of my desk drawer, a soft moan was heard from against the wall behind me. I turned my head to see Elliot Jr roll over in his bed before snuggling back into his blanket and resuming to gently snore. Mentally I expelled a deep sigh, for if anyone knew me well enough, they would know that I hated to be interrupted during my accounting. Even if 'twas by that little one who had squeezed into my stone heart over the past year.

I turned back around and resumed my work when a knock sounded on my door. I had made not a single mark on my paper, dash it, and already I was being pulled away. I rose from my chair, struggling to keep back a growl. For Ellie's sake. Because I was certain he wouldn't be able to sleep through what I was of a mind to do.

I jerked open the door to see Keaton standing there, his bare muscular arms folded over his chest. At near five years my junior and standing at an even six feet, the top of his head didn't even reach my chin, which caused him to have to take a step backward to meet my gaze. With tangled curls of raven black that danced with an array of colors in the sunlight and a calculating green glare, as well as strong features that only added to his rugged appearance, he could easily pass for handsome. But his skill was what mattered.

His uncle had been my father's quartermaster, and had dragged Keaton on board after his parents had died, when he was about ten and six. To my surprise, he had proved to be an excellent seaman, and I was proud to call him part of my crew. And my friend. Even if he always had the worst timing.

"Captain, I doubt you're in the mood to hear this..." Keaton began with a rough sigh. "I went back and counted the crates from our raid last week, and as it turns out, we happen to be down on the rum, and I found that a good portion of the—"

I held up my hand, already certain to where this conversation was going. And to whom it was going. "I know. Who do you suspect?"

"Roger Mansfield. We all know that he is a shifty character, which is near to everything that we do. I've wondered what had gotten into you when you let him on board," was his reply, a frown twisting his lips.

I jammed a hand through my thick brown waves, taking a deep breath. Rarely did one of my men question my judgment, as they had no reason to. But 'twas not the first time I had made a mistake—just the first in many, many years.

"That is only your opinion, not a fact,; however I have to agree. He was not my first choice, but you know how hard it has been since the storm last month. We've all been doing our share and more. If I hadn't secured him, Ellie would have had to man the helm for the past several weeks," I stated, crossing my arms over my chest and leaning against the door frame, casting a glance toward the still-sleeping babe over my shoulder.

Keaton shook a lock of hair out of his eyes, revealing the scar there and the swirl of thoughts behind the green haze. "I suppose you're right, but if I find that he has been causing problems, I shan't sit by and do nothing. And I don't expect you to either, Captain." And with that said, he marched away, leaving me to ponder the situation.

I couldn't risk losing *any* man, but I also couldn't stand having a sailor disobey my rules. I shoved those worries aside, walking back into my room and softly closing the door behind me. I had work to do.

Chapter 2

I parried his blow, even as an unbidden smirk turned my lips upward. It had been but a week since the fair-haired boy, whose name I now knew to be Billy Sandes, had stepped on my ship, and already he was growing. Though anyone with a lick of sense would know that I wouldn't dare to kill the poor fellow, I knew that the only reason he worked so diligently was for fear of death.

Despite his motives, I had to commend him for his hard work, training with Keaton whenever he had the chance. Which was practically the entire day and well on into the night, as not much had been happening thus far. It would be a long while until we would arrive at the Caribbean, and not a storm had passed since that last dreadful one a month ago, so my men and I entertained ourselves the best as one could while sailing across the Seven Seas.

And currently, our entertainment was a faux battle between Billy and myself. Grand excitement, indeed.

Though Billy lacked much in experience and intellect, he made up for it in physical ability. Beginner's luck, I would've believed his obvious skill to be, if I hadn't had the pleasure of participating in a swordfight with him myself. Though not a scratch grazed my skin, neither did one mar his. He may not have defeated me yet, nor would he manage to overcome one of my other men, but the fact that he had avoided the pain of a wound as of yet was a good one. Better to not defeat one's enemy and live rather than die and as their adversary survived. And I knew that firsthand.

With one more swipe of his cutlass against mine, Billy stepped backwards. A wrong move, yet I could not fault him for it. I was pressing too hard, I could see, from the fact that I had advanced forward three paces since we had begun a quarter hour past. Though he was going to be pressed up against the balustrade if he didn't make a move soon.

He did, taking not only myself but the rest of the crew by utter surprise. Not only did he remove himself from my crushing nearness, but he turned the entire battle around completely. Quick as a flash, he stepped backwards and slid feet first in between my legs, his blade coming exceedingly close to my inner thigh.

A collective gasp ran throughout the deck, followed by cheers of Billy's name. But just as I refrained from conveying my shock over his actions so similar to mine own, I hid the sudden flash of pride over his accomplishment.

As Billy stood, I spun around, shocking him when I struck his cutlass out of his hand, catching it and advancing forward, the tip of my blade pointed directly at his neck. He stumbled backward, and I let loose my grin, shoving him by sword-point to the opposite side of the ship until his back was pressed up against the railing.

Only then, with the young man's eyes wide and his chest heaving, did I relent. Returning my cutlass to its sheath, I stepped away and clasped Billy's shoulder before playfully ruffling his blond waves. "Good, Sandes. I'm impressed," I told him, handing him his cutlass.

Having finally regained his breath, Billy chuckled, tossing me a smile. "Thank ye, Cap'n. I was right scared for a moment there, though," he replied, his easy and truthful confession of fear showing an amount of courage.

I returned his laugh. "Use that fear to your advantage, my friend. You cannot allow your enemy to sense it. Is that not right, men?" I questioned, looking towards the proud group in front of me.

A hearty "aye" came from them before everyone returned to their duties.

Billy spun around to follow, but I caught him with a hand upon his slender shoulder. He looked to me, his smile fading and eyes dimming slightly as though afraid of whatever rebuke I had for him.

I had none.

"I commend you for your hard work. In good sooth, I'm surprised. And it takes quite a bit to surprise me. I want you to keep up the good work, but tomorrow I want you to come to me for practice. You've made it above Keaton's level, we'll say."

At that, Billy's ocean eyes grew wide, and I

could see for certain that his chest puffed up with boyish pride. "Aye aye, Cap'n! I'll do that!" And with that, he hurried off.

Starting to the hatch that led down below deck, I couldn't keep from grinning. The young ones were always the most fun. I could remember, albeit faintly, when Elliot and I were growing up, when we would have sword fights with scrap slivers of wood, as Father would rarely let me touch a blade until I was ten and two years of age. Then, once my friend and I had reached adolescence—when Julius was toddling around on board at five—we would truly battle each other, and we still had the scars to prove it.

Oh, how those times plagued me! The memories so sweet were now tainted by not only the troubles of real battle and the problems of piracy but by Timothy Wilde. I could not, would not, let go of that dreaded remembering. That evil Scotsman had ruined my life. And one day I would ruin his. Even if it was the very last thing I did.

Feeling my blood boil at merely the thought of that man and his devilish leer, I pushed the matter aside, locking it away in a proverbial chest in the back of my mind, before I began reliving the moments, starting with the sound of his boots clomping against my father's deck with a rhythm of pure condescension…

No! I would not let my mind trail off so easily. I had perfect control. Nothing could slip by me. Not even a thought.

I bounded down the stairs that led me below deck, the dimming light causing me to lift my hand up to move my eyepatch. But before my fingers grazed the rough leather, I stopped myself. Even now my instincts had led me away from the present and into the past. Back before my left eye had been blinded. Oh, blast the devil of a man who had dared to take so much away from me!

"Captain?" came the deep voice of Keaton from the bottom of the stairs.

I huffed, rubbing the sudden ache in my head away. "I'm coming." I hopped down the last few steps, taking in a deep breath of the sickly sweet smell of rum that met my senses.

Thanks to my one working eye being adjusted to the light rather than the dark, I could barely see a thing and felt ready to claw that eye out of its socket. I walked straight into a crate then, stumbling forward and having to catch myself before I was thrown over the box to the floor. A frustrated growl left my lips as I picked myself up and felt my way to where Keaton stood. Despite my lack of sight, I knew his hand was clamped over his mouth to hide his laughter. How I knew, you ask, because of the muffled sound escaping the confines of his hand and the way I could sense and feel his broad shoulders heave up and down in the faint light.

"Oh, shut up," I sneered, swatting Keaton on the forearm. Or at least I thought it was his forearm.

Keaton's chuckling dissipated and he cleared his throat before I did more than just swat him on the arm. "Very well. I trust you were impressed with Billy's cunning skill, were you not?" he questioned, stepping back, probably to lean against a barrel and cross his arms over his burly chest.

"That I was. You've done good with him, I say. But that's not why I've risked life and limb coming down here. What have you found?" I asked, placing my hands behind me to be sure a sturdy crate sat there. As one did, I leaned back in a more relaxed position, awaiting my friend's reply.

Over the course of the past few days, Keaton and Elliot had taken to spying on Roger Mansfield, the both of them hoping to find something to prove his guilt. I knew, though, that they were determined to catch him more for their own sake, as they practically despised the man. Even still, I was curious as to if the newcomer was the cause of my missing loot, as well as my money. Unfortunately, even my strongest lock could be picked. And I was determined to find whoever had done so and dispose of him properly.

"It's him, I tell you. I've watched him sneak up deck at night, and Elliot said that he almost caught him exiting your room. Every morning he's up half-drunk also, even once his ration has run out. Don't tell me that it could be anything," Keaton fairly growled, but my mind was caught on his earlier words.

Exiting my room?! I pounded my fist against the crate behind me before standing and beginning to pace as best as I could in the tight space. "You dare to tell me that he walks into my room while Ellie and me are asleep? Why, I'll show that man! You're serious now?"

I turned back to face him, feeling his head nod rather than seeing it. "Dash it all! Oh, do you know what he…? My word! Some people have absolutely no restraint! I lock that door for a reason! And you mean to say that Elliot and yourself cannot even keep him in his hammock at night? Oh, if I could just get my hands on him!"

I ceased my frantic pacing and arm-waving then, sensing Keaton's amusement. I spun on my heel, glaring at the man through the dark.

"Really, Captain? You are taking this a little too far, I trow. Why don't you just stay awake tonight, see if you might could catch the perpetrator? Perhaps you can do him more justice than Elliot and I."

I snorted, rolling my eye. "I say, Clarke," was all I managed to mutter before mine and Keaton's names were called from above deck in Charlie's deep voice.

"Coming, Charlie!" I shouted back, weaving my way out of the hold and bounding up the stairs, my quartermaster following behind.

Charlie stood by the railing to my right, a spyglass in his hand. "Ah, over 'ere." He ushered me to him, then handed me the glass. "Right nice, wouldn't ye say?"

I peered into the small hole, a smirk forming on my lips at the sight that met my eye. Huge, even bigger than the last, with even more cargo on board. And embedded on the hull beside the name was a symbol. A royal ship. Navy? Nay, it couldn't be. It was a merchant brig, I knew by its shape, but this was far from the average vessel. It was wonderful. I tossed the spyglass to Keaton with a smirk. "What do you say? Shall we?"

Keaton looked through the glass for a lengthy moment before nodding. "Aye."

Aye, indeed. For this would be quite fun.

Chapter 3

I knew good and well that Charlie's plan would succeed, but the idea of being attacked by pirates just to find Lady Catherina Winterbourne was far from appealing in my mind.

Never had I had the pleasure, shall we say, of having my ship, the glorious *Jessica*, raided by savage pirates, so I had not the slightest idea of what to expect. I'd heard stories, as all children of pirates—whether reformed or not—have, of the ruthless murderers that set fire to merchant ships after plundering and killing every last man. Which made it only natural for me to whisper a prayer up to heaven that Charlie would make certain that his men refrained from chopping my crew's heads off. Not that, if I remembered correctly, Father had ever chopped his victims' heads off. Perhaps I should be on the watch for an even more gruesome technique.

I had already discussed the matter with my men, and my younger brothers Jonathan and David were below deck reminding everyone that there was to be no bloodshed but to not surrender, yet still I had several doubts running through my mind. What if her ladyship had stayed behind on Charlie's ship? What if Charlie's men didn't heed his instructions and started pillaging and killing? What if Lady Catherina didn't come with me? Charlie had warned me that she was, well, more than a little feisty. Which, how would I feel if my birth father randomly appeared to claim me, ripping me away from my adopted father, Reverend Collin Bennet? I wouldn't fancy the idea much either. But I couldn't imagine a lady being so barbaric as to punch me in the gut and run off, even if she had been raised by a pirate. I mean, how bad could a young woman get? I supposed only the good Lord Himself knew what might happen today…

I pushed my worries aside as unbidden an image of the Duke of Rothsford, Richard Winterbourne, appeared in my mind. The man had not seen his only daughter and heir since she was but a babe, and the girl—excuse me, woman—couldn't even remember her father. I could only imagine the joyous reunion sure to occur should I follow through with this plan.

So I would do just that.

My gaze caught sight of the *Rina*—Charlie's ship, or at least I presumed that it was his, as he had never denied that—from where I stood leaning up against my cabin's door-frame, and suddenly a lump rose in my throat. Good grief, that ship was huge, bigger than any other vessel I had ever laid eyes on. Certainly larger than any of Father's. And if the ship was that ginormous, how big would the crew be?

I walked back into my cabin, shutting the door behind me with feigned nonchalance before sitting at the chair in front of my desk, and began to look over my papers. At the moment the pirates stepped onto my ship, Jonathan would enter my cabin, warn me, then continue on with his day as though nothing had occurred. It was really all up to me.

And Lady Catherina. I could only hope that she would cooperate. Maybe Charlie had spoken to her of our plan. Of her heritage. No, I doubted that. He wouldn't dare be the cause of ruining the only life that she had ever known, and he had in fact told me not to dare mention his involvement to her. So I had only to hope that I could get her to remain on my ship…

I'd probably have to tie her up to the mainmast for that to happen, if what Charlie had said was true.

The door burst open then, and Jonathan popped his head into the room. "'Tis time, Xavier. Don't do anything stupid, if you can," he said with a wink before turning and leaving.

Little brothers.

I rose from my chair and strode from the room as one of my men yelled "pirates," and rushed to warn the others. They were already playing their part well, I would admit. I watched almost gleefully as the buccaneers invaded the *Jessica*, waiting for Charlie, one of my father's old friends from their Royal Navy days. Hordes of men, young and old alike, landed on deck, drawing their cutlasses in preparation should we not choose to surrender.

Charlie stole away from his crew to my side, managing to sneak past without anyone noticing. The man sidled up to me, standing there in silence for a moment before opening his mouth to speak. "Now, Xavier, I need ye t' remember tha' Rina, she ain't like the ladies ye're with on land. She ain't one t' be messin' with. I trust ye, matey, but I'm t' warn ye not t' be layin' a hand on her or think about doin' so. She be like a daughter t' me, and I want her right safe, y'hear? And I want ye safe too, so whate'er ye do, don't ye be gettin' on her bad side," he stated, having to tilt his head backward to meet my gaze. "Ye lead her away from the crew and distract her whilst I sneak up b'hind. And don't do nothin' stupid, ye hear?"

I chuckled, nodding my head. "Aye aye, Captain," was my reply. I waited for Charlie to disappear back into the crowd of pirates before searching for my victim. She wasn't hard to find.

The toe of tall black boots secured by golden buckles tapped in some sort of rhythm, the motion then drawing my gaze up to the long, slender breeches-clad legs. Swinging by her right leg from its sheath on a loosely worn thick leather belt was a huge cutlass with an ornate gold hilt. Tucked haphazardly into the belt was a tight white shirt that hugged her ladyship's perfectly curved figure, its low ruffled collar revealing more than was necessary. A waistcoat tailored of a deep crimson velvet was what came next, the long tails of the coat probably covering a dagger and pistol hanging from the other side of the belt.

Clasped around a slender neck was a beautiful golden chain, from which hung three bright emeralds that matched the jewels embedded in the huge golden hoop earrings that swung from her ears. Little wisps of sun-bleached light brown hair tickled her neck there, the remainder of the thick curls tucked hurriedly underneath the black tricorn hat poised atop her head, the brim of the tricorn shadowing her face.

What was I getting myself into?

From where I stood there, that lump having reappeared in my throat, I yelled, "No surrender!" and the fighting commenced.

I drew my sword, but rather than fight against the pirates with rest of my crew, I watched as Lady Catherina fought her way to prow of the *Jessica*. For a lady, or a woman in general, she was an amazing swordsman—woman. A parry, a thrust, and she had one of my bosun, Horace Stern, backed up against the railing at sword-point. I had to admit, Charlie had been understating when he'd said she wasn't average. She was extraordinary.

Horace dropped his sword, then fell to his knees as he shouted a plea for his life. Suddenly I was filled with suspense, feeling as though I had a front row seat to a spectacular play back in London as I tried to figure out what Lady Catherina would do next. Slowly, almost mockingly, she let her cutlass graze his neck so gently that not even a drop of blood left his veins. She said something in a low voice that I couldn't hear from my position, but it must have been relieving, as Horace's chest heaved in a sigh and he fell to his face.

Goodness, if I had known that he was such a grand actor, I would've encouraged him to stay on land and pursue a career in playacting.

Then, as Horace stood and walked away trembling, I made my way towards the prow, glad when I realized that Lady Catherina stood there alone. I sauntered up behind her and let the tip of my blade rest lightly at the small of her back before questioning in a taunting tone, "So the captain let his little lady on board my ship, did he?"

I almost toppled over in hysterical laughter at the assumption of the man behind me. Captain's little lady, he called me, as though I were some silly girl to be teased. Truly, I had been called many things over the past twenty-some years: Sister, Goldie, One-Eye, Rina, Captain, Blackstone, Daughter, Cathy, Kitty, and so forth; but never, ever had anyone, not even Wilde himself, dared to deem me the captain's little lady. Ha, I'd show him a "little lady."

I spun on my heel, mindless of the sword he had pressed against my back, and faced the daft man. "I, sir, *am* the captain," I declared, unable to suppress the sense of pride that I had over the title I so gladly carried. I held my own cutlass up to his chest, then realizing that I didn't have to look down at this man, as he actually surpassed my height by at most an inch or two. He was tall, I could easily give him that, but rather than being lanky he was well-muscled with broad shoulders, though not quite as bulky as Keaton.

His gaze met mine, and immediately I was taken captive by his dark, fathomless glare. Mirth and brazen interest burned in his eyes, making me all the more determined to wipe away the smirk that formed on his lips. "Ah, that you are, I see," was his reply in the same derisive tone that went hand-in-hand with his perfect English accent.

'Twas obvious that this was no common sailor yet a man of high social standing, and by not only his voice but by his well-tailored clothing and overall appearance.

Pulled out of his face in a queue was shoulder-length dirty blond hair that had been bleached even lighter by the sun, his light hair contrasting with his sun-bronzed skin. Set just right in their sockets were those arresting black eyes, framed by thick lashes shades darker than his hair that could rival those of any woman. He had a strong jaw, not to mention freshly shaved, with high cheekbones and a broad forehead that was covered by wisps of hair that had escaped from his braid. His nose, though, was knotted and was the only imperfection in his flawless face, as well as the only battle wound he had—if one could really count a broken nose as such—for I saw no scars marring his face.

Humph. Not only was he daft but nobly handsome as well. A man of his appearance didn't belong on a ship, I'd say, but rather a duke's palace. Or, in other words, anywhere but in front of me.

Then, his sword was pushing against mine, the sound of metal scraping drawing me out of my thoughts and back into the present. I didn't wait.

Quick as a flash, I flipped backwards, landing on the railing behind me without so much as a wobble of instability. Before he could even realize my transfer of positions, so to speak, I grabbed hold of a thick rope that hung beside me and swung around him to the opposite side of the forecastle, knocking his sword from his hand in the process.

Countless times had I performed the trick, but never had it felt so satisfying. A devilish grin crept up my lips as I swung back to where I had originally stood before the daft man and released the rope. After only a moment of my feet being planted on the ground, footfalls came up behind me, bidding me to turn and see the owner of the sound.

And the very second that I did, I met the familiar weathered face of Charlie, then I crumpled to the deck beneath my feet as a painful darkness overtook me.

Good grief, did my head hurt. Deep in the back of my head was a searing pain that ached so horridly that I was of a mind to bang it up against the wall of my bedchamber, as though that could somehow rid me of the agony.

I rolled over onto my stomach, pressing my forehead deeper into the feathery pillow it rested upon. I took in a frustrated breath, allowing the delightful scent of saltwater, lime, and pine to flood my sense.

Wait. Pine? Why did my pillow smell like that? The *Rina* was, after all, made mostly from cedar wood, not pine. So why then…?

I raised my head and forced my eye open, glancing around a room that was most assuredly not mine. Where my desk sat pressed up against the farther wall by the windows, in this room a desk had been nailed to the floor on the left wall, where my bed should've been. And instead of green curtains there were red, as was the same with the Persian rug spread across the floor. A pine wood floor, at that. But what startled me most was not the odd décor but the two men in the room with me.

Sitting on the floor with his back pressed up against the wall was a man probably two years my junior with overlong blond hair, green eyes, and huge shoulders. Beside him in a chair was a man identical to him in appearance, though his shoulders weren't as broad. They had to be twins.

The one in the chair rose, walking over to my bedside with clover green eyes wild with worry. "M'lady, how are you faring?" he questioned in that same perfect accent as the daft man had.

That was it! The daft man must have taken me captive after our "discussion" over my rank. But how had he managed to get me without a fight, and why in the world did my head hurt so terribly?

I could remember swinging on the rope and knocking the man's sword into the water, then I had landed back on my feet. I'd turned. And someone must have hit me over the head. So that could explain my presence on this ship, but what it couldn't explain was why the green-eyed man referred to me as a lady.

Green-Eyes tilted his head, his brow furrowing as his gaze raked over my face. "Lady Catherina? Are you all right?"

I rolled my eye, sitting up in the bed. "Oh, shut up. Of course I am not all right. I'm lying a bed not my own with a severe headache and two random men watching me. Now ask me again if I'm all right, mister," I growled, moaning in pain as I lifted my arms above my head, stretching, and yawned. With a sigh to break the sudden silence, I dropped my arms and glared at him. "How long have I been unconscious?"

"Two days," was my answer, but not from Green-Eyes.

We both looked up at the doorway, where a familiar tall man with long blond hair stood leaning up against the frame. Dash it all, it was the daft man.

"Well, well, well. Look who the wind blew in," I mumbled sarcastically, reaching up to brush a strand of hair out of my right eye. "Pray, tell me why I happen to be stuck here, if you please."

The daft man chuckled, sauntering up beside Green-Eyes, who I supposed was his younger brother, as the family resemblance was easily noticed. "Why, my dear lady, you are far from stuck. Only detained for a short period of time," he replied, sketching a mock bow, though that blasted dark gaze never left mine.

"Now, Jonathan, when did she awake?" The daft man looked to Green-Eyes, or rather Jonathan, with a raised eyebrow.

"Just a minute ago, Xavier. You're right on time, I'd say," Jonathan stated. He took a step back as his brother, the completely aggravating Mr. Xavier Something, plopped down all nonchalant-like on the edge of my bed. Or mayhap 'twas his. I wasn't much sure of anything at the moment.

Out of instinct, I slid my hand by my hip, prepared to draw my cutlass should this Mr. Xavier Something make any unnecessary advances. But, as I should've known, my blade was not there, and had likely already been thrown into the sea, along with my dagger and pistol.

I stifled a huff, rubbing my forehead with my fingers. "Look here, Mr. Xavier, I refuse to be 'detained' and demand to be given my things and set back on my ship. Immediately!"

"Ah, poor girl, but I am afraid that is not something I can do, for the *Rina* has set sail and is not likely to cross our paths any time in the near future. Though I am sure that Charlie has everything under control. As for your things, I think I can manage that. If you'll just give me a moment, of course."

My fingers clenched into a fist that I longed to send flying my captor's way, but I only flexed my hand and opted for a quite satisfying smack on his cheek. His head flew to the side at the force as red crawled up his jaw. Ah, now *that* was a battle wound.

"I demand an explanation, and if I cannot get one, I'll see if one of your dear brothers would be of service," I sneered, reaching behind me to draw out from beneath my shirt a small knife. 'Twas not my first choice of weaponry, but it was the only available one. I pointed it directly at the man's chest, ready to plunge it straight into his heart should a response not come forth.

Mr. Xavier Something only chuckled, not even daring to rub his bruised cheek. "Well then, an explanation you shall be given. You see, I, Xavier Bennet, have been commissioned by the Duke of Rothsford, a very wealthy and prominent man, to find his daughter.

"Now, this poor girl had been kidnapped by ruthless pirate only days after her birth, and no one has been able to find her. But seven years ago a man who helped in the abduction of her ladyship and a friend of my father's contacted me, willing to assist me in my search even as it would cost him his life. Well, never had my path crossed with her ladyship until two days past. So, that is why you are here, my lady."

How daft could this man get? I glared at him, unsure if I ought to kill him on the spot or figure out his real objective. I chose the latter. 'Twould be, after all, a more adventurous prospect rather than risking my life spilling his blood so soon.

"Did Timothy hire you?" was my first assumption, as it seemed most likely. That Scotsman was relentless, and it wouldn't shock me to hear if he had finally caught up with me after all these years. Already he had ruined my life by killing my only family and taking my brother, but he wouldn't give up until every last Blackstone either danced the hempen jig or swam in their own blood.

He raised an eyebrow, his lips quirking upward. "And who might that be?"

"Oh, don't act like you don't know. Now tell me, and I might consider sparing your life. Did Timothy hire you?"

"No. I've told you, I was commissioned by the Duke of Rothsford. Your father."

I sprung out of the bed, a growl tearing at my throat. How dare this man declare someone else, a duke at that, be my father! My father was and always would be Captain Maverick Blackstone, and no one, most especially this Bennet fellow, would ever contradict that and live!

I leveled my knife at his neck, peering deep into those lying eyes of his. "If you ever belie my heritage again, I *will* kill you. Do you hear?"

But before he could reply, strong hands grabbed hold of my wrists, jerking my arms behind my back and yanking the knife from my grasp. I tried to wrench away before my wrists could be bound, but the fingers gripped them tighter. Having tied my hands up, the man—who I now saw to be the one with huge shoulders—removed the quilt that was tangled up in my legs, and bound my feet. My bare feet, come to think of it.

Oh, for pity's sake, don't tell me these men took off my boots and ogled over my feet, I inwardly moaned.

'Twas enough that they had sat watching me slumber. Leastwise they hadn't undressed me while I was unconscious. They were only sailors, after all, not pirates.

Once my feet were tied, Big-Shoulders sat me upright, replaced the quilt over my legs, and then stepped back to meet my sneer and his brother's smirk.

"Now, my lady, would you like to repeat that threat of yours?" Bennet's grin only grew as he stood and folded his arms over his chest.

"I will kill you. Every last one of you. Don't you doubt it," I said, having to shove my gaze to the wooden beams above me to keep from being blinded by those bright white teeth Bennet was now flashing my way.

My captor turned to exit the room, tossing over his shoulder, "Oh, I'm sure. Rest up, my lady. You've got a lot of killing to do."

Chapter 4

"Blast it all!" I kicked the doorframe of my cabin, where not a single pirate captain lay bound upon my bed. Not only had David tied up her arms and legs, but I had locked the door from the outside and set Jonathan to guard the room should Lady Catherina have exceptional lock-picking skills. I obviously didn't need either, for she had still managed to escape without detection. It was completely ludicrous!

Raking my fingers through my hair, I set to pacing across the threshold. How had she pulled off such a feat? The one door was the only means of exit and, unless she was hiding under the bed, she had all but vanished into thin air.

I stepped into the room, determined to figure out how she had disappeared so that when I found her, she would truly have no means of escape. I scanned the area, looking for anything out of the ordinary. The bed was rumpled; the mattress turned at an angle. Either her ladyship didn't know how to make a bed, or she had used that in some way. Aside from that, my desk drawer was cracked open just slightly… Oh, great.

I really should've remembered to remove the knife from where I kept it hidden inside my desk for safekeeping. Seemed it wasn't so safe under there anymore. Lady Catherina must have found the secret compartment that held my dagger, used it to slice through her bonds, then pried open a window. Charlie certainly hadn't be jesting when he'd said to be careful.

I dashed out of the room and up the stairwell, calling for my brothers. Surely Catherina hadn't climbed down the back of the ship. Or had she? But where would that get her other than drowned?

Jonathan met me in the middle of the deck, his cheeks red and chest heaving from probably having run at top speed all the way from below deck. "What's the matter?"

I waved my hand towards my empty room. "See for yourself," I replied.

Not even bothering to glance toward the cabin, Jon's jaw dropped, and he glared at me, his eyes wide. "You're serious?" At my nod, he continued, "And how? Don't tell me that you just let her walk right out. Did you?"

"No, of course not! She found my knife and pried open a window." I had started pacing again, the clomp of my boots grating on my already dull nerves.

"So you mean to tell me that we have a pirate captain climbing down the rudder of our ship?"

"No! I mean, yes! Oh..." I pinched the bridge of my nose in frustration, taking in heavy, labored breaths. This was definitely *not* going very well.

Lord?

"How do you propose we get her back?"

I glared down at Jon, ceasing to pace. "Any suggest-ions?"

He hitched a shoulder. "We could, um, ask her politely? Maybe swing down there and grab her?" Something flickered in his eyes, but I ignored it, about to reply.

"Ah, yes, as though she would dare to comply."

Though the words were the exact ones sitting on the tip of my tongue, the voice was not my own but rather the one of pirate in question.

I spun around, only to come face-to-face with the tip of a sword and one steel gray eye rivaling the blade in sharpness. "Well, I say, we were just speaking of you, my lady.

'Tis so good of you to join us," I teased in an irritated tone that bordered on a growl, as I drew from my side my sword.

Lady Catherina rolled her one eye, a sneered forming on those perfect, full lips of hers. She pressed the tip of the sword deeper, pricking the bare skin at my collarbone. "Look here, *Mr.* Bennet, I do not want to hear the word *lady* fall from your lips in addressing me one more time or I will kill you," she grumbled, moving her sword slowly, in that taunting way of hers, towards the end of my shoulder, slitting the top of the sleeve of my shirt.

I only nodded in reply, shoving the sword away from my forearm with the one I held. "I see you do not take your threats lightly, my lady. Now, would you like to inform me as to how you escaped my room?" I questioned, unsure how she could have climbed out the window, then around and up the hull of the ship in that small amount of time since my brothers and I had left the room.

She gave me a look with that steel grey eye, a cross between annoyance and hilarity. "'Tisn't that hard to climb out of a window and up onto the deck, sir."

From somewhere behind me, Jonathan snickered.

I turned my head just barely, gave him a dismissive glare.

"And not only am I not a lady, but I am most assuredly not *yours*." Following through with her threat, she pulled her sword away from mine and placed it against my chest, only mere moments away from killing me.

Up close, as we had been two days past, I could make out her perfectly proportioned features, her every scar. Her high cheeks, sprinkled lightly with freckles, both bore small white lines from battle. Adeeper scar ran down from the top of her forehead, through her patched left eye, and to her jawline. I could only imagine the pain that had caused. Her nose, bent slightly, looked exactly like her father's, while her rounded jaw resembled her mother Ana's. Her full lips, curved in a sneer now, would create the brightest smile if she was capable of such happiness. Her eye, though, was the biggest mystery to me. Glowing a shimmering silver now, it had been almost green the first time we fought. 'Twas almost as though it could change its color, which was absolutely absurd. And fascinating.

Aside from that, I was unsure if she was just ignorant towards the fact that I could easily slice her legs or stab her in the stomach, or if she was completely aware and prepared for both.

Either way, I would take that chance.

With a cruel grin that felt almost wrong on my face, I quickly took a step back, ducked underneath the sword, and jolted around Lady Catherina to her back.

Just as fast, she spun to face me and thrust her sword towards mine. I parried her blow, and before I knew it, we were engaged in an intense sword-fight, for the second time since she'd first stepped on the *Jessica*. And though I had already experienced her exceptional skills, I was still in awe of the way she acted so quickly, counteracting each move I made perfectly, protecting herself and yet managing not to scar my skin in the least.

But what bewildered me was just that, that she would refrain from killing me, though she had so easily declared that she would. What was holding her back?

One more step forward and my opponent would be backed up against the railing at the side of the ship. I could then knock his sword into the sea behind him, render him defenseless, and slit his throat.

But, I reasoned, what good would killing him do? I would have no answers, and his brothers would likely battle me back into the captain's cabin. And I, of course, would have no choice but to comply, as I was naught but a frail baby bird when it came to Big-Shoulders, whose name I had gathered to be David.

Perhaps I could bring this Xavier Bennet to his knees, and coerce out of him his true motives and who had *really* sent him after me. Then I could let him beg me for mercy. Aye, that would work.

I advanced closer, pushing Bennet back until he stood only an inch away from the balustrade. But he didn't relent, only pushed me back as well, his sword coming so shockingly close to my neck that if I inclined even slightly I would be dead. Without thought, I dove back, hearing the joints in my spine pop as I bent in a position completely unnatural. Then, jumping up, I threw my legs over my head in a flip, this one much riskier than my last when I had battled Bennet. His sword, still extended, barely grazed my shin, slitting the fabric of my breeches yet not touching my skin.

When I landed back onto my feet with a thud, I met the gaze of my captor and enemy, finding it hard to stifle a smug grin at the sight of the astonishment etched in his features. Though my plan had been foiled, I still had a chance.

Bennet then moved closer, continuing with his maneuvers, thrusting while I parried, but never making it close enough to cut me, let alone kill me.

Since adolescence, I had been training with my father, and if anyone had ever met Maverick Blackstone, they would know just how fierce I could be in my fighting.

But fierce or not, I was powerless against the strong arms that then wrapped around my waist and pinned me to a chest.

David. Oh, blast the brute! He could overpower me with one small touch, and I could only hope I could escape before he decided to do more than just tie me up.

David held me tight with one arm, while grabbing the sword from my hand with the other, despite how hard I clawed at him and tried to remove myself from his clutches. As he wrestled me into submission, Bennet stood before me, his sword sheathed, a blinding grin on his lips. Dash it all! How I hated that man and his sardonic delight.

"Well, my...dear, I shall see you on the morrow," he said, with a dangerous gleam in his midnight eyes and an equally dangerous tone.

Come to think of it, I really shouldn't have forbidden the use of *lady*, as it sounded much more formal than *dear*, or any other endearment this man had in mind.

As David all but picked me up off the ground and slung me over his broad shoulder, I contemplated my next escape. The window was no longer an option, but as long as I could find a moment when my door was left unguarded, I might could pick the lock and abscond before I was detected. Perhaps.

Slowly the door creaks open, slivers of daylight peeking through, blinding my eyes. Footsteps follow, the sound so familiar that it grates on my very last nerve. Clomp, clomp, clomp. It's a sound – no, a rhythm that exudes authority, arrogance, contempt. Pure hatred. Just like the owner himself.

The footsteps have come to a stop now, right in front of me. I can see the toe of the tall black Hessian boots, the sun's light glinting off of them in a blaze like fire. But that's not what has me shaking where I sit. 'Tis the knife that is extracted. Aimed. Then plunged directly into Father's chest.

Blood spills from the wound, trailing down Father's torso to the floor where it runs over my hand. There is no denying it.

Father is dead.

Dead.

I jerked up from my bed, my ears ringing with only one word.

Dead. What I would be when Wilde found me.

Dead. What my crew likely was by now.

Dead. Just like my father.

I pulled my hands up to my ears, realizing they were tied, then banging my head down on the pillow so hard that I might split it open. A scream, a sob tore at my throat, but it was closed shut, dry and hoarse. Sweat poured from my forehead, dripping down to catch in my lashes. And though my body was tormented by heat, I was cold. Freezing cold, chilled to the bone with despair. With hatred.

Hard, labored breaths left my mouth as I tried so hard to banish the nightmare from my mind. It had been years, seven years since I had been plagued by this blasted reoccurring nightmare. Why was it now that it was returning to haunt me? I had tried so utterly hard to forget, to keep control over myself. Why was I losing it now?

Then suddenly, filling me with a mix of dread, fear, and almost faint dizziness, the door opened to my room. But this time no light followed, only soft, nearly inaudible footsteps. No clomp, no dagger, no blood. Only a tall, well-muscled figure cloaked in darkness.

Bennet.

I had likely awakened him from his slumbering outside my door with my moaning and rustling. Ugh, hadn't he learned by now that I could take care of myself? That I needed no nursemaid to check on me, to coddle me, nor a shoulder to cry on? Obviously not, or he wouldn't be slipping silently into my room and seating himself beside me on the bed. Unless, of course, comfort was not part of his plan...

"Catherina," he whispered, the night's pain twisting his word to sound almost threatening, though only a sense of heartache could follow with my name, spoken just as Father had the moment he had taken his last breath. Not strained had his tone been, but peaceful, a strange, eerie peace that ought not to have mingled with the stench of death.

But Bennet's held only a wretched sense of soothing comfort. And I hated it.

"Are you all right?" he questioned, and through the dark I could see his brow furrowed in worry, his midnight eyes brimming with anxious compassion.

Oh, how I wish I could slap that expression off his face that very second! But, dash it all, my hands were tied. And if my ankles weren't as well as, I'd be of a mind to shove him off my bed. But despite even my inability to move, I could barely think except of Father.

My head hurt too terribly, my ears still ringing, my mind too foggy, to dare to think. Yet it was all I could do.

"Rina?" came Bennet's voice again.

That was it! I jumped up, wobbling on my bound feet, barely obtaining balance before I smacked my hands against his face. "Get out! How dare you charge in here like you own the place! Now get out!" I shouted, not caring if I woke up the entire ship. Not caring if I was acting like a fool. Not caring if anyone else cared.

Bennet made no move to leave, only tossed his head back and laughed. At me, the scoundrel. "Oh, my dear, dear Catherina! I do own the place," he managed to say between his howls of laughter. "I'd say I have a right, wouldn't you?"

My eyes widened, and I could literally feel my blood boil and my face warm. "You, sir, have no right. And I command you to leave this room and not return until I am back on my ship. Do you hear?"

Still laughing, Bennet stood, sketched a gallantly mocking bow, then exited the room, muttering something about domineering ladies. But just outside the door, he stopped and glanced over his shoulder at me. "I sincerely hope, my good lady, that the remainder of your night is less eventful." And with that, he disappeared into the shadows.

Chapter 5

Atlantic Ocean
August 1683

Fuming as he always was around that Blackstone brat, Timothy Wilde slammed his bottle of rum down on the barrel before him and met the taunting glare of Julius Blackie. "If'n ye say one more word, J-Julius, I'll be a-slittin' yer throat 'fore ye'd blink. Dinna ye be a-talkin' about tha' father o' yers, y'hear?"

He was standing now, he realized, though he swayed more than he ought to. And the ship seemed to be rocking quite hard. For a split second, he glanced up at the sky, but not a cloud was there with the flaming stars above.

Julius smirked as he stood, that expression so much like his father's that it made Timothy's stomach turn. Or maybe the feeling was from all the rum he'd drank tonight.

"Oh, can't be talkin' 'bout my father, you say? You mean you don' wanna be hearin' no stories of the greatest pirate captain to ever sail the Seven Seas, right next to Rina? Why, I'll be dogged! Well, I bet you're just jealous, ain't ya, Ole Timmy?" he questioned, his voice slurring even more the louder he spoke.

"Why, you slimy scallywag! I ain't no jealous. And yer father wasna no pirate, just a yellow-bellied coward, I tell ye," was Timothy's reply as he unsheathed his cutlass and held it up to Julius' collarbone. But just as soon as his arm was extended, a strong hand gripped it and tugged it back, sharp fingernails digging into the flesh of his forearm.

Timothy glanced at the person behind him, sighing when he met the blazing blue glare of his eldest daughter Crimson.

"I shan't be havin' none of this, Da. Yer both three sheets to the wind, and I ain't gonna be the one to cast ye o'erboard come midnight 'cause of yer stupidity," Crimson stated, her expression stern.

"Fer pity's sake, Crimmy, I ain't gonna die. But, if ye say so," he said, sheathing his sword before tossing Julius a deadly glare. "Yet if I 'ear one more word..." Timothy let his words trail off.

One day, he would have all those Blackstones dead, even if it were the very last thing he did.

I hated this. Completely, utterly hated this—being locked up in a room only to mope around, thinking up some nonexistent brilliant plan to escape from my confines, if only for a breath of salty air.

Bennet truly knew how to anger me, and not just with that arrogantly stupid smirk of his, but with his horrible treatment of his prisoners.

Bored out of my wits, with simply my nightmare alone to think of, I plopped down at the desk that sat up against the left wall, wondering why exactly Bennet hadn't placed it by the window. I mean, 'twas such a better view than this ugly pine wall in front of me. But to each their own, I supposed.

With a sigh, I sat, examining my fingernails as though they were the greatest things to ever look upon. My gaze caught sight of the glittering gold band that rested on my ring finger. I had worn it everyday since Father had given it to me, and kept it as a reminder of him and his love long gone.

Oh, really, why would someone go through so much just to capture me? And then claim I wasn't Blackstone's but another man's child? That Xavier Bennet had to be touched in the head, or at least I'd think him to be if every other thing about him didn't seem as sound as it did.

Oddly, I found it, that the more I wondered about Wilde having a hand in my abducting the more preposterous it seemed. If Timothy Wilde was actually behind this nonsensical situation of mine, then not only would I *not* be stuck on a merchant ship, I would likely be trapped with much less savory men than these Bennets, or would be dead even now. So then, who in Hades dared to do this to me?

My thoughts turned back to my first encounter with Xavier Bennet after my awakening. He had given his entirely false explanation, but hadn't he mentioned Charlie earlier in our conversation? What was it that he had said?

I had asked for my things and to be returned to my ship, and then he had said something about the *Rina* being too far away. Ah, yes, that was it! He had said that Charlie was taking good care of my ship during my hopefully short absence. But how, oh how, did he know who Charles Acton was?

Wait. Charlie had been in the Royal Navy at one time. What if Bennet's father had as well? It would explain the presence of the three Bennet men on the sea if their father was a seaman also. But if that connection was real, how would that help me?

Well, if I was going to figure this out, I would have to consider this from two different angles. This whole lie Bennet had created wasn't true, so then why did it exist? Someone was after me.

Mentally, I ran through my list of enemies. Wilde, of course; Captain Bryant Foxe of the *Raven;* Morris Goldwell, one of my ex-crew members that had turned against me after Father's death; and Roger Mansfield. Hmm...Goldwell hated me, but last I heard he had moved to Jamaica and settled down, or something of the sort. He had really no motive unless he was that vindictive.

Foxe could possibly be furious with me after not only my rejection of his proposal of sorts, but also after that ill-fated argument he and Father had gotten into eighteen years ago. Yet he really had no reason to hurt me after so many years.

Then there was Roger. Immediately I crossed him out. He was on the *Rina,* under Charlie's command and watchful eye. I highly doubted that he wanted anything more than money, never mind my death nor capturing.

And so that left only Wilde. But if that horrid Scotsman was the reason for this, I *would* be dead, of that I was completely certain.

So, what if—though it was totally and truly *impossible,* I would humor the foolish notion, only to grasp the idea of why I was here—Bennet was speaking the truth? Somehow, I was this Duke of Rothsford's abducted daughter. Then someone had to have informed Bennet, as he had said, of my presence on the *Rina.* Someone who would have known that and my 'true heritage.' Someone who would've been with Father at my abduction. Someone that Father either trusted enough to confide in him, or that was skilled at espionage and would have found out.

Someone with connections with land, connections with Bennet. Someone who…

Oh, dash it all! It *was* Charlie! I mean, it would have been, if this were true. And it wasn't, for that was entirely too crazy. But why would Charlie want to ruin my life so? Why would he let me be taken blindly from my ship, my men, by some unknown bunch of silly, fancy-pants Englishmen?

But he hadn't. Because none of this was true.

Suddenly, I jumped up from my chair, nearly causing it to topple over, and strode to the door. Locked, of course. But no one guarded it. Ah, splendid! I dug through the unruly hair that I had managed to pull into a queue and retrieved a small metal pin. A devious grin formed on my lips as I picked the simple lock on the door. It clicked, and I twisted the knob and slipped from the room.

Only to collide with the devil of a man, Xavier Bennet.

I bumped right into his chest, my hands flying out to grab a hold of his shirt. Purely out of instinct. But my right heeled boot caught on a crack in the wooden deck beneath me, and instead of catching onto Bennet, I stumbled backwards, one foot swinging helplessly in the air. I prepared myself to hit the ground, to twist my boot from its trap, but something caught me.

Hands—rough, calloused, hotter than fire—seized mine and pulled me upward. Again I hit Bennet's chest, but this time I stayed there. His hold moved from my hands to my waist, picking me up to free my foot and then setting me down. Except even once I had regained my balance, his hands remained on me.

Blast the man for his obvious ease with me! I wrenched from his hold, the touch that seared my skin like a flame. "How dare you touch me, *Mr.* Bennet," I growled, stretching his common title. 'Twould not hurt in the least to flaunt my so-called nobility, whether it was actually real or not.

Which it wasn't.

But he only grinned, that odious man. "Ah, yes, my dear lady. I probably shouldn't dare to touch you, should I? Oh, but I do have a bit of a right now, do I not?" Bennet raised a dark blond eyebrow over his black eye, his smirk only growing.

"Dash it all, y-you knave!" And with that I turned to walk away, but stopped myself as I remembered the reason I was in this predicament in the first place.

"Bennet, I want to see proof. Some piece of deuced evidence that I am actually this Rothsford's offspring," I demanded, then played my best card. "I want to see correspondence between you and Charlie."

For a moment—a wonderful moment, I might say—I could see a flicker of surprise in his eyes, disbelief over the fact that I could somehow have even the slightest clue towards Charlie's involvement. Or rather, lack of.

Even just the faintest hesitation in his response could reveal that this daft merchant ship captain was really a liar.

But just as soon as the shock appeared, it faded away and was replaced by Bennet's normal nonchalance. "Oh, but my lovely lady, you must know that your dear friend wanted no one but myself to know of his participation in your capturing. You see, he couldn't bear to suffer your wrath should you find out," he replied, a hand splayed over his heart in a dramatic display of theatrics.

I took in a deep breath, closed my eye for a moment, then met Bennet's mirthful gaze head-on. "Show me."

I knew that her ladyship was intelligent, a skilled swordsman, and as beautiful as her mother, but the fact that she'd figured out Charlie's involvement without any evidence—and in such a short amount of time—was definitely a surprise. But what I wasn't sure of was whether or not she actually trusted me. Her eye, glittering with silver and green, spoke of her doubt, but if she supposed my word to be false, then why would she have taken the time to even think about it? Unless, of course, she was softening up to the idea.

I glanced at Rina—er, Lady Catherina—from beside me, catching a glimpse of her frown, and immediately banished the notion. She most certainly didn't believe me.

"My lady—"

She jerked her head towards me, a sneer forming on her full lips that revealed a golden tooth.

Good grief.

"Excuse me, my *dear*, but might I ask why you are so adamant about seeing evidence if you don't trust me to be telling the truth?" I inquired, watching the play of emotions on her face.

She was a mystery for sure. I really couldn't help, it though, but make her angry. There was something about her that just begged me to tease her. Then again, I would tease even a tree if it were all I had with me.

"I don't trust you." She hitched a shoulder as though she was actually at a loss for words. Which would likely be a first for her. "But I want to know your true motives. Who you're working for. The danger I am to face. I shall ask you again, were you hired by Timothy Wilde?"

Ah, yes, this unknown Timothy fellow. Just last night I had overheard her muttering something about the man, whomever he was. I supposed I had to be on the lookout for this fellow, as she truly seemed almost, well, afraid of him. "Look, Rina, I know of no Wilde, I promise. And I also promise that I was commissioned by the Duke of Rothsford and none other," I assured her, having to resist the urge to set a hand on her shoulder.

As we started down below deck, where I kept Charlie's letter hidden carefully inside a crack in the wood, I noticed that Lady Catherina seemed to scowl at the dark. Odd, but there again, everything about this woman was just that. Odd.

She took a step down the stairs before me, tossing over her shoulder, "Was this duke tall?

"Yes."

"Well-built?"

"Yes."

"Flaming red hair?"

"A deep caramel. Unruly waves."

She huffed. "Dash it. Wilde's is red, and there is no denying it. Hmm. Perhaps he set Tomas up to this. How old is that boy anyway?" With a glance back at me, "Do you know the color of the man's eyes?"

"Green as the grass." I frowned, bounding down the remainder of the steps before Lady Catherina reached the bottom. Was she going to interrogate me about every little thing? Surely she could understand that this Wilde had absolutely no part in this whatsoever? Obviously not.

"Ugh, I'm but throwing blindly. So maybe Wilde isn't behind this. Foxe certainly isn't. Oh, for pity's sake, Bennet, how are you so blasted sure that I *am* this duke's child? Other than Charlie's alleged assistance, what gives reason?"

As she reached the last step, I placed my hands on her waist to help her down, and to my surprise she didn't shake them off. Either she was too deep in thought to pay me any mind, or she knew that she couldn't see a thing in this dark and would likely bump right into the crate Stern had so carelessly set at the end of the stairs. But even still, I relished the fact that she didn't bother to push me aside.

Just as the woman herself was odd, so was the tug I felt toward her. But there were many obstacles I had to face before I could actually consider being counted as her ladyship's friend. Gaining her trust, for one; getting her home to her family; the possibility of being killed before either of those things happened. And that was only the beginning. But deep inside, I knew that once I brought her home, my job would be far from done. I wanted to touch this lady in a way she had never been before.

With the love of God.

I placed her back on the ground, yet only held her hand once I released her waist and began to weave through the cargo hold. And she didn't pull away, only continued to prattle on about that Wilde fellow.

Finally she quieted down, then asked a bit less sternly, "Are you going to answer me or not?"

"Yes, I am. And there are multiple reasons. For one, you look like your parents. You have your father's abnormal height, his nose, and his hair. You have your mother's jaw, her bearing, and her figure. The second reason, Charlie not only led me to you, but rendered you unconscious and then carried you into my cabin. And lastly, you are the same age as her ladyship, and if I'm not mistaken, you bear the same name. Am I not right, Catherina Ana Dorcas Rosette?" I raised an eyebrow and grinned, even if she couldn't see through the dark.

At the mention of her name, she jerked her hand back, and then I heard a crash, bang, and a grunt. I spun around, and through the faint light, I could make out her form laying on the ground in an awkward position, her head against the sharp edge of a crate.

Chapter 6

Oh, but I didn't want to wake up. Not when I was having the most splendid of dreams. An angel was holding me. One of those strong, handsome, winged creatures I had heard people talk about every once and awhile. I'd had no idea what could ever fit their description of something so wonderful, but now, in the arms of one that very moment, I could understand.

And this angel smelled wonderful, like limes and coconuts and goodness. With a moan, I snuggled closer to this angel, nuzzling into his side.

Softly, I heard my angel chuckle, and oh, but it was a glorious sound!

But slowly, my eye opened, and I knew my dream was coming to an end…

Especially when I looked up to see Xavier Bennet. Dash it all! I knew angels were too good to be true. Immediately I jerked up, hating the realization that I, Rina Blackstone, had willingly enjoyed laying in *Xavier Bennet's* arms. And very muscular arms they were, but that was of no matter.

Unfortunately, the very second I attempted to move, a sharp pain struck through my skull while

Bennet held me in place. I reached up to feel my head, searching for a bump or bandage, only to draw my hand back and look directly at blood.

Now that got my attention. My eye wide, I sat up, no longer caring if Bennet was holding me, and struck him. "What in the deuce did you do to me?" I exclaimed, ready to hit him again just for the pure pleasure of it. Even if a mere slap couldn't do much good. What I wouldn't give for a cutlass. Or a pistol. Or just a little knife.

A sigh escaped Bennet's lips as he gently stood, placing me on the bed. Wait! I had been unconscious, in Bennet's arms, on my bed, again? Would this man ever leave me alone?

"Catherina, I didn't do anything, remember? We were going to retrieve Charlie's letter, and you fell and hit your head on a crate. I was waiting for Jon to bring me a clean strip of cloth to bandage your head. I had a feeling it would work a good deal better than a piece of my shirt," he replied, motioning to the ripped hem of his shirt.

But that wasn't what grabbed my attention. 'Twas his voice, soft and rich and calm. For pity's sake, surely he didn't take that angel thing seriously, did he? Because I wouldn't fault him in the least if he yelled at me and slapped me back for getting so riled with him over naught but his tender care for a dashed pirate. Not that I needed care, and certainly not from him. But still, the man was too good-acting for his own britches.

As I let the fact that Bennet's intentions were again honorable, I sunk deep into my mattress, careful not to let my bloody hand touch the white sheets I buried myself in. "So, uh, did you get the letter?" I questioned, hoping to steer the conversation back into my favor.

"That I did, my dear," he replied, and though I desperately hated it when he called me his dear, I let it pass. But only just this once.

"Well, show it to me."

Bennet pulled out from his waistcoat pocket a folded sheet of slightly yellowed and wrinkled paper. He handed it to me, and I snatched it from his hands and instantly unfolded it, scanning the scrawled out words as quickly as possible.

It was Charlie's handwriting all right, with a couple words smeared or crossed out. But, well—and I had a hard time admitting this to myself—I hadn't the faintest clue as to what the letter said. Almost embarrassed, I handed the paper back to Bennet. "Could you read it for me?"

He nodded, and not a single bit of hilarity or puzzlement over my inability to read flashed in his eyes.

> "'September 18th, 1676.
>
> "'Captain Bennet, I risked life and limb to get letter to you without her ladyship knowing, and I ask you don't take this information lightly.
>
> "'My name is Charles Acton. I knew your father from our navy days. Please trust me. I heard the Duke of Rothsford's search for his daughter, Catherina Ana Dorcas Rosette, and I want you to know that the moment you are reading this, that very woman is likely telling me to pass her another bottle of rum.
>
> "'I was there, Captain Bennet, on the day Blackstone captured Lady Catherina, and I want to see her back with her family, despite

what it cost me. Her ladyship is not the average lady, and she would kill me if she learned of my part in ruin of the life she knows.

"'Three year ago, her adoptive father died, and now she has taken over as captain of his ship, the *Rina*. She is hard. But I cannot bear to think of what His Grace might be feeling this moment. Please, search for her. You'll find her on the *Rina*.

"'Charles Acton.'"

For a long moment there was silence. Dead silence. But not in my mind. I was running through every possibility that Charlie had written that letter, that Charlie was right. I wasn't Maverick Blackstone's daughter, Julius's sister, an untitled pirate. I was a...lady. A noble born lady.

I couldn't think about it, as it only made my head hurt worse. I would think about that later, when I could actually comprehend the very idea. Or not at all, as Elliot would recommend.

Just then, the door burst open, and Jonathan dashed in, a bandage and vial of something in his hand. "Here you are, brother," he said, handing the materials to Bennet.

I gulped. Xavier Bennet was actually going to touch my head. My poor, bleeding head. Well, leastwise 'twas my head and nothing else.

Bennet bent down beside me, then carefully removed a blood-soaked strip of cotton fabric from my forehead before placing a few drops of a burning liquid on my wound. I quickly recognized the medicine to be alcohol, and I found myself relieved by that fact. At least these men didn't plan on poisoning me through a head wound.

After a while, my head was wrapped up securely, and I lay half asleep on my bed, kept awake only by the turning of pages.

I lifted my head just slightly, glancing at where Bennet sat against the wall beside my bed, completely immersed in whatever he was reading.

"What have you there?" I questioned, for a reason I knew not.

"My father's Bible," he replied.

As soon as the words were out of his mouth, I scoffed. "So you are one of those religious sort, are you?"

Elliot would've shot me a glare—Keaton as well—for speaking like that. But how could I help it? I suffered enough piety already on board my own ship. Enduring it on another man's was an entirely different issue.

Bennet only chuckled softly. "In my opinion, 'tis more a relationship rather than religion, but, yes, I suppose you could say that."

Rolling my eye, I turned on my side, bracing myself with my elbow. I was about to comment on Bennet's reply when came the terrifyingly familiar sound of rain. And not just any rain.

Heavy rain.

Immediately, I lept from the bed, shoved my boots onto my feet, then strode to the door and slung it wide open. Large drops of rain fell from dark grey clouds above my head.

For pity's sake, how had I not noticed the signs of a storm before? I marched from the room, prepared for whatever the sky desired to throw at me.

"Rina, what in the name of all that's holy are you doing?" Bennet called from behind me. "You've a serious head wound. You need to be in bed. And what if you were to faint out there from the loss of blood or something?"

I ignored the man's insistent pleas and excuses, as if they mattered much now that I stood half soaked in the rain. "Look, matey, we've a living gale out there, and you want me to lie in bed like a pampered princess?" I retorted, running out into the rain, yelling out orders completely out of instinct.

Someone *had* to do something, after all.

Men were climbing up the mast as quickly as possible to furl the sails toward the back of the ship, and for that I was grateful. At least someone knew what to do during a storm. But what had me extremely worried was that no one stood at the helm.

"Dash it all." As fast as I could without slipping on the wet deck, I ran up to the helm and, gripping the wheel until my very knuckles turned white, steered the ship to an angle. Unfortunately, the *Jessica* was smaller than my ship and was built slightly different, and it took me a moment to adjust to the change and gain full control of the vessel.

Wind whistled loudly through the sails that were still up, waves crashing down hard against the sides of the ship. And through it all rain poured heavily, the sound of the drops pounding against the deck like that of hail. It would be a miracle if even only half the crew made it out of this tempest alive.

Rain still pattered on the deck, waves still tossed my ship, yet after an entire day, the storm had begun to settle. I could only thank God that it had lasted such a short time. The sea was merciless, but the Lord was not, and He was certainly watching out for my crew and I. And Lady Catherina.

Night had fallen over five hours ago. The moon and stars were hidden behind the clouds of rain, yet it was a beautiful night.

Soaked, I sat on the railing towards the stern, my feet dangling overboard. Four hours ago the waves would've been brushing against my boots, but by this time the level of the raging sea had lowered, barely grazing the railing around the middle of the ship when a wave tossed.

I released a sigh, relieved over the fact that even during such a tempest her ladyship hadn't become worse, fainting from the loss of blood. Truly, I underestimated her strength, both physically and mentally. Easily could she spin the ship around, even while blood still seeped from the gash in her head. I could only hope that she was resting now, for the Lord knew she needed it.

And yet a smile turned up my lips. She had dared to confront me about Charlie, obviously having thought the situation through. Yes, she was coming, albeit slowly, to trust me. Leastwise while she was unconscious.

Now that very thought drew a chuckle from me. I could only revel in the amazement that she had been so, shall we say, willing during that moment while I held her. Innocent as it was. I had only picked her up and carried her from below deck into my room, bandaging her head as best as I could to staunch the flow of blood while I waited for Jon. Purely innocent indeed. Yet when she had snuggled up to me, I'd begun to wonder just how much that woman hated me. Obviously not as much as she'd let on. Not that I was using it to fuel my pride.

Although it could help.

The familiar sound of boots sounded from behind me, banishing thoughts that were only to be replaced by worries. Without turning, I knew exactly who walked up behind me and what they were holding in their hand. Why else would Lady Catherina's step wobble?

"You ought to in bed," I grumbled to her as she swung a long leg over the railing and settled in beside me.

"And I ought not be drinkin' either, eh?" Rina tilted her head back and took a swing of rum from the already half empty bottle that she held in her hand.

Crossing my arms over my chest, I looked towards her now. "Aye. And you're going to have to pay for that. 'Tis property of England."

She finished off the last gulp, then tossed the bottle into the ocean underneath us. "'Tis property of the sea now, matey," she retorted, mimicking my position by folding her arms over her chest with a frown that met mine and countered it in intensity.

Silence hung in between us for a long moment, broken only by the sound of drizzling rain. Finally I opened my mouth, one question that still racked my mind spilling out. "Why did you ask, Rina?"

She obviously understood my meaning, for her answer was a grunt followed by a hitch of her shoulder. "In good sooth, I don't rightly know. I wanted to know, even as I didn't. I s'pose ye think me to believe ye now, though, hmm?" She paused for a moment, though one not long enough for me to manage an answer before she spoke again. "Well, I don't. And I shan't. Ye've either lost yer bloomin' mind or I've lost mine. Wanna bet 'tis the first?"

I chuckled at that, resisting the urge to actually bet. With all those head wounds this woman had suffered as of late, she was likely the one to have lost their mind. "I would venture to say we've both lost our minds, my dear. Shall we make it even, then?"

All emotion, be it anger or mirth, fled her features, though she didn't move as I expected. "Ye make it whatever ye desire, Captain Bennet. I frankly don't give a fig."

My first thought was to see just how little she did give, but I shoved that one aside, choosing silence over what would likely end in bloodshed, knowing Catherina.

But she, probably the effect of the alcohol, seemed to be in a much more talkative mood, as she was now asking the question that had likely been racking *her* mind the last few days. "Why'd ye do it, Bennet? Why d'ye give a fig what becomes of me or tha' duke? Is he payin' ye or somethin'? Perhaps offerin' another daughter in return for this'un?"

That last part, though, was what had me chuckling, unable to answer her between my laughing.

Which irritated her, for she swatted at my arm, causing me to teeter on the edge of the railing. "I mean it, Bennet. Why?"

I took in a breath, calming myself. "Well, my lady, I shall tell you this, you are your parents' only child. I will be getting no bride out of this. And His Grace isn't paying me. I wouldn't take money for doing something that ought to have been done years ago out of pure kindness. Why I care about what happens to you, Rina, would be because God does." I knew I was jumping overboard now, yet I continued on. She needed to hear this. "God cared enough about you to send His only Son to die for you. If the King of kings can love someone that much, why shouldn't I?"

Maybe that fall had taken more than blood out of her head, because Catherina remained there beside me, didn't move except to breath, her face expressionless. And whistling through the wind and rain was her deepening silence. Was she going to say something or just sit there for the rest of the night?

Or perhaps she was plotting to kill me?

"D'ye really believe all o' that, Bennet?"

At the sound of her voice, dull and low, almost soft, I expelled a sigh of relief. No plots for my death, leastwise not yet. "Yes, Rina, I do. With all my heart I believe it. But why don't you?"

Again was that shrug, followed by a grunt. "Father didn't. Father believed tha' there ain't no supernatural being out there in the heavens, tha' life don't lie no farther than the grave. And who be I t' doubt his correctness? I live me life 'cording t' how I been taught: to steal and kill and revel in it. I ain't got no conscious, no sense of justice, of mercy. 'Tis all I know, all I'm gonna know. An' even if there is a God out there, who be I to care? I ain't some sinner beggin' to be saved by grace and mercy. I may rot in hell for all I care."

Callous couldn't even describe the indifference Catherina exuded as she sat there, giving her speech with all the emotion of a frog. Which has none, so you get the point.

Her voice so flat just fell over the sea, the calming waves, like a heavy, suffocating quilt. Her words seemed to fill the suddenly thick air, settling over me rather than the ocean.

Did she really subject herself to such a hopeless existence? Live and die with no hope for tomorrow? No eternity to await her? And did she really, truly have no conscious?

That I doubted. This was the same woman who let Horace crawl away rather than plunge her sword through his chest. The woman who slapped a man even if he really wasn't going to make any advances. And she said she had no conscious. Perhaps a lack of self-control, but certainly she had a conscious.

I could only frown, resisting the urge to wrap an arm around her tense shoulders, and sent up a silent prayer for her. Honestly, I had to thank God that he put me in her path, that the duke or Charlie hadn't chosen another man to find Catherina. And thank Him for the chance to minister to someone, for even if I wasn't standing at the pulpit as Father did, the Lord could use me. And use me He would.

Chapter 7

A week had passed by now. And though everything within me urged not to, I had given up on trying to escape. Why, you ask? Because if I did, where would I go? We were too far away from land for me to hop in a rowboat and make my way there, and too far away from the *Rina,* which should be setting sail from the Caribbean by now, for me to return there.

My best chance would be to wait until we docked, then I could disappear from Bennet's sights and commission myself safe passage to Spain, my crew's next stop. That is, if my curiosity didn't get the best of me and result in me traveling all the way to London to meet this "father" of mine.

Ugh, but it was an utterly bewildering situation I had so quickly and unwillingly been thrust into. If only I could find some answers. But even if I could, I knew without a doubt that however logical they may be, I wouldn't believe anything. Deep in my heart I knew I was Blackstone's child.

I had to be.

He was, after all, the one that had raised me, not this fanciful duke. And even if he was my birth father, Maverick Blackstone would always be my dad.

He was the one who'd fed me and clothed me, that had given me a home. He was the one who'd cheered me on as I took my first steps; who'd taught me how to survive on the sea; who'd set me on his knee and told me stories. He was the one who had given me my love for figures; who'd showed me how to parry and thrust, to gulp down a bottle of rum and still manage to sing a song that somehow made sense. This duke fellow hadn't done that.

For all I knew, he hadn't done anything at all.

No one could be Father, just as no one could ever be Julius. And dash it all, even if I could never have my father, one day I'd get my brother back.

I started back to pacing across my room, resisting the urge to stomp all over that fancy Persian rug spread out on the floor just as I wanted to do to every man who had ever dared to cross me, whether it be Wilde or Mansfield or Bennet. Just crush them under my heel like a maggot. Ah, but I could never have such a pleasure.

'Twas a shame.

It was humid in here, worse since the storm, and opening all six windows didn't help much, unless I was planning on baking myself like a biscuit. Yet I couldn't leave my deuced cage, thanks to Xavier Bennet, the rogue. I couldn't even scratch my itching nose.

One would think that after I had proved myself trustworthy by not disappearing during this past week that Bennet would allow me some fresh air, if only for a moment. But alas, his lordship had not granted me such an honor quite yet. And it was to be the death of me.

At least he hadn't confiscated my pins. All I had to do was figure out some way to untie my wrists, then a-lock-picking I would go. Well, I would be if Bennet hadn't tied my hands so blasted tight. I could almost feel my blood cease to flow through my fingers. Oh, and now my hand was going limp. And my fingers were turning purple, I could feel it…

Wait! Quick as a flash, the perfect idea flew into my mind. I had only to collapse upon the floor, and...

"Xavier!"

Rina's voice, sharp yet painful, pierced my ears as her scream set my heart to thumping. What had happened for her to shout my name out so loudly? And my Christian name, at that? She never called me by that, even as I took the liberty of using hers. So then something had to be wrong.

I jumped up, nearly knocking over a crate, and ran out from below deck, bounding up the steps into the daylight before charging into my room, the sight that I found stopping me right in my tracks.

She laid there across the floor, her head against the wood, blood spilling from the gash that must have reopened. A chair rested along her legs, likely having fallen over her. Goodness, but she was in some kind of a mess.

And I really should have nailed that chair to the floor as soon as I had bought it a week ago.

I stepped slowly into the room, set the chair away from her, then crouched down beside her. "Lord Jesus. Rina, what happened?" I reached out, letting my hand brush a loose strand of golden caramel hair away from the blood that trickled from her wound, the feel of her smooth skin underneath mine a pleasant one.

She coughed, attempting to sit up, though I stopped her with a hand to her back. "I was tryin' to stand from where I sat, but me legs got tangle up in the chair, and before I knew it, I was on the ground. I woulda been a'right if it weren't for this dashed hole in me head," she choked out, lapsing into a tone more like Charlie's that would've had me grinning if she weren't bleeding.

I could only frown, slip my hands around her waist, and pull her into my arms. And she didn't resist. Holding her against me with an arm around her back, I used my other hand to brush a drop of blood from her brow. Her eye glistened with shades of green and silver and blue, that alluring combination so prone to change, a tear threatening to slip free from its depths. "I knew I should've let Jon sew this up," I whispered, more to myself than to Rina.

Wait. When had she become *Rina*?

Rina's hands came to rest on my shoulders, her face so very near I could but lean down only an inch and touch my lips to hers…

I shoved the thought aside. "Is this all that hurts?"

She shook her head, her gaze falling to my lips as though she'd had the very same thought. Then she answered. "Nay. I believe I've twisted my ankle."

Involuntarily, a moan escaped my lips. "Come and sit. I'll take a look at it for you," I said, beginning to lead her toward the bed.

But then she grinned—that sort of devilish grin that would set anyone on edge—and pulled back. "Thank you for saving me, *Xavier*. But I think I shall be fine." And with that, she winked and sashayed straight out of the room, not so much as a wobble to her step.

Blast it. That girl was good. And had me wrapped around her little finger, obviously. I should've known she was playing me for a fool. I mean, since when had she been so helpless that she couldn't pick herself up off the ground? And even if she had been, Catherina Winterbourne wouldn't have called for me. Likely would've shouted for Jonathan if she had been so desperate as to need assistance. How stupid could I be?

She was probably going to find a knife now, free herself, then climb down the side of the ship to where the longboat rested that she could use to get away. And wouldn't forget to grab a bottle of rum before escaping.

And I would be left to mourn my loss.

"Catherina Ana Dorcas Rosette Winterbourne, you get back here right this instant!" I called out, charging from my room and out onto the deck, heading to the first place I expected her to be. In the cargo hold. There she could gather whatever goods she needed, possibly find the money I had stashed down there, and steal Charlie's letter, just for the sake of it.

I had made it halfway down the stairway into the dark hold when a sickly sweet voice crept up behind me.

"Looking for someone, hmm?" Rina whispered, and I almost expected a hand to cup my mouth or a blade to graze my neck, yet all she did was thrust her bound hands out by my shoulder. "Untie me, would you please?"

With a huff that would've awarded me a scolding from my mother, I pulled my knife from its sheath and sliced her free. "Were you going somewhere, m'lady?" I inquired, returning my blade to the case.

"I was sweltering in there, Captain Bennet. I needed some fresh air, and since you would not freely give it to me, I had to obtain it on my own. Believe me, I did not plan to leave you to your demise. I want to be present for that," Rina explained, tugging her hands back and starting up the steps ahead of me. "Surely you did not think me so cruel as to leave you ever so soon, did you, *my dear*?"

Oh, now I knew how she felt. I wanted to slap the smirk that she tossed me from over her shoulder right off her face...but I had more breeding than that. So I opted for the more gentlemanly approach.

I slid an arm around her waist and tugged her down the steps to me, holding her as tightly as possible.

And kissed her.

I wanted to jerk away, but his hold was too fast. I wanted to plant my fist in his face, but I was drowning in his touch. And I wanted to tell myself not to lean into him, to return his kiss, but the last of my common sense had fled me, and frankly, I didn't want it back.

Xavier's arms around me tightened, his mouth c]moving against mine in such a way that made me wonder if he had intended only to shut me up or if he had been planning to get his hands on me all along. Not that there was anything I was able to do about it, leastwise not when I was unwillingly enjoying kissing this devious scoundrel all too much.

My mind was spinning now, with warnings and objections and *him*. My heart was pounding, perhaps from fear of what the knave might truly be attempting to do or perhaps from sheer pleasure. And my hands, the utterly rebellious little limbs, were sliding up his chest to his shoulders, gripping onto him for dear life as I went overboard.

I parted my lips, deepening our kiss even as I told myself not to. Dash it all. What did it matter anyway? It was naught but a stupid kiss. I might as well make the most of it, aye?

But then, at that very moment, Xavier pulled away, his hands immediately slipping away from my waist as he stepped back.

Out of furious instinct, my hand shot out and whipped him across the jaw, yet for the opposite reason than usual.

And this time, he rubbed his jaw, his gaze colliding with anything but my own. "I'm sorry, Lady Catherina. I truly am. And you may have all the air you want."

I watched, arms folded over my chest, as past me he went, bounding up the remainder of the steps, either completely forgetting everything that had transpired over the last few minutes since he had swung open my bedroom door or sorely regretting it.

Coward.

Not that I cared. He was likely doing the better thing, while I stood here missing the delightful taste of his lips. Ugh, but I shouldn't have succumbed to such weakness as to actually let him kiss me...and like it. Though try as I might, I couldn't regret doing it. I had just given that "good" man a reason to keep his distance anyway. Perhaps 'twas not the worst of ideas after all.

I trudged up the last of the steps, shoving away any and every last thought of Bennet and kissing from my mind.

He could feel the misty air through the crack in the door, could feel the figure sneak into his cabin with all the same stealth as a fox in the night. Or, in this case, a *Foxe* in the night.

Timothy Wilde heaved a rough sigh, staggering out of his bed as Bryant Foxe, the captain of the *Raven*, shut the door to Timothy's room. He was far from accustom to uninvited visitors at night, but Foxe was known for his odd way of striking up business. He really should've been a merchant rather than a pirate. But if Foxe was on board, then he had information. Information that Timothy would greatly appreciate.

"Well, Wilde, ye canna say I've no skill. I found 'er." Foxe folded his arms over his broad chest and leaned his back against the door.

Timothy ought to have been taken aback by Foxe's quick search. But he wasn't, for he could only wonder if his scout was actually spouting truth or mere observation gathered from random rumors. Considering a lot was on the line for the other man, Timothy opted for the first. Foxe wouldn't risk his life over naught but inaccuracy, now would he?

"Right, then. Where she be?"

Foxe chuckled, though 'twas a dry, mirthless laugh. "On some fancy English merchant ship. The *Jessica*. I trow, the girl 'as lost 'er bloomin' mind. A merchant ship. Ha, the wench woulda 'ad a much better life on mine."

Timothy frowned. If the man could only be more vague. "An' where be this ship?"

"'Round about a 'undred miles from Lisbon. Shan't take ye but a few days to arrive at her side," was Foxe's reply in an almost agitated tone. Timothy knew what the man wanted, but he still had quite a ways to go before he gained it. Not that he necessarily would.

"Me? Foxe, I tol' ye t' *bring* her t' me. Not tell me where she be. Now, go uphold yer part o' the deal." Timothy inched closer to Foxe, sensing the man's fear and irritation rather than seeing it.

"I be wantin' tha' girl o' yers first. Then I'll brin' ye *her*." Foxe took a step forward as well, his hand coming to rest upon the hilt of the cutlass that hung at his hip.

"Blackie's first. Then we'll see 'bout discussin' the other," Timothy ground out, prepared to draw his knife from its sheath.

Gears turned in Foxe's dark eye as he stumbled back several steps. The man wasn't gòrach; he would know what was best for him. And what was best for him was to be gone before Timothy's bubbling anger boiled over.

Releasing his cutlass, Foxe sighed. "Right then. Ye'll have her directly."

"I had better." And he would.

Chapter 8

A scream tears through the humid air, ringing through my ears in its sorrowful tone. Only one person carries such a familiar voice. Only one person would call out my name. Julius.

From where I sit in my dank, dark prison, I reach out, grabbing at the air, wishing I could hold my brother close. But it is no use, for I know that Wilde has him in his clutches. And what can I do, chained here in a pool of blood? I could not save Father from Wilde's blade, and I cannot save Julius from Wilde's torment. I can only hope that the villain will not slay my brother as well. He is only eleven, still so young, with so much life and promise. He cannot meet his end so soon. He must carry on the Blackstone name. But that is what has brought this plague among us, is it not? Our prized name.

At the sound of Julius's next cry, of his final goodbye, I scream in anguish.

Anguish. It crept its claws up my back, sinking its long nails into my skin. I jerked up, shaking myself from my nightmare, though the horror of the day so long ago would not leave my mind.

Anguish. It was what I suffered from day and night.

Anguish. What likely held Julius himself captive.

Anguish. What caused those childish tears to spring to my eyes.

I never cried. Not since the day Father had died. But now, in the peaceful dark of night, I cried. I buried my head in my pillow and let out all of that anguish, all of those pent-up sorrows.

A soft *shh* whispered through the air as a hand found its place on my back, rubbing circles there. But I knew this hand. 'Twas not the hand of anguish, as was Wilde's, but neither was it Bennet's, a hand that would comfort. Nay, this was a hand that took. A hand that turned the oars of his rowboat and climbed its way on board a ship. A hand that silently unlocked doors and tied up wrists.

Immediately I ceased my infantile sobbing and reached slowly, carefully, underneath my pillow, allowing my fingers to close around the handle of my knife. Then I lunged.

A curse left Captain Bryant Foxe's lips as he grabbed my wrists, attempting to resist the feel of my blade. "What the deuce, Blackie?" he whispered into the night air, his voice for once untainted by rum. "Can't show yer fellow captain a wee bit more respect?"

I rolled my eye as I scurried off my bed and planted my feet on the cold pine floor, tempted to right then and there kill him. But what good would that do me? "I believe I am the one needing respect, man. Why are you here?"

Foxe, ever the thespian, splayed a hand over his heart, stepping back with a mocking sigh of disappointment. "Straight to the point, are ye? Well, surely I can least fish out an apology from ye b'fore we begin with the abductin'. Tell me, m'dear, why ye'd leave me, who be lovin' ye so much, for a landlubber?"

I wanted to roll my eye again over Foxe's incorrect description of Bennet, but I decided against it. Knowing Foxe wouldn't yet hurt me, and that the real reason for his presence was likely not entirely his idea, I remained still. And gave in to playing along with Foxe's dramatics.

"Oh, but you see, his lordship is just ever so much handsomer than you. I could not resist," I replied, trying—and failing—at infusing heartsick sorrow into my tone. I was no actor, after all.

Foxe frowned, his arms crossing over his chest, his beady black eye glistening with a combination of contempt and desire. Odd, I found it, how both his and Bennet's eyes were the same color, yet so very different. Not that eyes were of any consequence to me.

"I coulda offered ye more, a life like yer *athair*'s," was Foxe's reply, his tone dripping with lust.

I only huffed. The man wouldn't bother with his silly pleading if he knew that I was more than just a female, more than just something he could use for a time. "I have no need for you, Foxe. And I am not that landlubber's anyway. Now can we get back to the original subject—why you are here at this time of night?"

"Aye. That." Foxe pulled out his cutlass and leveled it at my throat, and I wasn't sure if he figured my capturing would be that simple or if he was naught but playing with me. I opted for the first. Only Charlie and Bennet knew I had to be rendered unconscious before I could be taken captive. And Bennet knew that all too well, I was sure.

I tilted my head back to avoid the cutlass, jumped back onto my bed, then reached down to grab the sword that I knew Bennet had hidden beneath the matress. As soon as the cold metal of the hilt touched my hand, I crossed the length of the mattress, jumped off, then positioned my sword at Foxe's back.

"Blackstone taught ye well, I see," Foxe said, disbelief belying the to-the-point statement. He spun around to face me, clashing his cutlass against mine with a resounding clang that might have aroused the entire ship.

A parry from me and a thrust from the opposer, and then we were in the midst of a miniature battle within the small space that was my temporary bedchamber. Oh yes, the perfect place for a sword-fight indeed.

I wasn't entirely certainly why we were fighting, for 'twould accomplish nothing. Foxe would want me alive, and I did not want a dead body in my room. But the least I could do was convince Foxe to return to the *Raven* before I slayed him. Not that I planned on killing him in cold blood. I was not that harsh.

But our battling did not last long, for soon I heard the door swing open, followed by familiar footfalls and a muttered curse from Foxe.

"I am in the middle of something, Bennet," I called over my shoulder to my actual captor. "You may return to your bed. My friend here shall be returning to his ship very soon."

Foxe raised an eyebrow at the statement, while Bennet's steps came closer. "So ye mean t' tell me tha' ye'll be a-comin' with me?" he questioned, parrying my next blow.

"Most assuredly not. You shall be returning empty-handed." I pulled my sword back before stepping backwards...and tripping over my bare feet to stumble right into the familiar arms of Xavier Bennet.

"Wilde will kill me."

Immediately, and not from his touch this time, I jerked away from Bennet's hold and walked up to Foxe as he sheathed his sword. "Wilde put you up to this?" Dash it, but I should've know. Foxe wasn't such a fool as to tangle with the viper again unless fueled by fire itself.

He cocked his head, his eye flashing almost fearfully. "Nay. I might have offered."

I could only sigh. Despite all the past Foxe and I had, we truly weren't enemies, and all I could feel for the man was pity. He had likely offered to find me in return for Wilde's eldest daughter Crimson. And, of course, that meant Wilde would get me, but I knew he wouldn't relinquish his child. Either from lack of honor on his word or from love. I opted for the first. That villain had no love in his heart, not even for the children of his youth.

Really, though, what had ever possessed Foxe to do such a fool thing? He might as well have hung himself from the yardarm!

"Why in all the world would you make such a stupid decision? Y'know I ain't gonna just hand meself over to the likes of ye to die at the hand of Timothy Wilde. My word, matey! Have ye lost yer deuced mind?" I was yelling now, and my speech was coming out rough and choppy as though I were drunk.

And Bennet was gripping my arm now, holding me back from trying to pound some sense into the head of that ignorant man before me.

And Foxe was wincing, his gaze darting everywhere but at me. He looked to Bennet, and a small smile crept up his lips. "She be a spitfire, don't she?"

I could hear Bennet chuckle, replying with a hearty yes, and I spun around and gave him a good and fiery slap across the mouth. "This be me conversation 'ere, Bennet. And I appreciate it if ye stay out o' it."

He only grinned, the rogue, and pinned me to his chest.

I ignored him and looked to Foxe. "Go home, Bryant. Who gives a fig about Crimmy Wilde anyhow? Go back t' the *Raven* and find yerself a ship to raid, aye?"

There was a small moment of hesitation, gears seeming to turn behind that single black eye before Foxe nodded solemnly, slipping past Bennet and I. "Aye, Blackie. I'll go. But when Wilde kills me, just know I did it for ye," he mumbled softly.

Oh, but the man was a wreck. "And I thank ye for it, Foxe. Have a good night now," I called after him as he made his way across deck before swinging himself over the railing to climb down the Jacob's ladder to where his rowboat awaited him.

Then he was gone, leaving me in the darkness. Suddenly, everything came flooding back, chasing away the adrenaline of battle and draining my veins of all my strength. Weary, I crumpled on the ground beneath me as my head began to spin.

Xavier said something, but I couldn't hear. I thought I felt arms slide around my waist, but I didn't care. Xavier was likely cradling me in his arms now, but all I saw was Julius's young face in my mind's eye.

I couldn't bear the thought...but what had Wilde done to him? Was Julius even now dead? And if he wasn't, was he lying in the cargo hold of the *Rogue Maiden*, sick and bleeding? Or had Wilde somehow bestowed nonexistent mercy upon him and refrain from hurting him? Perhaps even fed him and clothed him?

Likely not. The scoundrel had probably already slayed him, as he desperately wanted to do to me.

If only I could easily talk Timothy Wilde out of his nefarious plan to torture and kill every Blackstone as I could Foxe out of his stupid ideas to capture me. If only I could talk Bennet out of dragging me to England as well.

I was helpless. Completely and utterly helpless. I was bound for England, with likely no escape. I was bound for Davy Jones's locker, with no possible way to avoid that. Wilde would find me, sooner rather than later, especially if Foxe had told him where the *Jessica* floated. We were stopping next in Lisbon for a spell, I knew, and Wilde could easily catch me there.

With a moan of despair, I sat up, only then realizing I was held against Xavier's chest while he sat on my—his—bed. "Will you ever leave me be, sir?" I questioned, only half serious. I could not help it if I was crumpling under the weight of the world.

And Xavier couldn't help it if he was so good as to comfort me. Not that I was a simpering princess in need of comfort. He was just doing his duty as a gentleman, I supposed.

"I'm afraid not, dear," he replied with a rakish grin that had me, of all people, smiling back.

I would never admit it, not even to myself, but I had missed the captain over the past four days. Ever since our mistake of a kiss, he had grown rather distant. I supposed it took a five minute battle to bring him back, aye? Not that I would make the error of letting him kiss me again, or that he would think to kiss me to begin with.

Not that I hadn't liked it; I had. It was just that, well… Oh, what did it matter?

"Well then, I shall have to find a way to change that," I teased. Maybe I truly didn't want him to leave me alone. Or maybe I just liked having him wrapped around my finger.

Xavier only chuckled, situating me on his lap so that he could meet my gaze. Or at least that was the only reason I let him situate me on his lap. Because I really ought not to be sitting on his knee.

He reached out and brushed aside a small strand of hair that had fallen over my one eye, his fingers searing my skin. I needed to pull away, to demand he leave, then get some rest—but I remained still, as if mesmerized by him and those fathomless eyes of his. Dash it, but I was the one wrapped around his finger.

"What happened?"

His words were a whisper barely audible, one that floated through the air, breaking me away from my careening trail of thoughts. And his voice was one filled with compassion and something akin to heartache, something I certainly didn't want to dwell on. Just like the cause of my wound that he questioned so softly.

"A small mistake. 'Tis of no matter," I replied as truthfully as I could, though 'twas only obvious Xavier sensed my dishonesty.

"Then you can tell me, yes?"

Oh, but he was as slimy as an eel. How was I to back out of that? Just say no? As if Xavier Bennet would settle for a simple no. "'Twas Wilde. He cut my eye. Now please, go away."

He only grunted, as if resisting the urge to further interrogate me, and rose. "Not before you tell me what that was about and who on God's green earth that man was."

Ah, now there was that rough concern that was most assuredly safer than his lover-like heartache. "Captain Bryant Foxe of the *Raven*. He and my father had a bit of a feud going on nigh unto eighteen years ago. And after Father died, Foxe seemed interested in my taking up permanent residence on his ship. Of course I rejected that offer."

"And so he's come to fetch you after what, ten years?"

"Nine and one quarter. But no. He struck up a deal with Wilde, offering to fetch me—or more bluntly, drag me to the gallows that await me—for Wilde in return for Wilde's oldest daughter Crimson." I had folded my arms over my chest, having scooted across the bed to lean back up against the wall with feigned nonchalance.

In good sooth, I was shaking in my boots over the fact that Wilde could be only a few miles away from killing me. I didn't want to die. Deserved it, yes, as all slandering and thieving pirates did. But desiring the end of my existence, most assuredly not. But how was I to escape my obvious fate? I would die eventually; why not sooner and at the hand of my greatest enemy?

Xavier remained silent, his head cocked in deep contemplation. Then he began to pace, as I knew he did when worried. Just like Father. "Tell me, Rina, who is this Wilde fellow?"

I wanted to give him the vague answer, the one that didn't cause me so much grief, but once my mouth opened, I couldn't stop the words from flowing out. "Timothy Wilde, the captain of the *Rogue Maiden*, was the son of the chief of the Wilde clan in Scotland. Was, until my father's father killed every last member but him, woman, child, and all. That was, though, before my father was ever born, when Wilde was a toddler.

"But Wilde never forgot that day, and set out to murder every last human being bearing the name of Blackstone, innocent for his people's slaying or not. He killed my father in cold blood." I slammed my jaw shut, knowing what would follow. I would say how I sat there and watched him die, how my ears still burned from the sound of my brother's screams. I would tell Xavier of how Wilde had glared at me, his knife jamming so deep into my eye before my world went black. I would tell him of the hole inside my heart. And I wouldn't, couldn't, do that.

The words I had spoken already were enough. Enough to cause a tear to fall unbidden from my eye. Enough to cause Xavier to return to the bed beside me and wrap me in his strong, comforting arms and hold me close to his chest.

He was muttering something so quietly that I barely heard, but only enough to realize that he was praying. To his God. For me. Dash it all, but the man was too good to be true. And I was too vulnerable to think anything of it.

He held me there, praying over me in a soft voice for what seemed to be the entire night until he finally—much to my hidden chagrin—pulled away and looked me in the eye, his hands cupping my cheeks and forcing me to meet his gaze. Only love shined there. Something I hadn't seen in a man's eyes since the day Father looked to me before he took his last breath.

But I didn't deserve love.

From anyone.

And especially not from Xavier Bennet.

"Catherina," he began, his thumb swiping a tear away from my eye. "I won't let him get you. I promise."

Oh, how I wished I could believe him! But he could lock me in a dungeon a million miles underneath the ground, and Timothy Wilde would still find me. Of that one thing I was completely and utterly certain.

So I took this one moment to cast aside the worries and fears that I wasn't supposed to harbor, and leaned back into Xavier's arms, sliding my arms around his neck and laying my head on his shoulder.

But then the door creaked open again, and I knew this time 'twas Jonathan walking in, a person ever so much safer. It was his soft chuckle that gave him away. "Xavier, don't tell me that you and Lady Rina were the ones making all that noise?"

Though I didn't dare to release him, I felt Xavier shift slightly. "Not necessarily. We had a visitor by the name of Bryant Foxe. Fortunately, he has returned to his home just as you ought to return to your bed."

Jonathan only tossed his head back and laughed, a sound so pleasant and mirthful yet not as deep and delightful as Xavier's. "And leave my brother and a pirate alone at night without a chaperon? I think not."

Xavier rolled his eyes at that comment, tearing himself away from me. Which left me suddenly chilled and wishing for his embrace. "She was almost killed. I see that as a good reason to comfort someone, middle of the night or not."

At his extremely false explanation, I jumped off the bed and crossed my arms. "Killed? Comfort? Ha! Only one person has the courage to even think of killing me, and it certainly isn't Foxe. And I, of all people, need no comfort. So the both of you may carry your blasted behinds out of my room. Immediately."

Jonathan was chuckling harder at that, and Xavier was rising from my bed with a fierce grin. 'Twas the latter that blew me a kiss as he stepped out of the doorway and disappeared into the night that was as dark and mysterious as the man himself.

Ugh. I was going to need a drink after this.

Chapter 9

I bounded down the stairs to the hold, hoping against hope that I would find Rina there. After what had happened only five hours ago last night, I wouldn't much blame her if she had decided to leave. I probably would as well, but I was going to hold onto the hope that she was down below deck with the rest of my precious cargo. Not that I thought of Rina as cargo.

As I hurried down the last two steps, the sound of something akin to either bird-squawking or drunken singing met my ears. I wanted to opt for the first, but I knew the voice that was singing out some incomprehensible song in a rough English. Aye, 'twas drunken singing to be sure.

"Rina, what in the name of all that's holy are you doing?" I questioned as I rounded a crate to reach her. "Surely you don't plan on being staggering drunk all day, do you?"

The lady only chuckled, waving her arm around as rum sloshed out of the bottle she held. "I don't stagger, I 'ave ye know. I sway. Like t' music. Wobble a bit, mayhap. But I sure don't stagger. So I'd 'preciate it if ye didn't 'cuse me o' such."

She began to chuckle again, and I would have appreciated the sound if she weren't out of her right mind while doing it.

I sat myself down on the crate beside her, resting my elbows on my thighs as I examined her through the faint light. Goodness, but she was beautiful, even at eight and twenty, even after years of being hardened by the sea and burned by the sun. Her face, normally tight in that grim expression of hers, was relaxed, her features soft. Her lips were upturned in the slightest of grins, and her eye, almost green in the dimness, glistened in what light there was. Her hair tumbled over her back in long, silky waves, and I longed to run my fingers through the tresses, but I knew better than to do so. If she was huffy sober, then I could only imagine what she would do while inebriated. And if anyone knew the risk of drinking, 'twas I.

But even as I told myself not to, my hand involuntarily reached out and my fingers twirled around the soft curls. I expected her to jerk away, to slap me as she was wont to do, or perhaps to just scold me, but instead she leaned into my touch and nestled into my side. The feel of her against me was overwhelming, and it was all I could do to remain still. She smelled of oranges and rum, a sickly sweet scent that beckoned me to drown in it. Now I was really in trouble.

As if sensing my sudden discomfort, Rina shifted slightly so that she was facing me and cleared her throat. "Your father's a seaman, aye?"

For a moment I was taken back by her random inquiry, my thoughts still on our close proximity, but I soon snapped back into reality. "Was."

She cocked a brow at that. "And what d'ye mean by 'was'?"

"He spent three years in the Royal Navy. That was were he met Charlie."

At the mention of her greatest enemy, she snickered. "Three years o' service t' the King o' England don't necessarily make one a seaman."

"The next eight years he spent as a pirate captain. Mayhap you've heard of him. He was called Captain Ben of the *Justice*."

Rina jerked up at that, her eye widening. "Collin Bennet is your father? Ye jest!" She slammed her bottle against the crate underneath her. "The honorable Xavier Bennet, the son of a pirate! Ha, 'tis the greatest I've heard all me life. Ye really think I'm gonna believe tha', now do ye? 'Tis a wonder I didn't recognize the name. And the resembl-ance. Ye really do look like Ben, y'know. Spittin' image o' 'im."

Her voice drifted off then, her expression growing grim, and her fingers tightened around her bottle. "I s'pose that 'cause o' all tha' pirate blood in yer veins, ye'll 'ave a little mercy on a fellow pirate's child and won't be turnin' me in."

I startled at the question. Turn her in? Did she really think that I would up and have her hanged? She was a criminal and deserved to be hanged for piracy, I knew, but her father would have her pardoned, of that I was sure. And I had no right to turn her in.

All right, I had captured the most notorious female pirate captain that had ever sailed the Seven Seas, but I hadn't done so to have her hanged.

I crossed my arms over my chest and glared at her. "Do you really think so highly of yourself that someone would go to all that trouble to have you hanged?"

Rina chuckled, but 'twas a dry, mirthless laugh so unlike her earlier one. But that was all I could expect from her anyway. "I know a few people who would like to see me dead."

"As in all those poor people you stole from? All those whose family members you slayed?" I stopped myself there, knowing better than to press, to shove her sins into her face. For I myself had sinned, had ruined a family. And still it laid heavily on my conscience, the remembrance of that dreaded day, the guilt I carried. But Christ had forgiven me, and I had even sought out the forgiveness of the man's family. They might not have fully forgiven, but at least they knew I cared. And I was sure that Rina would understand how many lives her profession had effected, likely already did.

So I was not surprised when Rina jumped up, throwing her bottle to the ground, and wagged a finger at me. "The poor I stoled from? People I slayed? I'll tell ye, Mr. Perfect, tha' I ain't no worse than the rest o' ye high-an'-mighty folks.

"Those men I killed, they knew wha' was comin'. They knowed their fate. Those families tha 'lowed their menfolk t' be sailin' out on these dang'rous seas, they knew the consequences. Those tha' loaded up ships just like this 'ere with precious cargo worth plenty o' money knew tha' I'd be comin', knew somehow, someday, their ship'd sink, their cargo'd be stolen.

"'Tis the risk o' shipping, me good sir. Ye yerself know the risk, and yet here ye be, throwin' it in me face. Why don' ye tell yer father the same, aye? Let 'im hang for all 'is filthy sins! I say, Bennet, but I am not the only one who has fallen short of the glory of your God."

With that said, she stomped away, weaving through the hold until she reached the stairway.

Wisdom told me not to follow, not to bother objecting, for she was right. She was not the only one who had fallen short, for all have. Even the greatest of saints to the lowest of criminals. But I stood up and followed after her anyway. Halfway up the steps, I grabbed her arm and spun her towards me, only to find her one eye glistening with tears.

She crumpled against me, laying her head on my shoulder as she wound her arms around my waist.

I returned the embrace, pulling her to me as I slid my own arms around her. "I'm sorry, Rina. I truly am. I shouldn't have said anything," I whispered, rubbing my hand over her back.

How could I be so cruel? This woman had only just went through more in one night than most ladies did in their entire lives. How would I feel if I suffered day and night from nightmares or came so close to being taken to my father's killer? How would I feel if my entire world was falling into thousands of little pieces, and I had absolutely no control of the outcome?

Rina sniffled, shaking her head against my neck. "Nay, Xavier. You are right. I deserved to be hanged, and you ought to do the honors. I'm wretched, and I know it."

At the words, my heart broke.

I balled up the back of Bennet's shirt in my fist, scolding myself for being so dashed emotional. But when one combined drink with heartache, one could only expect the worst of outcomes. Such as holding on to Xavier Bennet as though my life depended on it.

Come to think of it, it likely did.

I shoved those blasted tears back into my eye, determined not to cry. Not again. Crying was a weakness reserved for querulous little ladies with absolutely no control. And I was not weak, for I had control over every thought in my mind. Or at least I had until Xavier came and shattered my world.

With one last sniffle, I pulled away just enough to met the gaze of my captor, only to be surprised by the wounded look in his eyes. This man was an enigma beyond all others. At one moment he was rebuking my every action, and yet now he looked at me with sorrow. Sorrow over what, my obvious lack of self-discipline and common conscience? I did not need his proud pity or his rebukes. I did not need him at all.

But I wanted him.

"Rina, I don't ever want you to think of yourself as wretched. Do you hear me?"

I raised an eyebrow at the infuriating man, resisting the urge to roll my eye. "Aye. I am not deaf."

Xavier sighed at that, his hold on me tightening. Oh, why did I continuously put myself into such compromising positions? I never behaved in this way with any other person, any other man, yet somehow 'twas Xavier Bennet that had managed to strip me of all my control and render me helpless.

"I know. And you are not wretched either," Xavier replied in a strained tone that would have pulled at any other woman's heartstrings. But not mine.

"And what makes you say that? You're the one who just reminded me of all those poor souls out there whose lives have been ruined by my horrid actions. Oh, but I have destroyed the world! Shoot me now!" Feigning distress, I bent back in his arms, splaying a hand over my forehead as though I were to faint as I slid my eye closed.

I remained still, slowing my breathing for a long moment before I peeked up at Bennet from under my lashes. He only glared at me, his midnight eyes swirling with mirth. Aye, I certainly was no actor.

I straightened and returned the glower. "Well, what have you to say for yourself, hypocrite?"

He reached up and brushed aside a strand of hair that had fallen over my eye, his touch searing my skin. "You may do some wretched things, Catherina, but *you* are not wretched. You were made in the perfect image of God. You just haven't realized that quite yet."

The words, spoken in that soft voice of his, sent a pang through my stone heart. I should have known he would say something all sweet and righteous like that. Should've known that no matter how long I had believed Father's philosophy I would still wonder if there really was a God out there. One that was full of love like Charlie and Mary had mentioned every now and then. One that forgave and cleansed and forgot. One that loved no matter what. But 'twas all a foolish fantasy. Of course Xavier would believe it, for he had never once missed the mark or made a mistake. He was the epitome of all that was good and perfect and honorable, and I despised him for it.

"And what are you, Mr. Perfect? A prophet or some sort of wizard that can see inside hearts, hmm?" I countered, wanting, no, needing him to falter.

Bennet chuckled, his thumb beginning to caress my cheek. "I am not a prophet, and I certainly am not a wizard, my dear. But neither am I perfect. There is only One who is perfect."

I rolled my eye then, desperately wishing I could wiggle out of his hold and vanish into thin air to keep from hearing all of this man's holier-than-thou preaching. But he held tight to me, his fathomless black gaze holding me captive.

"What did you do that was so terrible?" I questioned, unable to keep the sarcasm from dripping from my tone. "Steal an apple? Refuse to clean up your room? Oh, perhaps you told a lie! My word, what a sinner you are!" I threw a hand over my mouth with a gasp.

"I killed a man, Rina."

For a moment I stood there unmoving, the words still hanging in the air between us rather than having gone through my ears to my brain. Slowly my hand dropped, and my breathing grew deeper.

Xavier Bennet, a murderer! 'Twas impossible.

"Surely you jest." He couldn't have killed someone, not this perfect man. Not that it was so atrocious a thought, that I knew a murderer, for I myself was one. 'Twas the thought of someone so perfect having been the one to commit the crime. And that he thought one measly murder all that awful.

Xavier nodded in reply, his gaze tearing from mine and moving somewhere past my ear.

Ah, but I knew well the look in his eyes. 'Twas the familiar feeling of guilt. Of heartrending shame. I knew it all too well. It resurfaced every time I ported, every time money was exchanged, every time a ship came into view. But every time I reminded myself that this was my life, not a crime, not a mistake. And then the guilt, the shame, would disappear.

I placed a finger underneath Xavier's chin and turned his head back toward me. "And I have killed more men than one can count. Xavier, do not pretend as though one death on your hands is such a sin. You are making me out to be a criminal." I tried—and failed—at pasting a smile onto my face, at infusing a teasing tone into my voice.

He raised a brow, giving me that mocking look of his. "You *are* a criminal."

"And what did I, a sweet little innocent lady, ever do wrong?" I set my hands on his shoulders, arching my back, and grinned.

Xavier smirked, his eyes sparkling in that dangerous way. "You stole my heart."

My jaw dropped, and I squirmed in his grasp, but Xavier only held me closer, leaned in, and pressed his lips to mine. For the second time.

I ceased my squirming and melted into him. Oh, but the knave had me wrapped around his finger. And I only held onto that finger of his. I wound my arms around his neck and returned his kiss as he pressed even deeper, his mouth moving hungrily over mine. My fingers tangled in the few loose strands of silky hair that had managed to escape Xavier's queue as his hands crept up my back, his touch warming me even as it made my blood run cold. I should not, could not, let him touch me.

And yet I could not pull away.

Slowly, though, Xavier broke away, gentling his kiss before placing his forehead on mine. His breathing was slow and ragged, his chest heaving just as mine was. His delightful scent of lime and pine flooded my senses. And his eyes, so dark and coruscant, were all but smiling at me with that roguish gleam.

I could only remain unmoving, still twirling my fingers through his hair. "What happened to 'I'm sorry, that will never happen again'?" I questioned breathlessly, letting one hand move to cup his cheek, to feel the stubble on his jaw.

"Ah, but I never said it would not happen again." He leaned in and touched his lips to mine in a feather-light kiss that rattled me just as much as the one before.

I had to resist the urge to angle my mouth over his and drown in him once again, and instead shifted myself onto the next step, putting a safe distance between us. Although nothing was truly safe when it came to Xavier Bennet.

"But you regretted it, did you not?" I raised an eyebrow, hoping to get him to admit that he despised kissing me, that he would never again attempt such a feat, even as I liked the idea of feeding my pride with his desire for me.

Bennet cocked his head, his gaze raking over me with that same glint countless other men had in their eyes whenever looking at me. Perhaps he wasn't as honorable as he seemed. But then his eyes found their way back up to mine and he grinned. "Not quite. And I get the distinct feeling you didn't either."

He was right. I didn't regret a single moment of it. But if he ever tried something like that again, *he* would regret ever messing with Captain Rina Blackstone.

"What the deuce?" Timothy Wilde glared at the messenger who stood before him, shaking in his boots. "Wha' d'ye mean, 'Foxe ain't coming,' lad?! That man oughta get his bloomin' b'hind o'er here with tha' blasted chit b'fore I kill 'im too!"

He started to pace, his fingers itching to grab Foxe's neck and squeeze the ever-living daylights out of him. What had happened for the man to so quickly turn on him? Had he lost his dashed mind? Or what if Blackie had somehow managed to slit his throat? She was a Blackstone, after all. Killing was just like breathing for those infernal savages. Oh, but she had better not have killed that man. He was Timothy's only chance at catching her. Not that he was solely dependent upon Foxe. And not that he didn't necessarily know how and where to find her.

"Weel, lad, wha' happened t' Foxe, eh? Blackie 'ave 'im dance the hempen jig or somethin'?" Timothy ceased pacing and faced the boy, who was no more than ten and seven, he was sure.

"Don't rightly know, sir," the boy said, his voice's trembling stilling as he steeled his shoulders. "I can only say he just up an' turned his ship 'round."

Timothy cocked a brow, feeling the questions rattle through his brain. “Up an’ turned around, aye? No word t’ ‘is employer. Tha’ man be a coward, I say. A yellow-bellied coward o’ a man. An’ he calls ‘imself a pirate. Scared o’ naught but a stupid wench. Ugh, I shoulda killed her when I had the chance.”

The lad glanced up at him then, confusion etched in his brow. “Why didn’t ye, sir?”

Timothy could only sigh, berating himself for what was likely the fifty trillionth time ever since that fateful day. “Torture, lad. I figured a girl o’ only ten and eight wouldna stay alive fer long. Likely throw herself o’erboard in pain. She be a strong one, though. Much like me Crimson. And tha’ fact may be the death o’ me.”

Because if he saw a man with a cutlass at his daughter’s throat… But he wouldn’t think like that. Rina Blackstone was no girl, an innocent young woman. Nay, she was a killer. Had the blood of her ancestors flowing through her veins. And she was just as vicious.

And he would be rid of every last murderous Blackstone even if it killed him.

Chapter 10

I had been on the *Jessica* for exactly two weeks. My life had been ruined for exactly two weeks. All of my hard-earned control had been gone for exactly two weeks. I'd had the extreme displeasure of knowing Xavier Bennet for exactly two weeks. And I had been a wretched mess for an entire fortnight.

Just last night I had awoken to yet another nightmare, had been cradled in Bennet's strong arms, then had returned to my slumber. Morning had come, and I had hurried out of my stuffy cabin for a breath of fresh air and something to eat. Noon had arrived, and then I'd spent the rest of the afternoon watching the sea, my home, float away and land float nearer.

We were almost to Lisbon, our one and only stop before sailing straight to England, my one and only chance to escape before I was trapped on land forever. And I had never been happier.

'Twould not be long before I could return to the *Rina*. I had only to disappear from my captor's sights and find a way to Gijón, where Elliot should've been sailing toward now.

It was less my well-being that I was worried for, for which I was wishing to return home, as I knew I would be fine. Father or no father awaiting me in London, safety or no safety available near a man like Bennet, I would be fine. 'Twas my crew I was worried for. Oh, Elliot would have stepped up as captain, and would do splendidly, I was certain. Aside from passing out on deck and having no one to berate him for it later.

Keaton handled most everything anyway. Of course, he would take up the accounting, a job that was actually supposed to be his. And Charlie would be able to keep things running just as Father would have wanted. 'Twas not they in particular that had me worried.

'Twas Roger, Ellie, and Billy.

It would be much harder for Billy to adjust to being on board my ship without the rightful captain present. And if he was more of a troublemaker than I had given him credit for, problems could arise. Roger, troublemaker I already knew him to be, was continually on my mind. Had Elliot and Keaton found solid proof that he had been stealing? If so, had he been properly disposed of?

And then there was Ellie. Despite how much he loved his son, Elliot would not be able to take care of him as I could. Aye, he was the boy's father, but I had been the one to hold his hand as he toddled around the *Rina*, had fed him as a babe. 'Twas the motherly instinct females were equipped with. I could not expect the men to provide that same kind of care, especially not while occupied with their duties. And so he was the one that induced the most concern in my mind.

Which was why I had to get home. And quickly.

I shifted on the railing I sat on, wishing I could just miraculously float through the air back to my ship. But I was no more an angel than Bennet was.

The sun glinted off something, casting a bright glitter onto the ocean's waves. I followed the beam of light to where my hand rested on the railing. A grin turned up my lips at the sight of the sparkling golden ring placed on my ring finger. It had been my father's, and he had worn it on his hand every day of his life. Until he'd passed it down to me.

Even when I had asked, he had never told me where or when he had found it, if it had been a family heirloom or a stolen treasure, but I knew it to be important. I could remember clearly the moment when, breathing his last, he had pressed the band into my palm. It had not fit my finger then, at ten and eight, but it had soon grown on me. I myself hadn't taken it off once since then. It reminded me of who I was—Maverick Blackstone's daughter. A pirate captain that was unbeatable. A woman with a place on this earth of men only. And most assuredly not the daughter of a duke.

It was a simple band crafted out of pure gold. On the center of the ring was engraved a symbol—of what, I had never known. Yet another secret of Father's. 'Twas a mere cross-like shape with a single ruby embedded in the center of the emblem. What was odd, though, was that as I gazed at it for what was likely the one millionth time, the symbol resembled something that I had seen before. But I had only seen this sign on the ring… Or had I?

I looked down at where the name of Bennet's vessel was painted across the hull. Beside the red words was an engraving in the wood. A cross. With a small red dot in the center. A seal.

And yet I could not figure out what it could mean.

Either there was more to this "father" story than Bennet was telling me, or my father and Bennet's were connected. The latter was the most likely, I knew, as both had been pirate captains during the same time. Both had known Charlie as well. That had to be it. Perhaps I could ask Bennet about it later.

Then again, perhaps I ought to continue avoiding that odious man and concentrate on getting my behind back on my ship.

Two days had passed since we had been alone together—unless one counted last night, which I didn't—and I intended to keep it that way. I didn't want to see nor hear tell of that man ever again in my entire life. And I most assuredly did not want to feel his lips upon mine.

The sun slowly sunk behind the horizon, drowning in the ocean's waves, as the giant star sent forth a rainbow of colors. Pink and orange splattered the sea, purple tainting the blue sky above. The day was coming to an end, Lisbon drifting closer and closer by the second. We would be there by nightfall. And I could be home by the end of the week.

Ah, but 'twas so close I could taste it! I would be rid of this stupid myth, of Bennet, and of all those doubts and questions that floated through the back of my mind.

How could I help it, if I wondered? If I questioned everything I had ever known? It could still be true, I knew, that I wasn't Father's child. For there were subtle clues that pointed to this newfound rumor. Father had never spoken of my mother, for one, and had never mentioned a relationship—marriage or one-time—between himself and a woman. Julius's mother was the only person he had ever been with that I knew of.

And he had always avoided the subject of his early life, such as his parents and where he had grown up. All I knew of his life was that his parents hadn't married until he was ten, and that he had left for the sea at eighteen. Just like with the ring, he had never told me. But I had never questioned until now. Now, when it was too late.

I swung my legs off the railing and settled myself on the deck, wishing with all my might that I could banish all the uncertainty, that I could remain as trusting as I had been as a child. That I could retain that childlike faith I had once had.

Did Julius ever doubt? Did he ever wonder if perhaps Father had withheld something from us, whether it be about myself or us both? Was he perhaps sitting on Wilde's ship this very moment just wondering about his life, his future? Or was he content, never questioning his very existence or pondering the thought that there could be more to life than pirating?

Ugh. I was not supposed to doubt; I was supposed to trust. And yet 'twas so difficult to trust anything anymore. I could not trust Bennet or even the memory of Father. I needed answers. Yet for how long would I dismiss whatever answers I found only because they did not align with what I had always known?

No! I wouldn't think like that. When I found my answers, they *would* align with what I had always known. There was no other way.

Unless…

I did not know what possessed me, what fueled me other than pure curiosity, and made me head straight across the deck to where Xav—Bennet stood watching Portugal drift nearer. But whatever 'twas, it could not be helped.

As soon as I reached the man's side, a twinge of regret shot through me. I shouldn't ask, not when every other question that I had had given me an undesired answer. In fact, I shouldn't even stand at his side. Not when every look in his dark eyes made my heart skip a beat, or when every smile that graced his lips caused me to grin in return.

But I didn't move except to turn and face him.

"Bennet, have you ever seen this symbol before?" I showed him the ring and watched his reaction. A very disappointing reaction.

His eyes lit up with recognition as a grin turned up his lips. He grasped my hand and examined the band with obvious interest. "Now where, may I ask, did you find this, my dear?"

Aye, I really shouldn't have asked. "'Twas my father's. The same is embedded on your ship's hull," I replied with a huff, the feel of his hand holding mine ruining my concentration.

"You are right on both accounts. This symbol is your father's seal."

Immediately, I jerked my hand back, stunned with fury. Though I should have been prepared for such an answer, as everything these days was shocking and just plain unrealistic, the answer was surprising.

The only way Father could've gotten that ring was if he had stolen it when he had abducted me.

The *Jessica* turned sharply as we pulled into the harbor, the acute turn resembling exactly what my life had done. Took a dramatic turn into the abyss. An abyss I couldn't get out of.

Unless I ran.

As soon as the ship docked, I would leave. I would get as far away from Bennet and everything that pointed to this Rothsford being my father as quickly as was humanly possible.

I gave Bennet one last look, one last sneer, before I walked away. Just as I would from all this that had ruined my life.

Chapter 11

Lisbon, Portugal
Late August 1683

The solid land of Portugal rested beneath my feet, my future placed before me. I could either stay with Bennet and his crew, leaving my fate in his hands, or I could disappear from their sights and leave my fate in my own hands.

I'd made up my mind, and there was to be no turning back.

I had gathered all of my things, and had managed to find my dagger and pistol, though I still could not locate my cutlass. Both of those had been secured in the belt that hid underneath my waistcoat. Pirate or not, a woman could never be safe from those unsavory sort of fellows that preyed upon any unaccompanied young lady. Though I was certainly not young and far from a proper lady, I myself needed protection time and again.

But most important of all my possessions was the small letter that rested safely in my pocket. I had stolen, shall we say, Charlie's letter to Bennet from the latter's hiding spot. Aye, 'twould only remind me of this unfortunate journey that I had taken, but as soon as I confronted Charlie about it, I could toss it in the sea and forever forget the last few weeks. Or at least I hoped to forget them.

The remainder of Bennet's crew hurried off the dock, following behind Bennet and his brothers.

Regrettably, I happened to be flanked by said brothers, David doing the most flanking while Jonathan carried on a conversation with the worst of the three brothers in front of me.

I knew I would never be able to escape from David's view, as he watched me like a hawk, and I had the feeling that if I was to flinch, he would pick me up and sling me over his shoulder. Jonathan, on the other hand, likely wouldn't notice. As for Bennet… He might not watch me as closely as David did, but I had caught his glances my way, and I would most assuredly rather be thrown over David's shoulder than pulled into Bennet's arms.

So I had to wait for the right time to slip away. When that right time would come, I didn't know.

Thus, I waited, my heart pounding with anticipation, sweat beading under my tricorn from the heat of the evening sun, my feet growing sore as we walked through the large city of Lisbon until we finally reached a moderate-sized inn where we—nay, everyone but I—would be staying while Bennet and his crew stocked up on supplies and probably posted a letter to the duke declaring that he had found the long-lost Lady Catherina.

Ha, but I wished I could see the look on both Bennet and Rothsford's face when I never showed up.

The sun had finally set, and the shadow of night had fallen over the city, coating everything in black. Good. The cover of night always made escapes much more simpler.

Bennet held the inn's door open while everyone filed in, and as the crowd of men made their way into the building, I weaved my way through them and snuck around the opposite side of the inn.

I stood unmoving, back pressed up against the brick wall, until I heard the door slam shut, then I ran.

It wasn't until everyone had eaten and the table had been cleared that I realized someone was missing. I looked across the table at the faces of my men. Men, men, men. Every. Single. One.

Immediately, I jerked upwards, knocking my chair to the floor with a crash. Blast it all to the moon and back! I picked the chair up and turned to David and Jon. "You two. With me. Now," I grounded out through clenched teeth as I swung my finger between them.

They both rose without question and followed me out of the inn. We crossed the street, all but running to the livery, and quickly rented three horses and mounted them as I barked out orders for Jon to head east, David south, while I galloped towards the north.

I had to find Rina, even if it was the very last thing I did. I couldn't let that girl get away after all that I had went through to get her in the first place. Ugh, but I shouldn't have let her out of my sight! I had thought that after everything that had happened between us, after what she had found out about the ring on her finger, that she had come to trust me, if only a little bit. She hadn't tried to escape in over a week, hadn't attempted to kill me in a week and a half, hadn't jerked away from my touch in almost as long. I had thought that I had actually gotten through to her, even if in just a couple of ways.

Apparently not.

I nudged my horse into full speed, whizzing through the streets. If I knew Rina—and I figured I did, albeit somewhat—she wouldn't have stopped for anything until she was miles away from me. Though it was nearing midnight, she wouldn't have snuck into an inn or even an alleyway to rest before dawn. Nay, she would've charged full-on to wherever she planned to go. And as fast as possible.

But even still, her legs wouldn't have carried her very far, and she hadn't the slightest clue as to how to ride a horse. So eventually, she would slow. Unless she came to where she was headed before then.

And where was she headed? I'd sent Jon towards the docks, so if she planned on sailing away, he would hopefully be there to catch her. And if she wanted to avoid detection and find a way to leave without bumping into any of my crew, she would head to the south, where she could obtain passage somewhere. Why I went north, I didn't know.

I glanced up at the full moon above me and could only thank God that He provided me with light for my path. Then again, He was also providing light for Rina, which wasn't necessarily in my favor. But I thanked Him anyway and prayed that He would help me find her.

At least, though I couldn't be sure I would ever have her back, I knew God was watching over her. And maybe, just maybe, these last couple weeks had effected her in some way. It was only one more step closer for her. I could only hope that perhaps God had used me in some way to bring her closer to Him.

But if I found her, then I wouldn't have to just hope for something to happen one day. Which was why I was going to find her, even if it took me all year.

I turned down a darkening alleyway, moving farther and farther away from the rushing waves of the sea. It had been an hour before I'd noticed her missing, so she had likely left just as we were entering the inn. Smart. So that would have given her an hour and a half by now to get somewhere.

I heaved a sigh, doubts creeping into my mind. This was probably not going to work. Even if I rode all night and morning, I wouldn't find her. Not if I didn't know where she was going.

I pulled my horse around the corner of a building and pulled him to a stop in front of the first building with candles flickering through the windows that I spotted. The building looked to be some sort of shop, and through the dark windows I could make out the silhouette of cheese and bread. Good. There was food in there. If anything, Rina could've stopped there for something to eat to keep her going.

I dismounted my horse, tied his reins up on one of the posts holding up the building's roof, and bounded up the steps to the door. I swung it open and stepped into the shop, the smell of cheese and rosemary reminding me of when Mother would cook some big feast whenever I returned home from the sea. Ah, but I couldn't wait to get back, to see my parents and little Beth and Marjorie, to feel the warm, cozy feeling of home. And I knew David and Jon felt the same.

I walked up to the counter and peered into a room in the back. "*Com licença*? Is there anyone back there?"

As soon as the words left my mouth, a portly older man wearing a flour-splattered apron walked out from the shadows of the room, his bearded face alight with a grin. "*Sim, senhor*? How may I help you?" He waved his hand over a selection of cheeses set out on a tray in front of me. "I have plenty of varieties and flavors and cheeses for every occasion!" he declared.

"Sim, that you do. But I am afraid that I'm not here for cheese nor bread. I was wondering if you have seen a young woman over a score old wearing an eyepatch, tricorn, and men's breeches. She reaches about this high." I raised my hand up to my forehead, watching as the man's face flickered with recognition and a bit of amusement.

"Sim, I have seen her. She came in about a half hour ago. I will say, she told me not to breathe a word of her presence to anyone, but I see that you are an honorable looking man, and she seems to be quite dangerous. I would feel much better if you could contain her somehow. You are her husband, sim?"

I could only grin at the thought. "No, unfortunately I am not. But I will admit to being her guardian, shall we say. Now, do you know in which direction she was headed?"

The man chuckled. "Ah, sim. Just continue northward. I do not believe she plans on staying in one place for long, though. You might want to hurry, senhor."

"That I do. *Obrigado*, senhor." I made my way to the door as the man called out a *de nada*, and all but ran out of the shop and mounted my horse.

Thirty minutes. I was thirty minutes behind but had a good advantage, as, despite her long stride, a galloping horse could run faster than a pirate captain on land any day.

And I had much more motivation than said pirate captain.

I had finally reached the outskirts of Lisbon. Now, far enough away from the city and its temporary inhabitants, I could rest. 'Twas at least a good couple hours past midnight, and I could barely walk another foot. I needed sleep and better transportation come dawn.

But for now I would focus on the sleep.

I could not risk an inn or any sort of place where Bennet could ask about me. Fortunate for me, the streets were vacant and I had slept in worse places before. I ducked behind one of the last buildings that lined the city, which looked to be an inn itself, and settled in, my back pressed up against the wall.

My feet were smarting and said back was aching, but I couldn't lose even a second, and so refrained from removing my tight boots or finding a more comfortable position. I had to be ready to jump up and get moving as soon as the sun began to rise. If I was going to find a coach of some sort and make my way to Gijón before the *Rina* came and went, then I most assuredly need to hurry.

So I tipped my hat down over my eye and laid my head against the brick of the inn behind me and forced my eye shut.

I had to sleep. Sleep. Sleep...

The sunlight, so bright and blinding, glints off those dashed boots before me, and it only serves to make Father's blood seem redder, the knife in his chest seem sharper. Why? Why had Wilde killed him? Why had the man gone to so much trouble for revenge over something that my father had not done?

And why must I pay for the sins of my grandfather? Why must I sacrifice so much of myself for Wilde and his thirst for revenge?

Because the world is not fair. Because pain can pierce even the hardest of hearts. Because not even the most righteous of men can resist the hunger for vengeance.

Those boots clomp forward, though their work is finished. Those feet had carried Wilde this far. Father was gone now. What more must he do to me?

Before I can blink my eyes, I look up only to stare straight into the wretched face of my greatest enemy, of my father's killer. Oh, how can that man dare to smile so devilishly in my face when he had only just murdered my father in cold blood? How can he take so much? I am innocent. Purely innocent as a newborn lamb. And yet I take the brunt of this pain.

Dash it, but can the man not just kill me now?

Wilde sets a finger underneath my chin, lifting my face up to his scarred one. I jerk away, yet he only holds me still. His dark blue eye bores into me, his iris glistening with murder, with hate. His finger, rough and blood-stained, runs under my left eye.

"Ah, such a beautiful combination of blue and green and silver," the murderer says. "'Tis a shame that your precious father will never be able to look in them again."

No! I yank back, attempting to stand, only to get caught and pulled back down to the floor by my chains. "How could you?" I choke out, the only words I dare to speak.

Wilde's face goes blank, his eyes turning hard as stone. "You have no right to ask that, child."

And then the familiar glint of cold, hard metal creeps slowly up to me, slithering as a snake. A snake that bites with killing venom, that sucks the very life out of one's soul.

My world turns a black that trickles with scarlet blood.

Why?

"Why?"

The word, yelled out, jolted me awake. I glanced around, only to find darkness meeting me. No! No, not again. He was coming for me. Slowly, surely, as a slithering snake he would come. He would come and attack and leave me to my grave at the bottom of the ocean where Father forever rested.

An arm, strong and solid, wrapped around my waist and pulled me into a safe haven as I was lifted up off the ground. I burrowed into the solidness of this haven, sliding my arms around it and holding on for dear life. Wilde couldn't find me if I was here, safe and protected. I was safe now, forever and for always.

Chapter 12

"Father!" I reached out to feel my father's face, to see if he was real. Had he truly come back after all this time? Was he really alive? Oh, but my heart might burst!

My hand extended, feeling the dark air around me. Where was Father? I felt around, searching, yearning. He was fading, slowly but surely, away, floating off into the abyss. No! No, but he couldn't leave me. Not again!

"Father, come back!" I yelled, a sob tearing from my lips, a scream threatening to escape my throat. I had control, perfect control, enough control that I could only just reach, just reach a little bit farther, and he would come back. I would pull him back to me. He couldn't leave. He just couldn't leave.

Father's face vanished completely then, only the twinkle from his eyes remaining before darkness fell over me. He was gone. He had always been gone. And he wouldn't, couldn't come back.

I collapsed against the soft, feathery darkness beneath me, willing it to swallow me whole. If only the darkness would take me far, far away.

If only I could somehow disappear.

If only Wilde was not coming for me.

If only death did not await me.

If only Father could still protect me.

A tear slipped from my eye, splashing against the darkness, seeping straight into it as if it were home.

Home. I wanted to go home.

And where was home? Oh, but I didn't know anything anymore! I didn't know who I was, where I was, or what I was.

"Heavenly Father, send Your Spirit to comfort her," someone was saying, their deep voice falling over me like a warm blanket. "Let Your peace cover her. Show her that You are here."

There! A light! It broke through the darkness, pushing it away, vanquishing it like a shining sword.

"Peace, be still," another Voice said, one so very tender and soothing, low and resounding. The Voice sent a wave of peace rippling through the light, rushing over me like a soft billow of water.

I released a sigh, sinking deep into the light. This, this was home.

But then a hand broke through the light, reaching out to brush its fingers against my forehead. And I knew this hand. It wasn't the Hand of light, but neither was it the hand of darkness. It was the hand of my captor, for I knew it well. Knew how it comforted and soothed and seared and burned. Knew how I ought to pull away from that hand, yet only leaned into it more.

But wait! Bennet couldn't be here. I was outside that inn, asleep on the ground, was I not? And Bennet was miles away, tucked safely in his bed, without the knowledge of my departure. Oh, dash it. I knew he would notice I was gone eventually; I just hadn't expected him to know *where* I had gone.

Ugh, it must have been that deuced shopkeeper. I knew I shouldn't have given into my hunger and stopped for food. Stupid decision, as not even being sworn to secrecy could keep men from blabbing. Even when they'd been threatened with certain death.

I wrenched myself away from Bennet's touch, jerking upward in bed. "What the deuce, Bennet? Lock up me in prison?" I questioned, forcing myself to met his gaze...and instantly regretting it once I did.

His deep black eyes only smiled at me in the same way his strong mouth twisted up in a grin. He sat, elbows on his knees, in a chair by my bedside, his Bible resting in his lap. His beautiful blond strands of long hair where all in disarray, his clothes rumpled. Obviously he had spent the night in his chair, likely reading by the dark circles under his eyes. Disarray or not, though, he still looked just as handsome as ever.

Not that I thought him handsome, just that someone else might. Or because 'twas a basic fact of life that the man was good-looking. 'Twas truly a wonder the man wasn't married yet.

"Did you sleep well, my darling?"

My darling, was it? Why had I ever banned "my lady" from his vocabulary? 'Twould not be long before he was referring to me as his delightfully delicious love.

I could only roll my eye, pushing aside that rogue thought. "Aye, I slept like a babe." I paused for a moment, watching as Bennet lifted a brow in disbelief. "Of course I didn't sleep well. I'm locked up in a strange room with a strange man. How could I have closed my eye for even a second, hmm?"

Bennet just grinned, the rogue, as he rose from his chair, placing his Bible on a table against the wall. "I wouldn't call myself a strange man. After all, we have gotten to know each other quite well over the last few weeks, wouldn't you say?" His eyes twinkled with something akin to desire, his tone dripping with sardonicism.

And my blood began to boil with the need to see this man dance the hempen jig. Honorable as he composed himself, he surely played the part of a rake rather well.

"Nay, I would not. But I will kill you if you so much as a breath another word," I sneered, though I knew I could never bring myself to follow through with that threat. Why exactly, though, I didn't know.

"You continue to say that, Rina, and yet here I am. Alive." Bennet turned away from me and crossed the room. He grabbed my pair of boots from their resting place against the wall, as well as my waistcoat and belt. But neither did my dagger nor my pistol hang from the leather.

Dash that man.

"Here, put those on," he said as he tossed the latter items at me. "We've got miles to cover and places to go. I won't have you laying there all day."

I caught my coat and threw it over my shoulders, then secured my belt around my waist. "You expect me to come with you, do you?"

He grinned. "Aye."

I twisted in Bennet's grasp, wishing there was some possible way I could get comfortable. But I was in the knave's arms, and ease was not found there. All right, it was, but at the moment that thought was far from my mind.

He had been right; I was going with him. But it was only because he had slung me over his shoulder as soon as I had reached the door and had carried me straight out of the inn in his arms as though I were a sack of potatoes. And at times such as these, I wished I were.

Because sitting astraddle on his rented horse all but in his lap, my back pressed against his solid chest, his strong arms around my waist, was most assuredly distressing. Appealing, but distressing.

Oh, for pity's sake, why couldn't I get a grip on my senses? Twice had I kissed this man within two weeks of knowing him, and had been wrapped up in his arms countless times. And had enjoyed both! 'Twas so preposterous it nearly drove me insane.

I was supposed to hate Xavier Bennet, not love him.

Not that I loved him; I didn't. But I obviously didn't hate him either.

Silence fell between us, interrupted only by the sound of horse hoofs clomping against the road. 'Twas the same sort of silence that had always seemed to hurt worse than a thrashing after getting into trouble or one of Father's rantings and ravings. Odd how it seemed to fit Bennet well.

And odd how it seemed to make me even more uncomfortable.

"Well, um, tell me about your family, how your parents met," I urged, needing to break the quiet before it as well brought me to insanity.

Xavier let out a low chuckle, followed by a moment of contemplative silence before he began, "My parents met when Father captured the ship my mother was on. My mother is the daughter of the Viscount Turenly, and had been engaged to the Earl of Riveredge at that time. She was also pregnant with his child. She didn't want to face social disgrace nor her parents' wrath, so she ran off in hopes of finding safe passage to Jamaica, where her brother, my uncle, was staying.

"Long story short, the ship she was on was captured by Captain Bennet of the *Justice*, and she was taken captive along with the ship's cargo. She and the captain fell in love, and married as soon as they ported. And then I was born four months later."

Four months? So then, that would mean… "You're the earl's child?" I turned to face Bennet, surprised at the smile that graced his lips.

"Aye. Though no one but a few close family members know, other than myself."

"So you've never met your father?"

"My father is Reverend Collin Bennet. Nothing can change that," was his reply, his tone colored by sheer love for his adoptive father.

"Then you know how I feel about my father, don't you? And yet you strip me away from what is left of him anyway?"

Bennet sighed. "'Tis not like that. I had the blessing of knowing the truth, even if it didn't much matter. But you never knew. You were lied to and cheated out of a life that you could have had."

"I do not want that life!" I shouted the words, unable to stop the anger, the rage from seeping out of my tone. I fairly jumped from the horse, and the animal came to a screeching halt. I knew better than to yell, but I could no longer help it. This man, this devastatingly horrid man, had ruined my life, and he wanted naught but to rub it in my face. Well, he would get what he had coming to him, that was for certain.

"Listen 'ere, Captain Bennet, I don't want a duke or a palace or all of the deuced money in the world! I don't want no blasted life! I wanna go home." The last word came out strained, almost like a babe's whine, and it burned my ears.

Home. Truly, but it no longer existed.

Bennet's hands clamped down hard on my shoulders, pushing me back into my place in between his legs. Not a word of rebuke nor sympathy left his lips as he held me tight against him, just silence.

Dash that silence.

I situated myself in his arms and kept myself completely still. But then Bennet kicked his horse and urged him into a gallop, and I lurched backward and to the side, the only thing keeping me from tumbling to the ground being the arm that slipped around my waist and held me captive in Bennet's grasp.

I could only pray to Bennet's God that we could get back on board before this horse-riding thing became the death of me and hoped that He answered soon.

Fortunately, we arrived back in town at noon, and I gladly slid off that infernal beast and into Bennet's arms. He set me down on the ground in front of the inn and commenced to tying up the animal to a post.

My first thought was to vanish from his sight, but then he shot me a stern glare, and I immediately dismissed the idea.

"So, are you going to tie me up as well, or shall I be locked up in your room again?" I placed my hands on my hips and met his glower.

"I'm considering both. And if neither work, my last resort is to turn you into the authorities. I'm certain that Portugal would be glad to receive the fierce pirate captain that raids their seas into their prison."

Blast the man to the moon and back. "How about you let me come with you, and *I'll* consider not running again?"

Bennet sighed. "Fine."

After a quick meal of bread and soup to break our fast, Bennet and I managed to catch up with his crew and the twins as they began purchasing supplies. Of course the twins seemed very happy to see that I had been found, while the remainder of the men appeared to be a bit less enthusiastic. Though I couldn't blame them. If Roger Mansfield ran off with only the clothes on his back, I frankly wouldn't have given a fig if I never saw nor heard tell of him again.

Before long, supplies had been bought and placed on board the *Jessica*, the men had all eaten again—pigs that they were—and we were hoisting the mainsail and starting out again.

Now this would be the time to escape, while everyone was busy, and as soon as they noticed my absence, they would be miles from Lisbon, and I would be halfway to Gijón.

Except Bennet had somehow been able to tie my hands behind my back and bind my ankles despite my kicking and writhing, and then David had thrown me back into my room and locked the door. And this time the windows were secured, no daggers rested in hidden places, my pins were nowhere to be found, and that dashed chair had finally been nailed onto the floor. And, of course, all my wounds had healed by now.

Ugh.

I was destined for London, wasn't I? Destined for doom was more accurate. Oh, if only Charlie had never smuggled Bennet that letter. Then Bennet would've never known and never would've found me.

If only Quintus Blackstone had never killed all of Wilde's people. Then Wilde would have never need come after Father.

If only all the blasted signs didn't point directly to Rothsford. Then I could go on living the life I had always known.

I peered over my shoulder at the glittering gold on my finger. Why, oh, why had I asked? I couldn't bear to even look at the deuced thing anymore. It no longer reminded me of Father. How could it, when it belonged to another man, another family?

Family, ha. I could remember the days when I had dreamt of one, a mother and father, brothers and sisters. I had hoped for such when Father had met Lavinia, but then she'd left, and all those dreams had vanished.

Would I have a family with Rothsford? Would I have a father who I could call my own, a mother who would love me despite it all, brothers and sisters to entrust my life to and call my friends? Or would I be welcomed into the arms of a sire who despised me, a mother who loathed me, siblings who abhorred me?

But whether I would have such things or not, why should I care? I had a father and a brother. Their names were Captain Maverick William Blackstone and Julius Augustus Blackstone. My father had been a strong man, stern and tough, but he had a love in his heart for Julius and me that filled every crevice of our souls. Julius was a bright lad, full of spunk and life. He was always ready with a good joke to cheer up a down matey, and his laugh urged even the most serious of men to join in.

Whoever Rothsford was didn't matter to me, for I had Father's memory to carry along with me throughout the rest of my years. And I would always have Julius. One day he would come back to me, and I could wrap him in my arms and keep him safe forever.

And if that was not good enough, I had a brother named Elliot who had been with me through every step of life; a serious and intelligent younger brother named Keaton; a jolly ole uncle Charlie that had mentored me as his own daughter; a sweet nephew that snuggled up to my side and loved me with every piece of his tender, innocent heart; a bright and promising baby brother called Billy that reminded me of my youth; and so many others. They were my family.

But out of all of these, I had never had a mother.

The thought hit me right out of the blue, sending a sharp pang through my heart. What would it be like to have a mother?

Only Keaton had spoken at times of his mother, especially during those few hard weeks when he had first boarded my ship. She had sounded like a kind and generous woman, full of love for her two children, but not all woman were the same. Lavinia Shawe, the mother dear Julius had never known, was far from how Keaton had described Mrs. Clarke. A selfish woman, I remembered her being, full of desire only for Father. But whenever I was around, the tittering laughter faded, her bright eyes grew hard, and her seductive smile turned to a frown. She had despised me, and even the cheerful seven-year-old child I had been recognized such. 'Twas the opposite of Father, every look and word.

And obviously she had held little love in her heart for her own child. She had left Julius as soon as she could lift herself out of her bed, and the poor babe had as much of a memory of his mother as I did of this duke father of mine. None.

Hopefully the woman who had birthed me did not hold such resentment. After all, her husband had gone to so much trouble to have me found and she surely would have supported him.

But none of that mattered, did it? The duke and duchess were expecting their daughter, a sweet, tenderhearted woman longing for their love, to run straight into their arms. They were not expecting me.

Chapter 13

London, England
September 1683

London.

A city far from the sea, with cobblestone streets and horses and carriages and buildings and trees. Lots of trees. Not a forest necessarily, but when one was accustom to the treeless ocean, London resembled a timberland for certain.

But the worst part of London, beautiful and bustling city that it was, was the person that resided in it. Rothsford.

I could handle all the other men and women that crowded the streets, all the other people I might possibly meet. I only dreaded catching sight of Richard Winterbourne, the man that had to be my father. Or at least seemed to be.

Fortunately, his townhouse was located on the other side of London, and we—Bennet, the twins, and myself—were destined for the Bennet House before Bennet and I continued on with our journey.

Jonathan had spent the rest of our voyage keeping me company in my prison, regaling me with tales of his childhood and all the mischief he and his brothers had gotten into. To be honest, I was anticipating meeting the great "Cap'n Ben" and the woman who had converted him, the couple who had raised such interesting young men.

And I was certainly curious about this Marjorie and Beth that Jonathan had spoken of. The brothers had said nothing about sisters, and from what Jonathan had said, Beth was yet a young one. A million thoughts had flitted through my mind as to whom they may be, and half of them had certainly been unpleasant.

But I would rather ponder over whether or not Bennet was married to this Marjorie and Beth was his child than to try and figure out why Father would've abducted me. The former was much less taxing.

Our carriage hit a rut, and I went flying forward. Oh, dash these stupid horse-pulled carts. 'Twas a shame the entire world wasn't made of water.

After we had ported at Southend-on-Sea, Bennet had chartered a carriage to carry us into London, and for the last two hours we had been cramped inside this blasted box like fish in a sword sheath. And anyone would know how well a giant fish, a lanky fish, and two tall fish would fit into a sheath.

David took up the most of the seat, while Jonathan somehow managed to squish in between him and Bennet, whereas I sat all but in the latter's lap, which was becoming quite a natural occurrence. Both of our heads grazed the top of the carriage, and as I slung forward, 'twas only by Bennet's strong arm that I was kept from falling to the floor.

As soon as I was situated on his knee, the carriage came to a screeching halt, followed by the horses' sharp whinnies. Fortunately, Bennet kept me in my place this time, one arm reaching around me to jerk open the door.

"Well, here we are." Jonathan rubbed his hands together and took in a deep breath. "I can almost smell the roast from here."

I slid from the carriage and out into the fresh late summer air, the feel of solid land underneath me a surprisingly pleasant one. Finally, out of that coach and into the light of day. I chuckled to myself, turning to watch all three of those tall men squish out of the carriage like rats from a crack in a ship's hull.

Bennet was first to step out, slipping up beside me with that dangerously blinding grin of his. Though the last few days had been, well, tense between us—not that I should care, although I did—and it had seemed as though Mr. Perfect was angry with me, his eyes always hard, his ready smile always upside down, he now stood at my side, his eyes alight with dark joy, his hand in mine.

And I was unable to resist. How could I, after I had missed him as I had?

Once David and Jonathan exited the coach and it began to drive past us, we started forward to the small parsonage dubbed the "Bennet House." It was nothing compared to some of the opulent buildings I had seen all over the world, but it gave of a sense of home, of comfort. And I liked it.

Probably only two stories tall, squeezed in between two other buildings, the Bennet House was all red brick and stood proudly, in the same way I imagined Captain Bennet, whether it be on the deck of his ship or at the pulpit. And if the man was anything like his sons, I knew that would be true.

The house was matching in design of the others to its sides, yet with the boxes of flowers hanging from the windows on both floors and the small flower garden, along with the immaculate appearance of the building, showed that it was well taken care of and made it stand out a little bit from the rest of London. Of course, it could never be as grand nor as homey as the *Rina*, but for a house, it was rather nice.

Before the four of us could reach the door, let alone open it, it swung wide open and a sprightly little girl with strawberry-blond braids came dashing out of the house, yelling a joyous "Daddy!" as she ran straight into David's strong arms. The big, burly, serious man enveloped the girl in his arms and spun her around, a beaming smile on his face.

A daughter. David Bennet had a daughter. A relieved sigh left my lips as I watched the slightly odd display. So this was Beth.

David set Beth down with a hearty chuckle, the flash of delight and pure love in his murky green eyes reminding me of the very same look in Father's. Oh, to be young again and bask in my father's love!

I banished the thought and turned aside to meet Bennet's grin with a glower. "Why didn't you tell me he had a child?"

The man only shrugged. "You never asked." He slid an arm around my waist and ushered me across the threshold. "Come now, there are many more people who would love to meet my fierce little pirate."

I jerked away from his touch, stumbling over the doorstep. "I am not your 'little pirate,' and I forbid you to refer to me as such, thank you very much." I folded my arms over my chest as I righted myself, stepping into the warm and welcoming house.

The scent of onions and carrots and celery flooded my senses, proving Jonathan's statement to be correct. Mrs. Bennet *was* cooking pot roast.

"Xavier, is that you?" A woman's voice, light and happy, came from the back of the house, followed by heavy footsteps that I could easy imagine clomping across the deck of the notorious *Justice*. A figure appeared from the back room, likely the kitchen, and came quickly into view.

Tall—though I towered over him by more than an inch—with broad shoulders and a muscular build, with waves of greying blond hair pulled back into a queue and sparkling ocean blue eyes, was Captain, or rather Reverend, Collin Bennet. He looked just as Father had said, although with a few more wrinkles. And he looked, from the blinding grin he wore to the dark blond eyebrows that arched above his eyes, exactly like Xavier.

I glanced at my captor, unable to resist grinning just slightly as I nudged him in the side. "Not your sire, you say?"

Bennet only smirked. "'Tis true, but don't speak anything of it."

I rolled my eye and turned back to the captain, whose grin only broadened.

"So who might this beautiful young woman here be, son?" the captain questioned, his voice dripping with youthful charm and interest.

Before Bennet could give him my full name and noble title, as I knew he likely would, I stepped forward and extended my hand. "Captain Rina Blackstone of the *Rina*. 'Tis a pleasure, Captain."

The captain gripped my hand in his strong, rough one and shook it heartily, suddenly making me seem small and lowly. "Ah, but the pleasure is mine, my dear. I must say, you look just like your father."

My smile instantly diminished. "Which one?" The sarcasm slipped from my tone like butter, and I could do nothing to stop it. The captain would be on Bennet's side, and likely knew Rothsford well. And though he and Father had once been good friends, I could not count on him to defend me. He likely knew exactly where I had come from anyhow, whether that be Rothsford or Blackstone.

Captain Ben chuckled. "Both."

My ire disappeared. Both? So, I did look like a pirate whose blood was in no way my own? "Thank you, Captain," I replied, truly grateful. Seemed someone actually had some sympathy for a poor woman whose life had been ripped apart.

Unlike some people…

My gaze cut to Bennet, to the odd gleam in his eyes. Apparently he was just as confused as I had been for the past two and a half weeks.

Finally.

Bennet cleared his throat, tearing his gaze away from mine. "Now, where's Mother?" He raised his eyebrows, sending a cheeky grin his father's way as he marched towards the kitchen.

The captain returned the smile, motioning for me to follow as the men made their way through the front of the house. And a nice house it was, furnished comfortably and built sturdily inside and out. The front room was a simple one, a brick fireplace the main attraction, with a stairway lining the opposite side. Through a doorway at the left was the kitchen and dinning room.

In said kitchen stood two women wearing flour-covered aprons, one looking a score older than myself—Mrs. Bennet, apparently—and the other obviously Beth's mother, as she had the same strawberry-blond hair and twinkling blue eyes that lit up with curiosity as I stepped into view.

I ducked my head slightly, having to remove my tricorn to keep it from brushing against the low doorframe, and moved out of the way as Bennet leaned in to embrace his mother.

Mrs. Bennet chuckled softly, winding her arms around her son's neck and rising onto her tiptoes to kiss his cheek. "Finally, Zay, you've returned! You had said 'twould only be a short venture, yet you come home two weeks later… and with a woman!" She glanced over Bennet's shoulder at me, her thin brown eyebrows raised in interest.

I sauntered forward, extending my hand. Or wait, was I to curtsy? Mrs. Bennet was, after all, the daughter of a viscount. And I was the daughter of a duke, so… "Captain Rina Blackstone. I'm your son's prisoner."

Mrs. Bennet grinned, her green eyes lighting up as she grasped my hand. "Jessica Bennet. It's a pleasure to meet you. I've wanted for quite some time to meet Maverick's lovely daughter."

Oh, but this was the most confounding family! The son was calling me a lady, the father was on the fence, and the mother referred to Father as though she had known him all her life. And they all behaved as though I wasn't mad enough to kill them all.

"Frankly, Mrs. Bennet, I haven't the slightest clue as to whose child I am," I replied, having to force myself into returning her welcoming smile.

"Well, we all hope that will soon be relieved. Don't we, Xavier?" Mrs. Bennet shot her son a glare that spoke volumes.

Aye, I was certainly going to like Jessica Bennet.

And so far, I liked each member of the Bennet family, save *Mr.* Xavier Bennet, of course.

Dinner had been a delightful meal, much better fare than that of the taverns my crew and I ate at when at port, and certainly finer than what we had on the *Rina.* Although I still believed roast couldn't beat oranges and a glass of rum.

The company had been delightful as well. Little Bethany Bennet had regaled us all with tales of daring bravery out in her grandmother's garden, while David's wife Marjorie had put in a few words and answered all the questions I hadn't dared to ask the brothers.

Jorie—as I had heard her called—was a pleasant girl no more than ten and nine, with a bright countenance and polite personality. Fortunately, and I cast the blame upon having Captain Ben for a father-in-law, she certainly wasn't the least bit uncomfortable dining with a pirate. The unease was reserved for her, David, and Jonathan.

One would have to be blind not to notice the tension between the two, or the gleam in the young man's eyes whenever he looked at his sister-in-law, nor would one miss every sharp glare David shot his brother from across the table. 'Twas no wonder the twins were rarely seen together unless with their older brother as well.

Captain Ben himself was quite the jolly older man, who managed to squeeze in a couple words to me while Beth paused her story to eat. He truly wasn't one that appeared to be a reverend, all staunch and boring standing up in a pulpit. Not that I had actually met a preacher, necessarily, but I had been told many a story.

And the stories Father had told me of Collin Bennet certainly didn't do the man justice. Tales of his bravery and then of his "downfall" all excluded the man's character. His love for his family and especially his wife was evident, and his strength and kindness put sword-fighting to shame. The only thing that bothered me was that the joy in his blue eyes and the smile on his face resembled Bennet all too much.

And the man wasn't even his father.

But neither was I Maverick Blackstone's daughter, and yet how many times I been said to be just like him?

Mrs. Bennet was certainly not the sort of woman I had expected to have raised a man such as Bennet. For one, she was not the grey-haired, hit-you-with-my-spoon kind of matron that would've mothered someone so blasted *good*. Secondly, she wasn't a tie-you-down, judgmental prude of a woman that would have forced a pirate into being a preacher. She was bright and energetic and quirky and brazen. I couldn't imagine her as a viscount's daughter or a reverend's wife any more than I could see the captain wearing some sort of priestly robe and reading from a scroll.

And the way she loved her children! I had known her for only three hours, and yet the love she had for her sons and daughter-in-law and grand-daughter was so obvious it caused some sort of hole in my heart to ache.

Lavinia had never loved Julius like that. She'd never had the time to even hold her son, let alone love him. And I had never had a mother.

But I did now.

I banished the thought, determined not to dwell on it. That matter I would leave for the morrow. But for now, I leaned back in the settee I sat in in the Bennets' parlor and tried not to look at the infuriating man beside me who wore such a relaxed smile that reached all the way up to his dark and dangerous midnight eyes.

Of course, I failed at that.

He looked so at home here, an arm thrown around the edge of the chair, his head tossed back in laughter as he listened with delight to another one of those daring tales of garden bravery told by his niece. He was no longer the flirtatious captor of mine, but a brother, a son, an uncle. And all three of those titles fit him well.

Bennet reached out and dragged his niece into his lap, twirling his finger around an escaped sliver of red-blond hair. "Now, Beth, tell me about that toad you found. What was it that you had named him?"

Little Beth certainly did not return her uncle's grin, instead sticking her bottom lip out in a pout. "Not a toe, Unca Zay. Pwince Percival was a fwog," she countered, the mispronunciation of her words coupled with the replacement of *w*s for *r*s only adding to her adorability.

Bennet's eyes flickered with a mix of stupidity and hilarity. "Ah, a 'fwog,' you say. Well, forgive my error, would you please?" He tweaked the girl's pug nose, eliciting a chuckle from her.

Oh, but he was so good with children. He would love Ellie, and the little one-year-old would certainly love to snuggle up in Bennet's strong arms and listen to his rich, soothing voice as…

I was going off course, diving into depths that I didn't desire to swim in. So I pushed up from my seat, grabbing the waistcoat I had flung over the edge of the settee, and cleared my throat. "You wanted to speak with me, nay, Captain?" I said, shoving my gaze from Bennet to the elder, who rose from his chair as well.

"That I did, Captain." He grinned, his eyes twinkling with amusement.

I probably ought to call him reverend, as there were already two captains in the room, and the man had lowered his Jolly Roger years ago, before I was even born.

Then again, how did I even know that I had truly been born on the eighteenth of April in 1655? Father had lied about so much, it seemed; what would a discrepancy on the date of my birth matter?

For pity's sake, if only my mind would just quit storming with questions and raining down fury! I could not blame Father for anything, abduction and lying aside. The man had raised me and done a dashed good job of it as well. He had taught me all the skills I needed to know, had protected me from all sorts of things until he felt me old enough to face them myself. And even then, he had stood beside me, ever at the ready to rush to my aid.

'Twas not Father I ought to blame, but every real and working power out there that insisted upon ruining my life while I still had it, plaguing my mind while it was still lucid, and breaking down my control while I still needed it.

Captain Bennet set a strong hand on my shoulder and led me from the parlor and through the doorway to the kitchen and dining room. He brought me to the table and motioned for me to sit down.

Ah, so 'twould be a long conversation, would it?

I pulled out a chair and plopped down into it, leaning forward and propping my elbows on the table. Perhaps he, who had known both my fathers, could give me some insight, something more than the cruel and blunt "you're not your father's daughter" that had spilled from Xavier Bennet's lips like poison.

I could only hope.

The captain seated himself as well, dwarfing the wooden chair with his bulky frame. He looked like Keaton sitting there, a stoic yet seemingly content expression on his chiseled features. "Tell me about your father," was all he said, the words striking me like a hand across the jaw.

He wanted me to speak of Father when all I wanted to hear was words of the very same man from his lips? Where was he going with this?

I clenched my jaw so hard I could've sworn I felt my gold tooth shift. "Well," I began through my tight mouth, unsure where to begin. Perhaps the beginning? "He was my father. And he raised me well."

There. That was all the information anyone needed. And all the information I dared to let slip past my teeth. I couldn't let any other words filled with soppy emotion come forth. I had control anyway; 'twould never happen.

The captain—reverend—nodded contemplatively. "I see. Tell me more."

Years of sitting in taverns playing cards and feigning indifference toward rewarding information of ships and their cargo was what gave the man such a straight face. Even more years of reaching out to "lost souls" gave him a calming, searching air. An odd combination indeed.

"He was strong, the same tough man the sea had made him, yet there was always an essence about him whenever I was near him." *'Twas love,* I wanted to say. But that galling voice in the back of my mind whispered continually in my ear, *control...control.*

Deuce that control!

"When I was little, he would always set me on his knee and tell me stories." Fairy-tales, old stories of battles fought at sea, but never anything about my mother, about Father's parents. Never anything that actually meant something.

"As I got older, he taught me how to do advanced arithmetic, how to decode secret messages even. He always said I surpassed him at each. Once I turned ten and two, he began to teach me how to wield a sword, and for hours we would practice sword-fighting and shooting. He would always let me beat him so as not to wound my childish pride. But soon I would come close to beating him as I got older.

"My brother Julius was born when I was seven. And I watched his mother walk away from him when he was still a nursing babe. Father truly didn't seem to care about Lavinia. He just spent his time nurturing Jules and me. He cared for us—for me. He may have been a wretched pirate and a child-abductor, but he loved me, Captain. He really did."

A tear threatened to fall from my eye, but I banished it, as well as the image of Father's deep chocolate eyes and his comforting arms.

A small smile appeared on Captain Ben's face, and he reached out to grip my hand. "I believe he did, Rina," he said before his tender gaze left mine and found the ring on my finger. Something sparked in his eyes, and he chuckled, lifting my hand to his face.

"I never would've thought he had kept this," he muttered in astonishment.

A million questions raced through my mind. Kept the ring? Why would it matter if Father had kept the ring? And how did the captain even know of it?

Slowly, I eased my fingers from his hand, examining the glistering gold as if the answer to all my problems was etched into the metal. "Father gave it to me when he died. 'Tis all I have left of him, save my ship. He wore it every day of his life. I never saw him without it."

"But he never told you about it?"

Finally, perhaps this would bring some sort of answer. "Nay. Never a word."

Captain Ben shook his head. "He must have had a time dealing with the truth himself." He looked up at me. "I suppose you're wondering what I'm prattling on about. 'Twas your grandfather's."

Perhaps I ought to gasp in shock, or frown in disappointment, mayhap even smile in joy. But I didn't see any reason to express emotion over the statement, other than outright confusion. "Do you refer to Quintus Blackstone, or some other grand-father of mine?" I questioned, raising an eyebrow.

And here I had hoped Captain Bennet wouldn't be as bewildering as his son.

He only chuckled. "Blackstone wasn't even of Maverick's blood. I'd be surprised if Maverick even spoke of the man."

Father hadn't; Wilde had done all the speaking needed. "So you mean to say that even Father had confused his heritage?"

"Nay. I mean to say that Maverick was never a Blackstone."

I shot up from my chair, knocking it to the floor with a *bang*, indignation causing my blood to boil and my ire to rise. First, they said I was not my father's daughter. Now they said that even he was not a Blackstone. What did these deuced Bennets hold against my family that they conjure up such lies?

And all this, my father's death and Julius's taking, had all been for naught? The scar on my face was the punishment for a crime someone not even of Father's blood committed? *I* had paid the price for some random man's iniquities?

Ah, but they played a cruel game, Bennets did. They lied and tricked and deceived and somehow expected one to believe it. Instinctively, my hand sought out the hilt of my cutlass. I ought to kill them all now, let them slowly drink from the cup of my wrath as so many others had. 'Twould teach them to cross Captain Rina Blackstone.

All that anger poured out as I turned to face Captain Ben, my fingers clenching into a fist. Not that I was as skilled in boxing as I was swordplay.

"Look here, Cap'n, I'm sick and tired o' all this nonsense! I watched my father die, and now ye tell me I ain't his. I heard my brother scream bloody murder as he was ripped out of my arms, and now ye tell me he ain't mine. And now ye wanna prance around saying Father ain't the only one with a befuddled heritage! Explain this to me!"

I banged my fist against the table, causing it to shake, as I longed to pick the whole thing up and throw it against the wall.

The captain only sat still at the table, a troubled look on his face as he scratched the top of his greying head. Then he rose and sauntered towards me, his hands reaching out to grasp my shoulders. He tugged me into his arms, and I fell willingly into his strong, fatherly embrace.

Sobs wracked my body, and try as I might to stifle them, tears trickled from my eye. “Why? Why is this happening to me?”

Chapter 14

Captain Bennet sighed, his hands rubbing comforting circles on my back. This must be a family trait, comforting. For it seemed both father and son were experts at the trade. Then again, Bennet had said the captain wasn't exactly his birth father, although I found that quite impossible to be true.

"I don't know why this is happening, Rina," the captain was saying, "But I can assure you that God knows. And if you will only trust in Him, I know all will work together for good."

Bilge. I pulled away from Captain Ben, having to resist the urge not to roll my drying eye. He was a reverend, after all; I couldn't expect him not to speak of his God. Even if the idea of a supreme being ruling the world was more than a little absurd. And impossible in Father's mind.

"Yes, yes. 'Trust in the LORD with all thine heart; and lean not unto thine own understanding. In all thy ways acknowledge him, and he shall direct thy paths,' so says your Holy Word," I replied sarcastically.

I had heard many of those scriptures spoken in my day, mostly by Father's childhood friend Charlie, of all people. With a preacher for an old friend, I couldn't blame the man for knowing the scriptures, though he had drifted away from religion and into the world of piracy when Captain Ben himself had deserted the Royal Navy long ago. And even Elliot's late wife Mary had dosed me with religious words of faith and grace. How I had ended up captaining a band of pious pirates, I only wished I knew.

The captain obviously was surprised, though, by my easy recitation. "You know Proverbs?" he asked, an eyebrow raised.

I indicated a small amount with my fingers. "Very little. Charlie had never forgotten them, I suppose." I heaved a sigh and directed the conversation back to where it needed to be. "Pray tell, if Blackstone is not my father's surname, then what is?"

He smiled, sitting back down. "That, my dear, is a very long story. Shall I shorten it for you?" His eyes sparkled with knowing.

I returned to my seat as well, having to pick it up from the floor. "Nay. Details seem to be much needed these days."

"Very well, then. Your father had never spoken of his past; Charlie was the one who told me. You see, Maverick was born in Yorkshire to a powerful duke of royal blood and one of his maids. Although he grew up with knowledge of his parentage, his father never claimed him. The duke did just the opposite: he dismissed the maid and sent her off with not a pence. The woman made for herself and her unborn son a home by the seashore, and it remained their haven for ten years, until the woman married.

"The man she wedded was Quintus Blackstone. A cruel man, she and Maverick suffered many a beating and foul word, and it wasn't long before Maverick left home to pursue a career in pirating.

"Maverick had been adopted legally by his step-father and wasn't acknowledged by his birth father, so he went only by his step-father's surname. He quickly became a feared and notorious pirate, and he raided the Seven Seas for seven years before a plan began to form in his mind.

"His birth father had died not long ago, and the dukedom had been left to the duke's younger son, a man newly married. Soon, word had gotten out all over England and its colonies that the young duke and his bride had a child. And 'twas the perfect chance in Maverick's mind. If he could abduct the child, then his half-brother would have no heir to the dukedom, and his birth family would have a taste of grief for all the pain they had caused him. And if there was no heir, then perhaps he could finally obtain the dukedom that should have been his if only his father had done the right thing and claimed him. So, he abducted the child, only to find out once he had set sail that the babe all bundled up was a girl."

Girl. The word echoed through my mind. That was me. I was the girl, the means of revenge, the duke's daughter, Maverick's… *Niece*?

It all made sense now: the secrets, the ring, Father himself. All the pieces formed together in my mind, finally completing some sort of puzzle that I had been struggling to figure out ever since I had awoken on board the *Jessica*. 'Twas the most outlandish story I had ever heard, and yet the pieces fit.

I was actually Father's niece, and Julius was my cousin. We at least shared a bond by blood, if not by our hearts and lives.

And we both shared a noble birth, a royal heritage. Ha, who would have thought of it, a lady pirate! Odd, how even before this revelation, people had referred to me as such already. Prophesy, perhaps?

I roll my eye at the thought with a chuckle. Leastwise now I could go on about my life knowing that I would not diminish Father's memory nor his place in my heart by accepting the duke as my sire, for Maverick Blackstone—Maverick William Winterbourne Blackstone—would always be my uncle.

Not that I would like this Rothsford, or love him as I did Father, or rather, Uncle. I would accept him just as I had accepted my fate at Wilde's hand. It didn't mean I desired it, or even liked it. But I accepted it, for 'twas the inevitable truth.

I grinned to myself, leaning back in my chair as a thought crossed my mind. "Xavier doesn't know, does he?"

"Nay. 'Tis the first I've heard of it."

Both the captain and I craned to see the bearer of the familiar rich voice, who stood in the dining room doorway, leaning against the doorframe in the most nonchalant of positions with his arms folded over his chest.

Ah, but he looked so handsome, I admitted to myself—albeit reluctantly. He was wearing simply a pair of black breeches and a white shirt, as he always did, the fabric stretching across the expanse of his chest. His long hair was slung over his shoulder, the thick waves of blond and brown glistening in the light that streamed in. I could only wonder if those waves were as silky as they looked, and I longed to run my fingers through them as Bennet had through mine only days ago in the hold of his ship.

But most attractive of him all was the broad grin that formed on Bennet's lips, reaching all the way up to his gleaming black eyes.

Oh, dash the man for spellbinding me so! Not only had he held me captive on his ship for over two weeks, but now on land he held me prisoner by that smile and those arresting, fathomless eyes.

And I truly didn't mind my chains, nor my captor, despite my better sense. Sense that I had lost from the day I had first glanced into those dancing eyes and still couldn't seem to find.

Said captor pushed away from the doorframe and sauntered into the room. "Why didn't you tell me, Father? Things probably could've gone a great deal better with her ladyship here if I'd had more substantial information to give her," Bennet said, though his gaze remained trained on me.

The captain looked between us both and smirked. "I don't see how things could've gone any better, information or not."

Aye, Bennet really couldn't be the earl's child. He and the captain were far too much alike.

Bennet returned the smile. "I suppose you have a point there, doesn't he, Rina?" He lifted his brows at me in a haughty manner. One I could easily counter.

"If you two are referring to all the times I hit you, almost killed you, and managed to escape you, then, yes. Things couldn't have gone better." I gave Bennet my charming and most seductive grin, the one I wore only when fishing information out of drunken merchants at port, the one that always worked.

And certainly didn't stop now.

"Ah, and all those times you fell into my arms and kissed me."

Captain Ben's eyes grew wide from where he sat immersed in our banter, and he sent his son a chiding glower. "Xavier Collin Bennet, don't tell me you've been taking advantage of Lady Catherina." His voice came out in a low growl, the words sending a shiver through even me. And I was not the one in trouble.

That was the tone I imagined the captain using to berate a crew member or growl out orders, not to scold his adult, and completely innocent, son. But I supposed the man was strict on drilling honorable traits into his children, and I couldn't see where he'd had failed. Well...partially.

Bennet, on the other hand, cleared his throat, running a hand through those wild waves of his. "I promise you, Father, no such thing happened. And I made certain Jon didn't overstep his boundaries either."

Jonathan? Surely he wasn't such a rogue. He had been nothing but kind and perfectly civil, unlike his older brother. In fact, all of Bennet's crew had behaved themselves impeccably. Unfortunately, I could not say the same for *my* crew, which would have to be put under lock and key if a woman other than myself stepped on board.

I could remember when Mary Lynde had first boarded the *Rina*, her angelic blond curls framing her perfectly fair face, her bright azure eyes flashing kind looks every man's way, her generous figure attracting the gaze of every man on board.

I could only thank Father that he had made an example of what would happen to anyone who so much as looked at me, keeping all the men at bay even after his death.

Fool Elliot, though, had dragged his new wife on board as though she were a harden sailor, accustomed to lustful glances and drunken brawls and illegal piracy. Whatever had possessed my best friend to marry such an innocent child, I would never know. And what had made said child marry a pirate, I could only wonder. I, unfortunately, had been left to keep Mary from my crew's clutches—for only few I could trust, such as Keaton or Charlie—and was now left, or was supposed to be, in charge of her son. I almost pitied the deceased woman, whose last year of life had been spent with pirates and confined to her room in sickness.

But all that was over now. I was stuck currently with a still-skeptical captain, a frowning knave, and past, present, and future that had suddenly changed drastically.

Said captain looked towards me, obviously trusting my words more so than his son's. "Is he speaking the truth?"

About whether or not we had kissed, or if he had taken advantage of me? I longed to say no, just to anger my captor. But I also didn't want to be dishonest. I was known across the Seven Seas, after all, for my honesty. Which was a bit of a stretch of truth in and of itself.

"Yes, Captain. Your son has been nothing but a gentleman, along with his entire crew. Not that I am not accustom to unscrupulous characters, mind you. I live with pirates, you see. Downright horrible fellows," I replied with more than a little teasing sarcasm in my tone.

Captain Ben grinned in relief. "Aye, horrible indeed. I know a certain wife of mine who can attest to that. And speaking of that wife, I think I hear her calling me just now." He rose from his chair and left the room, but not before turning to his son and whispering something in his ear.

I watched as the older man disappeared from sight and Bennet came to sit in his father's seat, that bright and blinding grin back on his face.

"What did he say?"

"Oh, just that he'd expect us back shortly." Bennet let out a deep breath and propped his ankles up on the table. "It's nice to see you two getting along."

I frowned, feeling the ice shoot from my eye rather than seeing it. "And why would we not? Am I that disagreeable that your father would not find me pleasant company?"

"'Tis not you I was worried about, other than you not liking Father."

I hummed in reply, fingering the band on my finger. It had been stolen after all, but instead taken by my father, it had been taken *for* my father, who should have been the rightful heir to the dukedom of Rothsford.

"I want to apologize."

I had barely heard the words, but had been draw from my thoughts by the tone, so soft and uncertain yet so rich and confident. Xavier Bennet was the most enigmatic person I had ever met, and yet he made so much sense.

"Apologize for what, might I ask?"

Bennet removed his legs from the table and leaned forward, grasping my hand just as his father had done only moments ago. "Oh, for being an ogre, for ruining your life, for appearing to be more brutish and roguish than I truly am. Honestly, I didn't want to go after you, Rina. And I still don't want to take you to your father." He ran his thumb over my knuckles, sending a shiver of awareness through me.

Though sincerity colored his voice, disbelief crept its way into me. Apologize, for everything he had done to me? For every word, every action, every look that had caused me pain? He was apologizing for it all? Surely he was growing dafter by the minute. Apologizing, and he expected me to forgive him?

"Rina, I don't expect you to forgive me."

Had I spoken the words out loud? Or had the knave just read my mind? "Good, because I do not plan on doing so for a long, long time," I stated with too much certainty. "But why do you not want to take me to Rothsford? Am I that much trouble?"

He grinned, ever the rogue, and laughed, just like the odious man he was. "Don't pride yourself so, my lady. You certainly do not cause me enough difficulty to not manage shipping you to your father."

"I disagree." I rose from my chair, having had my fill of this man and his mockery, and started from the room.

Bennet stopped me, grasping my arm and tugging me back to him. He wrenched me down, and I fell into his lap. Oh, dash it all. I squirmed against his arms as they wrapped around my waist, but he held me too tight, and without ground underneath my feet, I could only go so far. So far as to pull back to slap him, only to be stopped by his hand gripping my wrist in midair.

"I was wrong, I see. You do cause me difficulty," he sneered, though his eyes glistened with a smirk. "I am not done with my apology. At least grant me the time to finish."

I studied his face, searching for something, anything, to belie his words. This man wanted more than an ounce of time from me, that I could see. But what exactly it was that he wanted, I could not determine. So I relented, relaxing in his hold, and allowed him to finish.

"I don't want to be the cause of your grief, anger, or hatred. When I first volunteered for this, I hadn't expected a pirate captain to greet me. In fact, I didn't know what to expect. Call me stupid, call me reckless; but I had no plan nor idea of how I was to capture you, let alone reveal to you the truth. And so I give to you my most sincere apology for my actions."

He smiled, although faintly, and I was suddenly wishing for that infernal grin to grace his lips. He looked far too sad at the moment. His hand reached up and he brushed a strand of hair from my face, his rough fingers grazing the scar on my cheek, sending a flame blazing through my entire body.

Immediately, I jerked from his touch, and he released me with a sigh. I cleared my throat, returning my feet to the floor and regaining my balance, both in my footing and my mind. "Yes, well, I accept your apology," I blurted out, despite my earlier refusal of his words.

How could I not accept, when he had said the very words I had longed to hear? Perhaps it did not change my fate, my past, my parents, but it certainly chiseled away at a small spot of hatred in my heart.

Not that I replaced that hatred with admiration or love or any sort of good thing.

Bennet's grin returned. "Thank you, Rina."

I rolled my eye, finally able to leave the room and return to where David, Jonathan, and the captain and his wife sat. Jorie and Beth were not present, though I could hear their soft voices from upstairs. The mother had to be laying her daughter down for bed, then.

Mrs. Bennet was the first to glance my way, her bright green eyes sending a grin my way. Ugh, were all of this family so...smiley? "Glad you could join us again, Captain. Come, sit." She patted the cushion of the settee beside her.

I followed her directing and settled in beside her. "Please, call me Rina. We've already two captains in the house."

Mrs. Bennet chuckled. "Very well, then, Rina."

A door shut softly, and Marjorie reappeared, her light strawberry-blond hair floating around her fair face.

Jonathan's face lit up from where he sat in the corner, his clover eyes alight with—desire?

David, on the other hand, shot his brother a glower, obviously noting the man's pursual of his wife, as Marjorie slipped into her husband's arms. Well, at least someone in this family didn't smile.

And speaking of smiling, Bennet entered the room at that very moment, jamming a hand through those blond locks of hair. "'Tis getting late, and I believe Beth isn't the only one who needs their sleep." He tossed me a wink. "Her ladyship has a big day tomorrow."

And I dreaded tomorrow.

Chapter 15

Light—blessed, cursed, and right now my greatest enemy—seeped in through the window of …

Wait, where was I?

I lifted my head and glanced around the unfamiliar room. Simply furnished with naught but a dresser, a desk, and a chair filling the room other than the bed I slept in and the small lamp table at my side, the room held a cozy feeling.

Perhaps 'twas just the softness of the mattress beneath me and the warmth that radiated from the quilt over me, or perhaps it was the certainly familiar scent of lime and saltwater that enveloped me and pulled me back into reality. A very harsh reality.

I was in Xavier's room, I now remembered, for sleeping in the same chamber as he used to was becoming quite a common occurrence. I had argued against the infuriating man, saying I could sleep on the settee in the parlor last night, or even on the floor in Beth's room. Well, the Bennets had won that argument. A lady needed a real bed, after all.

And for some odd reason, the man who had spent the last two weeks sprawled out on the hard wooden deck of his ship didn't need to rest his sore muscles on his own bed in his own house. Not that I was going soft with generosity; 'twas just that sleeping in the man's bed was a vexatious thought. And a disturbing actuality.

But 'twould be my last night slumbering with his scent, as I set out for Rothsford's home this very morning. There I was to have my own bed for the few nights I would stay there—without Xavier Bennet—and then would soon be back in my own bedchamber with Ellie's gentle breathing and the scent of oranges and rum and the ocean.

That very thought, tantalizing and relieving, was what urged me from the bed and dressed me in my freshly clean black breeches, my once-white, bloodstained blouse, belt, boots. Then I perched my tricorn atop the hair I had pulled up into a queue and tied at the nape of my neck. My stolen earrings hung from my ears just as the golden chain dangled from my neck with its three emeralds.

I most assuredly looked a pirate, and not just because of my attire. My scar stood out a pale pink against my sun-bronzed cheek, so I saw in the mirror laying on the dresser. My eye glinted like steel, and every marking on my hardened face, every jagged line on my knuckles, and every callous on my skin attested to the violence I had endured.

How could *I* be of noble heritage? How could the same drops of blood that coursed through the king's veins flow through mine? 'Twas impossible. And yet everything bespoke the truth of that reality. Even the ring on my finger's bright red ruby seemed to scream at me, *royal blood, royal blood.*

Royal blood. Bilge. I'd show them royal blood. I would show the duke, my father, and all the Bennets just how much of a lady I truly was. For 'twas obvious that they needed a reminder.

The door flung open, and Bennet appeared in the doorway. "Are you ready, dear?" His black eyes raked over me, something akin to desire flickering in his gaze. Dash that man.

I scowled into the mirror before turning to face the endearing captor of mine. "You had better be glad I was dressed, *darling*." I shoved past him and bounded from the room and down the stairs to where Reverend and Lady Bennet sat awaiting us in the parlor, a chuckle following me.

I glanced around the room, looking, I supposed, for the twins and Jorie and Beth. Of course, they were not there. I turned to the elders of the family and nodded. "Good morning."

They both smiled, repeating the greeting. "David and the girls went down to the docks, per Beth's request. And Jonathan's gallivanting through town," Mrs. Bennet said, her bright eyes suddenly dimming, as she rose and started towards the kitchen. "I hope you don't mind cold eggs, Rina. I'm afraid we've already eaten."

Cold eggs. Sounded better than the sludge Dorian fixed up back on the ship. I really ought to leave the man at port and cook myself. Or perhaps the crew and I could just live off of rum and oranges. I myself had already switched to that particular diet long ago, even as it left me with an empty stomach half the time.

I waved my hand through the air, dismissing the apologetic expression on Mrs. Bennet's face. "Not a problem. I'm not much hungry anyhow. How long have I slept?" I turned to Bennet, whose gaze itself looked hungry enough for the both of us.

"'Tis almost noon, your ladyship," he replied with a bow as mocking as his tone. At least he referred to me as a lady rather than his dear.

Goodness, I had never slept so late! It had to be the still land and bland air that had kept me in slumber's grasp for so long. Fortunate enough for me, my sleep had been far from fitful, and not a nightmare had plagued me. Perhaps 'twas some calming effect that this place, filled to the brim with Bennets, held. Then again, I hadn't had a nightmare since that last one in Lisbon.

"Well," I began, returning from my thoughts, "perhaps then we must not tarry any longer. I thank you for the offer, Mrs. Bennet, but you may save your cold eggs for another time. 'Twas a pleasure meeting you and your husband." I looked to Captain Ben and bowed slightly in acknowledgment. It truly had been a delight to meet the great pirate captain Father—Uncle—had told me many stories about, and to meet his wife and the mother of such interesting, and exasperating, men.

The captain returned the gesture, reaching out to grasp my hand. But instead of shaking it, he lifted it to his lips and pressed a kiss there. Men, they were all the same. Impudent.

And I was not the only one who thought so, for Mrs. Bennet swatted at her husband's arm as he lowered my hand. "Collin, always had a weakness for the ladies."

Captain Ben chuckled, winking at his wife, who he tugged to his side, pressing a kiss to her nose. "Ah, only *one* lady."

Bennet wrapped an arm around my waist then, pulling me to his chest. "So, Father, does that mean I get this one?" He leaned in and buried his face in my neck, his breath warming my skin like a flame.

Before the captain could answer, I wrenched from Bennet's arms and sneered. "Absolutely not. I thought we had already determined that I am *not* the 'captain's little lady.'"

"Perhaps. But not for long."

I huffed, tipping my tricorn towards the captain and Mrs. Bennet, and started towards the door of the house. I swung open the door and stepped out into the daylight.

The sun hung above the clouded summer sky, precisely at noon, as a breeze rippled through the air, carrying with it the scent of land, horseflesh, and the faint odor of waste that had been dumped into the streets. Unfortunately, there was no vast ocean to devour those stenches here on land. And unfortunately, there was no aroma of rum, salt, and cedar that the sea's wind blew.

Resting at the edge of the street was a carriage, not two yards away from where I stood. This carriage, unlike the coach I had arrived here in, was large and bespoke its owner's vast riches. Newly polished wheels with golden spokes; ornately designed doors; red velvet curtains peeking from behind the window; and two healthy mares with freshly brushed black coats to pull the carriage along. Even the driver, wearing a top hat and sitting perfectly still, looked a far cry better than the other coach's driver.

But what really caught my eye was the very familiar and very real symbol embedded on the side of the carriage. 'Twas just a simple cross, its crevices filled in with gold, and a small ruby glistening from the center of the seal.

Father's. I held up my hand and glanced between the two. Exactly the same.

"'Tis yours, you know," a deep voice said from behind me.

"I'd rather have a ship," I replied, folding my arms over my chest as Bennet moved to my side.

"Your father has those as well. Where do you think the *Jessica* came from? A man named Williamson crafted a few for him."

I only laughed. "Aye, my father commissions ships built by an ex-pirate. I most assuredly saw that coming."

At the glimpse of confusion etched in Bennet's brow, I added, "Terrence Williamson built the *Rina*. He sailed with my father—uncle—for several years before finding his calling to be building rather than sailing."

Bennet nodded. "Interesting. Now, come along." He stepped ahead of me and opened the carriage door before the driver could even shift in his perch, and extended his arm to assist me. As if I needed assistance.

I hopped into the carriage and situated myself on the red cushioned bench. Bennet, on the other hand, remained outside, holding the door open.

"Are you quite sure this is Lady Catherina?" I heard the driver say in a cultured voice that was colored by disbelief.

"Of course she is, Edmond," Bennet responded, his tone so overly confident it would have angered me did I not agree with him.

"I hope that you are correct, Captain." I could almost see Edmond shake his head, his eyebrows raised.

I slid to the edge of the bench and leaned out of the door. I extended my hand and flashed my gold ring. "Wha' say ye, matey? Look familiar t' ye?" I said in my crudest tone, flashing the driver a bright grin. "Y'see, I be's the lady ye's is a-lookin' fer, but I didn't be's a-knowin' it till this 'ere cap'n came right along an' tol' me. I's a pirate cap'n meself 'fore all o' this 'appened. Ah, grand ole days, those were, piratin' along with me mateys." I released a sigh and sent Bennet a wink before disappearing back into the carriage.

"Egad, Captain, you have captured a pirate, and claim her to be Lady Catherina? His Grace will not tolerate such. He will have the pirate hang, I tell you," Edmond stated, a shiver in his otherwise cocksure tone.

Bennet chuckled, saying, "We shall see, Edmond. We shall see," and slipped into the carriage beside me, shutting the door with a click. "I declare, Rina, that was perfect. Ye 'ad tha' there man fooled, matey."

I only smirked, tossing my chin into the air. "An' ye doubted me fer a second, d'ye not?"

"Ha, I reckon I mighta. But only fer a second."

I stifled a chuckle at Bennet's perfect, or rather, imperfect, accent. He had some pirate in him, after all. I just hoped I had enough lady in me to pass so I could return home as soon as possible.

It was huge. And this time, it rivaled even my beloved *Rina* in grandeur.

'Twas a tall, possibly four story house built just on the outskirts on London that added to the city a sense of nobility which the remainder of buildings in the heart of the city did not possess. It was a simple tan color of brick, with a roof shingled in a bluish-gray that resembled the bottom of the ocean, but the design of the house was certainly not simple.

The grounds were freshly trimmed, along with the tall bushes lining the pathway to the house. Two tall trees blew in the breeze at the house's side, swaying whereas the house remained perfectly still, in control of its very posture.

All the windows in the house glowed with light, beckoning me to come forth. And, oh, how I wanted to do just that. But I could not run into the house of my father any more than I could run into his arms.

The carriage pulled to a halt in front of the Duke of Rothsford's townhouse, and the horses neighed as though welcoming the familiar sight. After a moment, the door burst open at my right, and Edmond came into view. He eyed me warily, a frown appearing on his thin lips, but he extended his arm for me nevertheless.

Instead of continuing with my charade, I laid my hand on his elbow and slid from the carriage, muttering as sweetly a thank you as could. I tilted my head back, gazing upon the house.

It was mine. Or 'twould be, I supposed, whenever I chose to accept it.

Would I? Would I accept this turn of fate, this new journey I had embarked upon? Would I open my arms to receive the truth, or would I push it away in disgust?

I was unsure, which was a rarity for me. I didn't know whether or not I should plunge headfirst into this new existence of mine, or if I should give it no more than a cursory glance and then return to my thieving, murderous ways.

Father would have loved to have seen the wealth he had been born into, I knew, despised it though he may have. He would have wanted to somehow embrace his heritage, his family, hate them though he had. He would have wanted to be welcomed into the nobility and abundance of the Winterbournes.

Except he had never had the chance. But now I did. I had a chance to know the only family—Father's family—I would ever have. I had a chance to get to know Father's half-brother, my birth father. I had a chance to actually have a part in the life Father had never had. Perhaps he would want this, for me to carry on his memory as I journeyed through this place. Perhaps he would have desired that I meet my parents one day, that he could too have been invited into the family.

So perhaps I would welcome this change, if only for a while. I would experience what Father never had, and I would do it for him.

Only for him. Not for any other man on this fateful earth.

Bennet suddenly appeared beside me, offering his elbow. "Shall we?"

Instinct bid me not to, but I rested my hand in the crook of his elbow anyway. I was a lady, after all. And ladies received the escort of gentlemen, though I couldn't necessarily refer to Bennet and myself as such highly regarded folk. I *was* a killer, a thief, a drunkard, and a criminal more than had I ever been an aristocrat. De jure, I ought to be hanged just for carting my pirating behind into London.

Slowly, we walked from the carriage down the paved pathway to the house, the light streaming in from the glass door drawing me in like a rushing tide. Once we reached the door, it swung open to reveal a tall and distinctively young man dressed impeccably and boasting a pair of curious cinnamon eyes that lighted upon me instantly.

"Captain Bennet. Miss." He ushered us in and removed Bennet's topcoat before reaching for mine. I allowed him to pull the velvet coat from my shoulders, having to stifle a laugh at the sight of his bulging eyes as he caught a glimpse of my shirt. That single irremovable spot of blood from that one battle ran down the side of my blouse, and my lacy collar dipped down to reveal much more than was considered ladylike.

I tipped my tricorn and curtsied slightly. "Captain Blackstone at your service, my good man," I said in a throaty voice that belied my gender.

The man shot Bennet a glare, as everyone seemed to be doing these days, and shut the door behind us. "A pleasure… Captain."

Bennet only chuckled, taking my elbow and leading me farther into the room

And what a ginormous room it was. Round and ornately carved pillars held up a vaulted ceiling; beautifully designed carpet led the way to a staircase; lights glistened along the railings of the stairs, urging me to step onto the rug and follow the path of the stairs up into this beautiful palace. Windows at the wall in front of me poured in light, casting shadows along the stairwell as it split in two. Everything glistened in gold and red, and I held up my hand and watched as the light danced on the ruby ring.

Then footfalls, light and airy like a lady's breeze, pitter-pattered from the right of the foyer, and I looked up to see a billow of pale blue float down the stairs in a cloud. The billow became a gown, and the lacy gown appeared in full view, exposing a petite woman no more than fifteen years older than me.

The little woman all but flew down the stairs in a surge of blue and chocolate brown before halting at the bottom of the steps. She was certainly older than me, but her face, fair and smooth, bore no markings of age aside from wrinkles around her blue eyes, nor did her dark brown hair sport a single strand of gray. She stood there, hand poised on the railing, in the most graceful position, her head of curls held high. She wore a sparkling grin that revealed straight white teeth and dimples in her cheeks, and her perfectly portioned features were colored by a smile.

I wanted to turn to Bennet and ask who she was, but before I could even the swallow the lump in my throat over my own assumption, the woman flew down the last step and ate up the floor between us with small yet quick footsteps.

Her smile only grew at the sight of Bennet, but her gaze landed on me as she tilted her head back. Those bright blue eyes bored into me like a nail into wood, and yet nothing but love glistened in them. "You look just like your father," she whispered, the words penetrating the air like a blade.

I stumbled back, only to be caught by Bennet's strong arm. This beautiful—and extremely short—woman was my mother.

How could someone so graceful, so gorgeous, so absolutely, well, everything that I wasn't, be my mother? Here I stood, dressed in men's attire, an eyepatch strapped to my head, innocent blood on my hands, with a mother that looked up at me with such adoration that it broke my heart into a million shards. How could someone such as her find it in her heart to even look at me without collapsing in heartrending shock? How could she say I looked like my father when she did not know who I was, what I did, how I lived? I would break her heart.

And I couldn't do that.

"Ana? Where have you gotten off to now?" The voice, deep and yet light with teasing, boomed from the top of the staircase. I did not know that voice, and yet something about it pricked my heart with familiarity.

Father.

My mother turned toward the stairs as black boots came into sight. "Oh, Richard, come here and see! Our daughter has returned! Xavier found her!" She spun around in glee, clasping her hands to her heart. Suddenly, she stopped, and glanced back at me. She reached up and took my hands in hers.

I swallowed against the lump in my throat and blinked back that dashed moisture that formed my eye. "M-mother?" No, no, she couldn't be mine. She couldn't have carried me inside her for nine months. Not this delicate little fairy. She wouldn't want me either, not for long. Not when she and my father learned of my crimes, my habits, my sins.

My mother only smiled, tears falling from her eyes. "Yes, dear Catherina, it is your mother. You are home now."

I forced myself to look into those eyes, feeling my heart wrench from my chest. I knew those eyes. I had looked into them long ago, had seen the love radiating from them. I knew those hands. I had felt them long ago, had experienced the comfort they brought. And I knew that voice. I had heard it long ago, had listened to it as it sung to me a lullaby.

My fingers had once clasped that chocolaty hair, my body had once lain in those arms. I knew it. I could feel it.

But that didn't mean I *should*.

"Ana," a voice croaked, certainly not the same voice that had boomed through the house only moments ago, and yet somehow it was.

Both Mother and I looked up to find an imposing figure standing at the bottom of the stairs.

He was tall, just as Bennet had said. He was strong; I could tell by the muscles in the arms that hung uselessly by his side. He was brave; the clenched jaw that bore a small scar bespoke that. And he was kind, for I knew by the glint in his eyes. And he was mine.

With an intimidating height and well-muscled figure, His Grace, the Duke of Rothsford, Richard Winterbourne was a noble looking man with sandy brown hair sprinkled with silver that fell to his collar in slight waves, piercing green eyes, a slightly crooked nose, a firm jaw with a small cleft in his chin, high cheekbones, and thick eyebrows. He was certainly a handsome man, still in his prime at only a few years past two scores.

He had the same dimple in his chin that my uncle had, the same wave to his hair, and the same bearing that spoke of courage, pride, and intelligence. The family resemblance was certainly noticeable, and that observation slowed my racing heart. But only a little.

My mother stepped to the side as the duke, my father, moved slowly toward me. His gaze, such a beautiful green, met mine and never left. "Rina."

Chapter 16

"Father."

It was not a question as it sprang from my lips, but neither was it a statement. It was an agreement, a revelation, and a plea all at once. It was agreeing with him and all the others who had said I was his. It was revealing to myself that such was true. And it was pleading with my very last breath that somehow, someway, he would love me.

But he couldn't. I didn't deserve it.

From anyone.

And certainly not from my father.

I bit my lip to keep back the tears as I closed the space between my father and me. I could not let myself get too close to them, whether they were my parents or not. I would only be a disappointment, I knew, and likely already was. So I cleared my throat and pasted on a small smile, the most I dared.

"You've grown up quite a bit since I last saw you," my father said with a mirthless chuckle, his gaze flickering with sorrow and regret.

I suppressed a laugh of my own, having to look away from the sadness in his eyes. "And you as well."

Silence enveloped us then, not even normally chatty Bennet opening his mouth to speak. Finally, after a long, tense moment, a soft hand slipped into mine.

"Well, I suppose we ought to show Catherina to her room," Mother said, breaking the quiet with her gentle voice as she tugged me with her up the stairs.

For a split second, I thought I heard footsteps following behind us, but when I glanced back over my shoulder, none of the men had moved.

I knew it. My father was repulsed by me. 'Twould not be long before he kicked me out of his home—or worse, had me hanged. Not that I blamed him. If I were a noblewoman whose long-lost daughter had returned after nearly thirty years as a pirate, I'd deny even the fact that the child was mine.

Perhaps that was it. Perhaps the duke just didn't believe I was his child. I hadn't believed him to be my father until Captain Ben had told me of my uncle's true heritage. And if Charlie had told him that story, then assisted with my capture, how could I not believe it?

But if the duke, my very real father, didn't trust Bennet's word, then how could I prove it to be true? My ring was no evidence, leastwise not to Rothsford. I was a pirate, after all; 'twas not *that* hard to steal a simple ring.

Ugh, I would ponder that later. Later, when I was not such an emotional wreck.

Mother dragged me up the stairs with surprising strength for someone so small, pulling me into a hallway adorned with painting upon painting, candelabra after candelabra, red from the walls blurring as we hurried through the hall.

Suddenly, Mother stopped and faced me, the tears that streamed down her cheeks belying the smile on her lips. "You don't know how long we've searched for you, Catherina. We've missed you so much. And we love you. We always will." She pushed up onto her tiptoes, though the top of her head still barely reached my collarbone, and cupped my cheeks.

But as soon as her soft fingers brushed against my skin, I jerked back. The touch was too loving, too kind to be real. She could not love a pirate, child of her youth though I might be. I turned aside, forcing my emotions away, willing myself to listen to that voice in the back of my mind and take control.

Mother obviously sensed my discomfort, and spun around to leave, her gaze pointed at the floor, which was likely more receptive than me. "Here is your room, Catherina. I'll give you a moment to freshen yourself. I shall be in the foyer should you need me," she called over her shoulder as she started away.

But then she stopped, tossing one last look to me. "Ignore the bassinet."

I wrinkled my brow, unsure what she meant, as she disappeared down the hallway, carrying her light and love along with her. It didn't register in my mind, what she'd said, until I opened the door behind me and peered into the room.

It was a beautiful room, even more glorious than I had expected, but a coat of grief seemed to cover it along with the dust that filled my nose as I stepped into the room. A bassinet was placed in the center of the room, cold and alone. Like myself.

Except I was cold and alone only because I had chosen to be.

I walked straight to the baby bed, disregarding the rest of the room. A simple little lacy thing it was, with one small pillow tucked inside. But what caught my eye was the thin red blanket pushed into the corner in a ball as though kicked away in anger. I pulled it from its prison and held it up to my nose, breathing in a scent of baby and love and lavender. It fit perfectly in my hand, and a sense of remembrance surfaced in my mind.

A thumb plugged in my mouth, the softness of the blanket against my cheek, arms around me, lips warming my brow.

"Oh, she's so very beautiful, Richard. I hope she never grows older," Mama says, rubbing her cheek against mine, cooing sweet words into my ear.

Daddy chuckles from where he lays in his bed. "But then you will never have grandchildren to snuggle with, love." He leaves the bed and steps up beside Mama to lean over her shoulder and look at me.

I grin, and he pops his finger in my mouth. "Ah, she's cutting a tooth. Your little baby is growing up, Ana."

How did I recall a babe's memory from so long ago? I shoved it aside. I had control. Control over every memory, every word, every thought, every…

Nothing. I had no control any longer. I could not control the nightmares, my capture, my fate, nor even the simple thoughts inside my head.

And yet I could have control over how I responded to them.

Pacing the floor, Richard Winterbourne jammed a hand through his greying hair, avoiding Xavier Bennet's gaze at all costs. Her image, both past and present, was embedded in his mind. Gone was the chubby, fair face of his daughter. Gone were her sparkling blue-green eyes filled with life. Gone was her innocence, her youth.

Now she stood an inch taller than he, proud and strong, with a muscled figure befitting a man, the scars of a warrior, the pain of a thousand deaths etched into that steel eye of a wolf, her skin as tan as a Carib's.

"She's a pirate." The words left his lips, ringing hollow through the air. He should have known. Should've realized that once his wretch of a half-brother had gotten a hold of his daughter, he would've ruined every last bit of her in the process.

Why had it been now, almost thirty years later, that she was found? Why hadn't it been when she was still a babe, or perhaps a child, before the world had tainted her?

"Captain Rina Blackstone of the *Rina*. She's the fiercest pirate captain to ever plunder the Seven Seas." Xavier's voice held such admiration that it nearly tore Richard to shreds. If Xavier could hold her in such high esteem, then surely she was not all bad.

Not that badness mattered. The thought of her sins, her crimes, was not what tortured his mind. It was the very fact that she had been thrown into the hands of the devil himself.

"What is she like?" Richard turned to Xavier, accustom to the smile he wore yet not to the flash in his dark eyes.

"I believe that is for me to know and for you to find out, Your Grace," the younger man said, his tone almost taunting.

Perhaps he didn't want to find out. Perhaps there was not even a sliver left of the baby girl he had once known. Had all the life, all the love, all the brightness she'd once held been drained away? She was still so young, with so much promise. She could've had such a better life here, if only Maverick had not stolen her from him. She would have grown up in love and laughter, frolicking through the grounds in their home in Yorkshire. She would have made friends with all the servants and tenants, would have known and loved them all. She would have married, likely to some earl or marquess that had caught her eye. She would have had children, sweet little young ones that gazed up at their grandfather with those same glittery ocean eyes.

But she hadn't had that life. She'd spent her days raised by ruthless criminals, her childhood with killers and thieves. Her only memories would be of blood and stolen treasure, of revelry and debauchery. She had never known love or laughter, friends or family. She had only known pain and heartache, evil and sin.

A thought flew into his mind, one so very wrong that it made him long to plant the fist he now formed into his brother's face. Richard drew his gaze up to Xavier's and asked the one question he wasn't sure he wanted an answer to. "Does she have any children?"

He shook his head in reply. "Not a one. Or at least none that she has told me of."

Yes, that was reassuring enough. "And how much has she told you?"

Xavier grinned sheepishly, rubbing the back of his neck. "Not enough. But I know she has spoken time and again of an Ellie and Julius." His sparkling eyes dimmed. "I think Julius was her brother."

Something stirred inside him at the statement. A brother. Oh, how many times had he longed to have a son, a sibling for his long lost Catherina? But after Ana had given birth to their daughter, the chances of her having another were slim. Very slim.

Richard unclenched his fist and rubbed his suddenly sweaty palms on his thighs. "She has no brother," he spat. Maverick's child was no brother of hers and no nephew of his.

He knew the hatred boiling inside him was not Christlike, but neither was the apathy towards Maverick's actions that Ana so strongly held to. But perhaps what he called apathy was indeed God's blessed forgiveness…

Oh, what did it matter?

"And you were not her father until three weeks ago." Xavier sighed, leaning up against a pillar. "You cannot expect her to so easily let go of Blackstone. He was her father, the only parental figure she knows. And from what I've heard, he was quite the good one. The hurt you see in her eyes, that is because of him. He was murdered ten years ago, and now his killer is after her. She still loves him, Rothsford. And he loved her."

Richard could feel the ire coursing through his blood. Maverick and love did not belong in the same sentence. If the man had loved Catherina, he would have returned her to her rightful father and never saw her again. "How, Captain Bennet, can a pirate love?"

"The same way all humans love: with their heart. A criminal is no more incapable of love than you are. God loved Maverick Blackstone just as much as He loves you. And if God can love all people, no matter how evil, then why shouldn't we?"

He was right, as always. And Richard was wrong, again. *Father, help me to let go of the anger and unforgiveness in my heart. Help me give Rina the love she needs*, he silently prayed, lifting his gaze up to the ceiling above him.

Ana's footsteps flew down the stairs then, and Richard turned to see his wife bound down the steps towards him. Her smile had dimmed, her eyes had dried, her joyous light seemed as though it had been doused by water.

Richard hurried toward her and held out his arms as she fell into his embrace. She wrapped her arms around his neck, her gentle frame fitting against him perfectly. "Oh,

Richard, I don't know what to do, what to say. She's just so, so...distant." A tear slipped from her eye, and she sniffled as she tangled her fingers in his hair as she was wont to do.

He held her tighter and whispered up yet another prayer. "Well, we'll just have to change that, won't we?"

I could only pace back and forth through this new bedchamber of mine, trying to determine what I ought to do. Should I collapse onto the soft canopy bed and sink into the silky green comforter, allowing myself to disappear from this odd world if only for a moment? Should I examine every nook and cranny, searching for more buried memories? Or perhaps I should leave the room and do what? Apologize for my actions?

I had sent my own dear mother, a woman I had never known yet always yearned for, away without a word. The very thought pierced my heart even deeper than Wilde's blade. I should not feel such emotion, such pain, but this entire experience had opened up some hidden well of feeling from inside the stone wall I had tried so hard to erect around my heart.

After my uncle's death, I didn't want to love, to feel, to even breathe. I wanted to die and get it over with. But I knew that I couldn't. I knew that I would have to go after Julius, that I would have to carry on his memory. And then Keaton had arrived two years later, dragged on board my ship at ten and six, buried in a grief that only I could understand. His parents had both died within a year after the loss of his baby sister. How could I not connect with the boy?

I'd taught him how to let go of his grief just as I had. To let go, forget, toss it into the sea. To live in the moment, direct one's own path, overthrow fate and take the helm of one's own life. And it had worked for a time. But now, something even greater than fate took my helm and steered me far off course, into a current I could not control, that I couldn't pull out of.

And now look at me. I was lost, confused, and drowning in a hurt that I hadn't felt before in my life.

Was this what that loving God of Bennet's did to His creation? Toss them into Davy Jones's locker and leave them to figure life out for themselves? Ah, but I deserved so much less than this. I deserved death and hell. Confusion and hurt was the most delightful sort of punishment I could ever endure.

Perhaps I should savor this gift from God, should thank Him for allowing me to live my wretched life this long. Perhaps I should thank Him for giving me parents that I would only disappoint.

I should've been better. I should have given up on my life, left the sea when Uncle died, and forged a new path. I had been so young then, still at least a little innocent. My name was not known then, and I could have settled into England without needing a pardon. I wouldn't have made it very far in life, not much farther than a tavern wench or a maid at the best, but at least I'd known enough to protect myself and make a living. Perhaps then I could have gotten married and had children. Perhaps then my parents could have loved me. Perhaps then I could have been deserving of more.

But it was too late, and whining over what I could never have would only make things seem worse.

Yet it was not too late to start over.

The thought appeared into my mind unbidden, though I couldn't dismiss it, no matter how much I wanted to.

So perhaps I could start over, could at least soften my heart enough to welcome my parents into it. Perhaps I could prove to them that I was more than a criminal needing to be hanged.

And I knew just where I needed to start.

The door to my chamber creaked open, and a petite woman—or perhaps she looked so only because I towered over her by nearly two feet and weighed probably seventy pounds more than she—stepped into the room. She bobbed a curtsy, never meeting my gaze. "Milady, Her Grace bid me to come and be sure you were comfortable with this room. There are gowns for you inside the wardrobe, in case you are in need of a change. Will there be anything else I could get for you, milady?"

I had to suppress a laugh at the young girl's trembling tone. Well, if I was to prove myself, who was to say I could not begin with the servants? "Ah, no thank you. I believe everything is to my liking. And, please, call me Rina. All of my crew does."

Then did the girl glance up at me, her wide eyes sizing me up in one swift look. "Edmond said you were a fright." She gulped, fingering with the hem of her apron. "I suppose I did not know quite what to expect."

I threw out my hands with a chuckle. If she had met Elliot on one of his bad days, she would then know the true definition of *fright*. "I can assure you, the fright is only skin deep."

She seemed to find that sufficient, for she curtsied again, this time the hints of a smile turning up her lips. "I'll pass it on, then. I'm Delphie, by the way. Your lady's maid."

"A pleasure. Tell my mother I'll be down in a trice," I said, the words rolling off my tongue as though I had been ordering around servants all my life. I supposed a crew of pirates wasn't much different, cruder though they may be.

Delphie nodded, then hurried from the room.

I pivoted about, coming to face the enormous wardrobe up against the wall behind me. Gowns, Delphie had said. Of all the things they expected me to wear, it had to be gowns. Goodness, I could only hope that Mother didn't force me into wearing a corset. Not that someone so little could force me into anything.

I grabbed the golden handles, the feel of them reminding me of the handle on the door to my cabin. Cold and slick, yet inviting. I yanked open the doors to the wardrobe and found hanging within exactly seventeen dresses—aye, seventeen; I counted them all—each bedecked in jewels and golden embroidering. But shoved away into the corner, still hanging all by its lonesome, was a small lacy baby gown. *My* baby gown.

Tears stung my eye even as I wondered what I had looked like as a babe, all chubby and white, I and immediately shut the doors to the closet.

Just at the same moment the bedroom door banged open. Footsteps charged into the room in the same way they had charged into my life only weeks ago. Except this time they charged in without the hurt as they had before. This time the steps pounded almost sorrowfully, as if their owner could sense my uncertainty.

And then they ceased to pound, scraping just slightly across the floor as though the toe of his boots was grazing the wood, and then the only sound in the room was that of breathing.

I spun around to find Bennet leaning up against the doorframe, his eyes following my every movement, and then trailing to the blanket I still clutched in my hand. "Come to think of it, you look quite at home in here. As if you were made for this place."

I met his gaze, hoping to find some bit of mirth sparkling there, yet sincerity was the only thing I found. Which must have been what forced the most childish and helpless sounding question from my lips."What am I supposed to do, Xavier?"

Chapter 17

I didn't know how long I sat there on the edge of my bed, just listening to Xavier's breathing and wishing there was some way I could voice what was on the tip of my tongue without sounding as desperate as I truly was. Perhaps it had been hours, or only just a few moments. I could no longer remember, could barely think except to note how at home I felt in Xavier's arms.

It had only taken that one hopeless question to bring Xavier across the room and lure me into his arms. We had sat, just waiting, Xavier likely praying. And me just wishing for an answer from some unknown Voice that I wasn't even sure existed.

How had Xavier done it? How had he returned home with blood on his hands and yet was still welcomed by the love of his parents?

I lifted my head from where it rested on his chest and looked up at him, at the peaceful, serene expression on his handsome face. I could ask. It wouldn't hurt. Perhaps open up an old wound in his heart, but then it might help him to talk about it. And help me to know that *someone* could be forgiven for their sins, even if I couldn't.

"How did your parents forgive you?"

The words spilled out even as I just convinced myself to say them, jerking Xavier's head up and suddenly tensing his entire body. "You mean after I killed him?" His tone was calm, though his eyes, swirling with remembrance and hurt, were far from such.

I nodded.

He heaved a rough sigh, tearing his gaze from mine. "I don't know, Rina. I just, well… I suppose that since God has forgiven all of us our sins, then Mother and Father knew they should bestow the same mercy and grace on me. And Father has killed probably as many men as you have, so he understood guilt and forgiveness more than I ever could. But not everyone understands that forgiveness, you know? After it had happened and I had sought out God's forgiveness, I found the man's family an-and apologized. They weren't as accepting, but it lifted a huge load off my shoulders."

I could only frown. It was all centered around God for him, wasn't it? Xavier's very life was based on Him, it seemed. And I was what? Nothing, because I didn't believe? Just dust, because I knew that there was no such thing as a supernatural being, that it was the will inside men's hearts that controlled their lives?

A will that I obviously no longer had, for my life was out of *anyone*'s control, and most assuredly mine.

I returned my head to his chest and shut my eye against the realization, the truth. "How did it happen?" I had to steer this conversation back into at least somewhat safer ground, somewhere away from God and His mercy.

Apparently this new ground was much safer, for Xavier chuckled, albeit mirthlessly, and relaxed a bit. "It was six years ago, when I had just boarded the *Lady Jess* and set out with a good bit of expensive cargo to the colonies in America. Turns out I had a few pirates on board, for my crew began a mutiny and took over the ship, leaving me in Charles Town, and sailed off somewhere else with all that cargo.

"I still don't know whatever happened to my ship or the men, but I myself ended up in quite the predicament. I had a lot of trouble with my temper back in those days, and it was no surprise when I winded up in a tavern. To summarize things, I got drunk and challenged a man to a fight. To the death."

Xavier, drunk and fighting. What a sight that must have been! I could hardly imagine the seemingly perfect man sitting beside me in a drunken brawl, let alone beating a man to death. And yet the idea that he'd resorted to such violence and had killed a man in cold blood sent a shudder through me. Odd, seeing as how I myself had run my sword through so many men only for their treasure.

And yet he had been forgiven, had confessed that he had sinned and laid all his guilt and shame down and had been given mercy and grace. Perhaps there was something to this God thing after all.

Or perhaps it was all a fantasy, just as Uncle had said, for the simple and weak-minded who needed a crutch to get through life. Except Xavier was certainly not simple nor weak-minded. Perhaps a bit delusional, but not quite weak-minded.

I sighed, sitting up and rising from the bed. Truly, I put myself into such compromising positions that it was a wonder I hadn't been ravished yet. Not that Xavier was the sort of man to force himself upon a woman, or that I was the kind to allow such.

"How would you feel if, say, you had a child that you hadn't seen nor heard from in almost thirty years, and the next time you see them, you realize that they have been a pirate captain for the last ten years and have done countless things that any respectable person wouldn't dare to dream of?" Something creaked just as I spoke the words, and I glanced towards the door, only to find it shut. But the sound of footsteps fading met my ears regardless.

"I would do just what your parents are doing, Rina," Xavier said as he stood up as well and came to my side. "I'd love you with my whole heart."

"You mean the heart that I stole?" I raised an eyebrow, having to suppress a grin.

"Ah, but of course."

If I were to be honest with myself, I would admit that I felt out of place and like an unnecessary second helm. If I were to be extremely honest, I would admit that I frankly didn't care.

It had been an odd family reunion, but needed nonetheless. After Rina and I had spent about an hour holed away in her room talking and thinking and praying, I had prepared to leave, to bid her ladyship farewell for good—unless I would have seen her at church on Sunday before I set out again—but Her Grace had stopped me. Things were awkward enough between Rina and her parents as it was, and I supposed that all three of them in the same giant house for only the Lord knew how long would be even harder until they got things straightened out. Until Rina opened her heart.

Until Rothsford let go of the past and embraced the present. Until both of them learned the power of forgiveness.

So I stayed. Likely only for the remainder of the day, but I would savor these last few hours with Rina. I didn't know how I was going to be able to walk out of this grand manor, knowing I might never see Rina again, unless she decided to finish what she'd started and raided the *Jessica* once we both returned to the sea. *If* she returned to the sea. One could never know what the future held. But if I were to be completely honest with myself, I would admit that I wanted Rina in my future.

Not that I was in the mood for honesty.

The afternoon had come and gone by now, and the day was coming to a close. The duchess had obviously been certain that Rina was to come home today, for she had planned a lavish dinner to welcome home her daughter. Now for that I knew Rina would be grateful. The woman did indeed have an appetite. Or at least she did when she wasn't preparing to meet her parents for the first time in forever.

I knocked my fist against the doorjamb of the sitting room, where Her Grace sat on the harpsichord bench, her fingers poised on the keys as though she were about to begin playing. For a moment I was unsure where Rina was until I glanced up at the tall and slender figure leaning against the harpsichord.

At the first glance, one would immediately think that she didn't belong here, all bedecked in her tight breeches, low-necked blouse, and knee-high boots. But there was something about the way she held her head to the side, her nose up in the air, her one green eye glazed over as though she were staring into a world I could not see. There was something in the way that she folded her arms over her chest and crossed her legs at the ankles, as though completely at home in this place. And then when she turned her head and shot me a steel grey glare that seemed to slice through the air and pierce my soul, something flickered in her eye, something akin to acceptance.

Suddenly, the duchess turned around, breaking through my reverie and causing my gaze to leave Rina, and smiled. "Ah, Xavier. I was wondering where you had gotten off to."

I returned her smile and took that as my invitation to step into the room. "I have come to escort her ladyship to dinner, and your husband should be right behind me, Your Grace," I replied with a bow. I glanced towards Rina, only to find her staring at the harpsichord as though it were the most interesting thing she had ever laid eyes on. And it likely wasn't. I made my way to her and extended my arm, though I was certain she wouldn't take it.

She didn't.

Pushing away from the harpsichord, she brushed past me as though she had never even noticed my existence and walked to her mother's side. "Mother was going to demonstrate the harpsichord to me, Captain Bennet, but I suppose that will have to wait until you finally decide to relieve me of your obnoxious presence." She spat the words like a curse, only then looking over her shoulder at me, an eyebrow raised. "That will be soon, will it not?"

Before I could answer, the duchess set her hand on her daughter's arm and said, "Actually, I was going to ask Captain Bennet if he would be so kind as to remain with us a few more days. But if that does not sit well—"

"I would love to," I interrupted before Rina could manage a response, who fortunately did the right thing and kept her delicious mouth shut once I had uttered the words.

My, but the woman was the most fickle human being I had ever met. One moment, she was content in my arms. The next, she gave me no more regard than one did a stray dog.

The duchess clasped her hands in delight. "Good. I will have Hanna prepare one of the upstairs bedrooms for you. Now, I must admit I'm starving." She looped her arm through Rina's. "Let's be on our way then, shall we?"

"We shall." Rina followed her mother from the room, leaving me to trail behind like said dog at her heels.

I turned into the hallway just as Rothsford walked up alongside me. I copied Her Grace and slid my arm through the duke's. "I suppose we'll have to escort ourselves. Won't we, Your Grace?"

The older man grinned, revealing a pair of childish dimples, yet his smile didn't quite reach his eyes. "That we will." His gaze then left mine and found its way to his daughter.

"Don't worry. She'll come around. It only took a week before she and I became the best of friends," I assured him as best as I could, although I was lying for certain. We had overcome our differences to a degree, but friends I was convinced we would never be. And certainly not within a week.

Rothsford seemed not to notice my dishonesty, but sighed nevertheless. "I'm afraid we will need much more than a week, Xavier. But at least she and Ana are getting along."

We continued down the hallway in silence, except for the clomp of our footsteps, until we reached the dinning room, which was a smaller space than the most of the rooms, but was just as grand. It certainly rivaled my family's dinning room.

I watched as Rina slid into a chair at the end of the table, sitting as rigid as humanly possible, her hands in her lap. Her head turned only slightly as she took in the entire room, likely noting every single detail through only her one eye.

I left Rothsford in the doorway to find his own seat, and slipped in beside her ladyship. "I hope you're hungry, for your mother's cook prepares quite the meal. And I hear tonight is extra special."

Rina only grunted, shifting in her chair.

Yes, 'twas to be a long, long evening.

It wasn't necessarily considered often that a knock sounded on the door to Richard's study, but almost always Ana stood outside waiting to be called in and to bestow upon her husband one of those bright smiles of hers. So when Richard heard a knock just after he had settled into his study for the evening after dinner, he put down his quill and called her in.

Except it wasn't Ana's slight figure that appeared in the doorway, but rather the tall, imposing figure of his daughter. She stood, arms behind her back, her eye darting back and forth across the room. "Very nice study, Your Grace. I can see why you chose this room to work in," she stated matter-of-factly, her voice flat and emotionless.

"Thank you, Rina," he replied, sweeping his gaze over her long legs and the broad shoulders that seemed to slump in—dejection? Surely *she* did not feel cast out, the one who had just gained wealth and security and a family. For it was he who had been rejected by the woman that now stood before him, her eye almost blue in the candle-light.

But perhaps there was more to her facade of disinterest than he realized.

"I see you and Ana are getting along well." Richard stood from his chair and rounded the desk, his gaze not once leaving his daughter.

She turned her head toward the opposite side of the room, a hand coming up to adjust the strap of her eyepatch. "Aye. Mother is certainly a pleasant person. Kind and loving I have found as well." Her feet shifted, and Rina spun on her heels to face him full-on. Her face was a hard, cold mask, devoid of any emotion. Except her jaw moved back and forth in perhaps contemplation, her silvery-blue gaze studying him like an astronomer did the stars.

"I'm a pirate, you know." She spat the words like a curse...a curse upon her life.

"I do."

"A right good one at that."

"So I've heard."

"And I am your daughter."

Finally, it all fell into place. Richard knew where she was heading with her words, why her gaze suddenly went steel grey, why her fists remained clenched at her sides. "I would have it no other way," he replied, wanting only to know that somewhere deep down inside her she would accept the truth. The truth that he frankly didn't care what she had done, that he forgave her and loved her with every ounce of love in his heart. Just as God did as well.

Unfortunately, it seemed that it would take some time before such happened.

Rina raised a dark brown eyebrow over her eyepatch, the action appearing to question him even as green sparked deep in her iris. "Would you really?"

He stepped towards her, coming close enough that he could reach out and place his hands on her shoulders, to assure her that, yes, he longed for nothing more than to have his daughter, no matter what she was. But he didn't. Instead he clasped his hands behind his back and gave her a soft smile. "Catherina, you are my daughter, my only child. And I would give everything I have to hold you in my arms one more time. I love you more than life itself. And nothing you could ever do would change that."

Suddenly, a tear trickled down her cheek as her countenance softened and her bottom lip began to tremble. No words left her lips as she closed the space between them and slid her arms around his neck, but no words were needed. Her embrace was all he could ask for.

Chapter 18

I was beginning—albeit slightly—to wonder if perhaps there was more to land than dryness. There was something about the solidity of land that countered the tossing of the ocean's waves, that seemed to describe the consistency and reliability of the feel of something hard beneath one's feet. One knew that nothing could toss them like a storm or shake their foundation when their feet were planted solely on the earth. And should tempest or quake come, one could always rely on land to remain steadfast, to always support.

Perhaps that was what love was like. A solid rock that would not wash away with the next wave nor drown in a storm. It could not fade over time and leave one stranded. It was not unpredictable, where one was left to wonder where they would be if a wave crashed over them and pulled them into the blue depths of the ocean. It forever remained, through trial and tragedy and storm and danger. And nothing and no one could ever take it away.

This concept was completely new to me, countering everything I had ever known. I had lived my entire life on a foundation of water and tossing waves that had no rule or way. And I was beginning to see the error in such. But it was a painful realization, diminishing every belief I had once held—or rather, hadn't held.

The waves had always represented fate for me, always taking me places I did or did not wish to go, moving upon their own accord. And I was at the helm, trying to redirect my ship and pull against fate's current. But now I realized that I could never escape the current, struggle though I might.

Land had no waves to drag me to and fro. It was still, although filled with so many hills and valleys that one would always be left to wonder where they were going. But land didn't move so quickly or drag one away. It allowed one to wander through its caves and mountains and forests and plains. And no matter where one wandered, land would always be there.

Don't get me wrong, I still loved my ocean. I would always love the challenge and the exhilaration of the waves. But I was finding that I loved the land as well. What I loved most of all, though, was not the land itself, but its fidelity.

Xavier would compare the land to his God, I knew, and His faithfulness and steadfast love. He would say how no matter what, God was always there. God had no mountains and valleys or storms and quakes. He could not erode or wash away. Eventually land would do that, I knew. But while I roamed the earth for my short life, I could rely on land to remain as it was.

I could rely on God for all eternity. He never changed. He was the same yesterday, today, and tomorrow. And His faith never faltered, His trust never faded, and His love never failed.

But what I was unsure of was whether I believed in such amazing love and faith. If I believed that Someone so great could actually forgive someone so wretched. Xavier would tell me He would, if only I let Him. Yet how I would reply to that, I knew not either.

A butterfly whizzed past me, its bright yellow wings carrying it through the air to a flower that grew on a bush a few feet away. The creature seemed to slice through the wind even as it blew in the opposite direction, defying the current of the air.

I had escaped the confines of my room—if one could call a palace a prison—earlier this morning, after I had wolfed down the bread and butter one of the maids had sent up and donned my clothes before Delphie could shove me into a dress.

I now walked through the garden at the back of the house, unable to keep from admiring the still-vibrant flowers and the beautifully designed landscaping, even as my thoughts attempted to drag me away.

It was oddly quiet, and though the silence was welcoming—as I rarely ever enjoyed such while living with a band of reveling pirates—I almost longed for a companion. And so when familiar soft yet quick footsteps found their way into my hearing, I smiled to myself.

I turned around to face Mother, still amazed at the fact that this sweet woman actually loved me and called me daughter. I had lain awake all night after my bath just thinking about it, about how Mother had so easily opened her heart before she had even met me, about how Father loved me despite it all. Of course, life was not all sweet. I was still a pirate and desperately needed to be pardoned—which meant abandoning Billy and Elliot and Charlie and Keaton and Ellie and the others—Wilde was still after me, Julius was still out there somewhere. I had nigh unto a million problems that needed solving. But for now, as I began my first whole day in my father's home and heart, I would dwell on the good things. Which did not include the fact that Xavier Bennet was still following me around practically everywhere I went.

"Why, you're up early this morning," Mother stated, making her way to my side.

I hitched a shoulder and drew my gaze back to the butterfly as it landed on a wilting rose. "I've been surprising myself at how *late* I've been awakening," I replied.

"Either way, 'tis good to see you. Your father was afraid you would stay locked up in your room all day."

"I wouldn't mind doing so." If only to avoid Bennet. The man unnerved me, unraveled me, and seemed to have cast some sort of spell over me. I never opened up to anyone, rarely even talked at all unless it was important. And yet yesterday I'd had the sudden urge to tell him everything, all the thoughts that swirled around in my head. I never permitted a man's touch, and yet I had enjoyed kissing him twice. And wouldn't much mind if I did it again.

Which is why I had to stay away from him at all costs. Funny how I had told myself that same thing at least five times but still ended up at his side. I truly was the most indecisive person.

"Well, I am glad that you chose not to." Mother slipped her hand into mine and pulled me down a brick pathway that led to a small stone bench sitting underneath a wisteria-covered arbor. She gracefully situated herself on the bench, then motioned for me to sit beside her. I plopped down and leaned forward to rest my elbows on my thighs, not quite caring about the impropriety of my position.

"So, tell me about your childhood. Maverick raised you well?"

I could hear the strain in Mother's voice, yet out of the corner of my eye I saw her peaceful expression as she leaned over to meet my gaze. Her sapphire eyes glistened with a mix of love and concern that made me long to regale her with stories of palaces and dollies and goodness and safety—things I couldn't truthfully say.

"My uncle raised me well, yes. He kept me safe from his crew and from the reality of pirating until I was about twelve years of age. During my younger years I spent most of my time either getting into trouble or studying my numbers. Uncle desired for me to have as good an education as I could. But unfortunately, I never could learn to read or write. A problem with my eyes, I suppose.

"Once I reached adolescence, I began learning how to sword-fight and such. My uncle wanted me not only to learn how to protect myself but to carry on the Blackstone name and captain my own ship one day. He was a very strict man and loved me very much, so he had rigid rules on board his ship concerning his men and me. Any man who so much as looked at me in a way he didn't like, he killed. I still uphold those same rules to this day."

I gave my mother a reassuring smile before I dove back into my tale. I told her of those good years with Elliot, of when Julius came along. I told her of how badly I had felt when Lavinia left, how hollow my heart was. Then I came to the hardest part of my story, of when Uncle died. I didn't want to bother with the gory details, just cut to the quick and say simply that my uncle had died. But the words spilled out like a waterfall.

"Wilde hated him for what happened to his family. It wasn't a hate that just boiled his blood for a few years, but a hate that still consumes him to this day. A hate that breathes fire over everyone he comes in contact with. A hate that fueled him to capture my ship and hold Julius, my uncle, and I prisoner in the brig. I don't know how long we all sat there before Wilde came in. He drew his knife and plunged it into Uncle's heart. I watched the blood trickle from his chest, watched him breathe his last. And Wilde only smiled.

"Not long after, Wilde returned, this time to slice me open, or so I had hoped." I swallowed against the tears that burned in my eyes, reaching up to remove my eyepatch. "He left me with a reminder."

Mother's eyes widened, and she slid one hand from mine and trailed her fingers over the scar, seeming to mend it anew with her touch. I never took the patch off, not even to sleep. But now I realized I ought to let that wound heal as well as the one in my heart.

A tear splashed onto Mother's finger, and I fell into her arms as the dam burst.

Eventually, my sobs dissipated, and I pulled back, swiping at my tears. I slid my patch back on and gave Mother a soft smile. "I had a father all along, though I had never known it. And I can assure you, I am not going to lose my father again."

I was also beginning to wonder if perhaps it would take more patience to become accustomed to my newfound ladyship than I had originally figured.

We had only just finished our midday meal when Mother grabbed my hand and began to drag me up the stairs to the second floor, leaving Father and Bennet to whatever they had been up to all morning. I had absolutely no idea what had Mother in such a tizzy or what had Bennet seeming to avoid me. Not that I cared if I ever laid eyes on him again. In fact, I found the idea of never seeing him quite appealing.

Or at least I wanted to find it appealing.

I picked up my feet to refrain from tripping over the stair steps as Mother carted me away. "I beg your pardon, Mother, but could you explain the rush?"

She tossed a glance at me over her shoulder, but didn't dare to slow her pace. "Your father just informed me that the Duke of Mayshire is planning a visit this afternoon. And I will not have my daughter meet a duke in breeches."

Ah, so that was what it was about then. My frightening appearance. "I'm afraid I've already met a duke in breeches," I replied, unable to keep from teasing her, nor to keep from wishing that all those seventeen fancy gowns wouldn't fit.

"Perhaps, but that was your father, and there was no way around that. At least now we can have you looking like a proper lady."

Proper lady. The one phrase that could never describe me. But how was I to refuse Mother? I released a sigh. "Very well then."

A thought flew into my mind, and though I wanted to banish it, I couldn't help but wonder. What would Bennet think of me in a dress? Childish, I knew it sounded, and completely stupid. What did I care about what Xavier Bennet thought of my appearance? But even as I didn't want to care, I did.

Ugh, rebellious, uncontrolled mind of mine.

We reached the top of the staircase and continued down the length of hallway to my room, where Mother swung open the door to reveal Delphie already setting out a green gown adorned with white lace and little diamonds shimmering along the collar.

I gulped, glancing down at the ruffly mangled collar of my blouse that hid a tear and a few bloodstains, then at the stripe of blood that accompanied the scar running down my side. Just another constant reminder of what Wilde had done to me.

Perhaps it wouldn't be so bad to be out of the clothes I had worn for the last three weeks. Well, so long as Mother didn't insist upon me wearing one of those crushing contraptions. My waist was small enough as it was.

The door clicked shut behind me as Mother ushered me farther into the room. "Now, let's see about getting you out of these breeches," she said, beginning to rip my shirt off my head. I was undressed in a flash, and before a breath could leave my mouth, a shift was being thrown over my head, followed by layers of ruffles and silky soft fabric that slid onto my rough skin like a fluffy cloud. Then Delphie assisted me into the gown, the emerald silk falling from my body to the floor in a long flow of green. Everything fit, from the long sleeves that dripped with lace to the bodice that hugged my waist to the skirt that didn't so much as reveal my toes. Toes that were then being slipped into soft little slippers.

Now I remembered why I never dressed so fine. I wouldn't survive an hour on board my ship like this. And not just because I would rip my skirt.

Mother led me across the room to the vanity, where the mirror above it bounced back my reflection to me in an array of greens and browns and white. I looked, well, different, to say the least. I could barely recognize the figure in the mirror, although my face was most assuredly mine. A lady. That was what I looked like. A noble born lady with royal blood.

And once I had thought the notion impossible.

Mother came up behind me, her lips upturned in a bright smile that revealed straight white teeth. "You look gorgeous, Catherina. I cannot wait to see the men's faces when they lay eyes on you."

I snorted, even as I returned her smile with one equally bright. "I highly doubt their faces will convey much more than utter horror."

Mother chuckled, a soft yet hearty sound that matched the lilt in her cheerful voice. "We shall see," was all she said before she rose on her tiptoes and reached up to tug my hair free of its messy queue. She ran her fingers through the long strands, brushing them down to my waist. "Delphine, what do you say we should do with this beautiful bundle of curls?"

More like an unruly bundle of snakes in my mind, but I kept that thought to myself.

I watched from the mirror as the petite lady's maid, who happened to be shorter than Mother herself, tilted her head and *tsk*ed. "Let me see." She came to Mother's side and pulled the sides of my hair behind my head. The tresses flopped over the strap of my eyepatch and made for quite the interesting style.

Delphie frowned, then shoved me into the chair beside me. She gently removed my patch, and I shut my good eye against the image—and the horror—that would appear in the mirror. But instead of a gasp of fright coming from little Delphie, I only heard a muted whimper, as though she felt my pain. Sympathy, I believed that was called.

So I peeked open my right eye only to find Delphie's face hidden behind my hair. I glanced at my other eye, prepared to see skin torn and marred or mutilated even after all that Stark, my ship's surgeon, had done to it. But 'twas only a pinkish white line running from my forehead to my jawline that I saw.

Until I looked directly at my eye. A bright turquoise shade it was, with a line going straight through my pupil that gave me the look of a dangerous wolf. And perhaps that was what I was, naught but a dangerous wolf. A wolf that stole and killed without a thought for the people I hurt. But that part of my life was over now, was it not? I had made up my mind. I would not go back. Ever.

But how could I abandon my crew, my *family*?

I pulled my mind away from my thoughts and my gaze from my scar, only to glance up at two tiny braids wrapping around my head in a simple style, adorned only by a small glittery diamond headpiece. Now even my head was unrecognizable.

"Ah, that is positively beautiful, Delphine," Mother declared, tucking a wild curl behind my ear. "Oh, Catherina dear, you look splendid. So much like your father. I mean, your face. Not the gown. Because Richard wouldn't be caught dead in a dress, you know." She sighed, exasperated by her own stammering. "Never mind it. You are wonderful! And your jewels match the dress to perfection."

I glanced at the rings hanging from my ears and frowned. They had been a gift, so to speak, from my uncle when he had captured a French merchant brig laden with treasures of all sorts. Including the jewels I'd so proudly worn for years. Now they weighed heavy from my skin, reminding me of all the times *I* had taken advantage of other people's blessings, their money and possessions, their family.

If only I could somehow make up for everything I had done. Apologize to all those I had hurt and killed and plundered just as Bennet had apologized for his wrongdoing.

But I couldn't.

A knock sounded on my bedroom door, followed my mother's "come in." A portly maid with greying hair peeked into the room. "The Duke of Mayshire has arrived, Your Grace," the older woman said before disappearing into the hallway.

Mother all but squealed with delight. "Oh, come now, Catherina!" And with that, she jerked me from the chair and dragged me back down the stairs into the foyer.

In the foyer stood Father and a hefty man of average height, Bennet leaning against the railing of the staircase, all three immersed in some deep conversation. I tore my gaze from Bennet before he realized my presence and sent me that infernal grin of his, and looked towards who had to be the Duke of Mayshire.

He was certainly much shorter than Father and distinctively younger—probably not much older than me—but with the same noble bearing and aristocratic features of any positioned Englishman. With curls of black hair that reached his collarbone and chocolate eyes that glistened with the same smile his lips wore, he was certainly handsome. And married, by the simple gold band on his left ring finger.

"Ah, Ana, there you two are," Father said, turning to face Mother with a look of pure love as she moved to his side. "Edward, I would like to introduce you t—" His voice trailed off as I bounced down the last step, trying—and failing—to walk with the same grace Mother had.

I stepped past Bennet before I caught sight of whatever glistened in his dark eyes, and extended my hand to the duke. Oh, wait. Wasn't I supposed to curtsy? Well, 'twas too late, for the Duke of Mayshire gripped my hand in his and shook it heartily. "Lady Catherina Winterbourne, Your Grace. 'Tis a pleasure to meet you." I infused as much cheer and courtesy into my voice, even as I wondered at the feel of my new name and title on my lips. How many times had I shook hands with a man, spewing out in a gruff or drunken voice my name? A different name that had never belonged to me in the first place?

More times than I could count.

"The Duke of Mayshire, Edward Covington at your service, my lady." The duke's tone sparked with a playfulness that resembled Bennet's, his dark brown eyes glittering with interest as he pulled his gaze up to mine.

"Tell me, Rothsford, where you found such a beautiful young woman," the duke urged, a dark eyebrow raised.

Father only chuckled, wrapping an arm around his wife's waist, yet his eyes were focused solely on me. "I am afraid only Xavier here has the answer to that."

Bennet stepped forward then, all nonchalant and handsome and dangerous. "And I, Your Grace, am afraid that I cannot divulge such information to you. You see, she comes from a long line of beautiful pirates, and I can't risk you discovering their hideaway." He flashed me a grin and winked, something swirling in his gaze that set me on edge. And sent a delightful shiver up my spine.

Dash it.

The Duke of Mayshire shook his head with a laugh. "You have a point there, my friend." He then turned back to me, a dimple appearing in his cheek as his smile broadened. "I believe, Lady Thirwick, that you will quite like it here in London. And if you're ever in need of any sort of companionship, I have a wife at home and two rambunctious boys who would love to meet you."

I couldn't help but return his smile. "Thank you, Your Grace. I hope I shall." And I hoped that I could find a way to return to the sea without ruining everything I had only just found.

Chapter 19

I loved her. I loved every rare smile, every light chuckle, every frown, and every scar. And I wanted nothing more than to love her the rest of my life. Which was probably the most absurd thought that had ever crossed my mind in the twenty-nine years that I had been alive, but it was the most true.

When I had first laid eyes on Rina Blackstone, I had known she was different, was special. Perhaps that was because she was wearing breeches and sword-fighting, or perhaps it was a knowing. A knowing that once I got to know this highly dangerous and extremely wonderful woman, that I would never be able to forget her nor forget the feelings that simply being in her presence induced.

I had never known anyone quite like her, despite the fact I'd been raised by a pirate myself. Nor had I ever felt this way about a woman before. Likely because I had never actually known a girl as well as I had Rina. And I had known her ladyship for only twenty-one days. Which just goes to show how much I knew about women.

Of course, there was Jorie. But I had always viewed her as the little sister, even before all that had happened between her, Jon, and David. When she had found out that she was with Jonathan's child and then he refused to marry her, I had offered to marry her and claim the child as my own. But only because that same kindness had been done to me, when Father married Mother and gave me a name much better than any other. But fortunately, David had taken that place, and though at first his and Marjorie's marriage had been just an arrangement, something deep and abiding had sprung forth from their friendship, something that I knew would only grow over the years.

Other than Marjorie, I didn't have much experience with the opposite gender. Unless you included Christmas with my cousins and the toddlers from the orphanage.

But then there was Chloe, except I really couldn't boast such a relationship with my sister.

Yet Rina wasn't just another woman that I had met in church one day, all bedecked in ribbons and fluff. Nay, Rina was someone that I would give my life to protect, someone that I wanted to spend the rest of my days just learning how to love even more. I wanted to be there to hold her whenever she had nightmare. I wanted to be there to see that extraordinary grin on her lips. And I wanted to be there to wipe every tear that dropped from her eyes.

But most of all, I wanted to be there to show her every day that someone loved her, that someone cared about her and forgave her every wrongdoing. I wanted to watch the doubt disappear from her eyes and be replaced by belief. Belief in love, belief in forgiveness, belief in God.

I had never thought of myself as a marriage-minded fellow—as I had never met a woman that I was that interested in—but I was seriously considering the prospect at the moment.

As if in tune with my thoughts, Rina appeared within my clouded view, the frown on her tanned face as deep as the ocean.

It was only her second full day at Rothsford's, but she had grown so accustom to the place already that it hadn't surprised me when I found her outside in the garden before the morning meal. The morning meal that was now finished, which meant Rothsford had disappeared somewhere along with his wife, leaving me with her ladyship.

Blast it, but she was beautiful. Rather than wearing breeches and a shirt, she wore the most becoming royal blue gown that hugged her generous figure tightly and accentuated the blue in her eyes. Eyes that shot flaming darts at me, rivaling the intensity of her frown. Aye, she had to have read my mind.

I extended my arm and gave her one of those smiles that had always gotten me out of trouble. "My lady, might I offer myself as an escort through the garden?" I cocked my head, awaiting her answer.

An answer that couldn't come soon enough. Rina raised a thin eyebrow over her left eye, her gaze raking over me in such a manner that reminded me of the time Mother caught me as I was about to put a frog in her dresser. "And whatever makes you think yourself so wonderful that I would willingly give up *my* precious time to spend a few meager minutes with you, a common sailor with nothing to offer me but your bony elbow?" Her voice rang with disgust, yet she could not disguise the teasing tone deep in her voice.

I splayed a hand over my heart, turning myself away from her feigned rejection. "Alas, but you are right. I have nothing but myself to give you, and that can never be enough. I flatter myself in thinking that I could ever be so good as to spend but a moment in your presence."

A laugh, light and cheerful, escaped her lips, filling the air with a sudden brightness that made my heart soar even as her hand slipped into the crook of my elbow. "Ah, I suppose you cannot be *that* bad. At least you are not proposing marriage."

I lifted an eyebrow and glanced at her ladyship. "Would you accept if I did?"

She snorted in the most unladylike way, waving away my inquiry as though it were a fly. "Absolutely not." And yet something in her voice belied her easy reply.

"Well, I count it as a loss, my lady."

Huffing, Rina swatted my arm. "I though I banned that word from your vocabulary."

"That you did, my love." And with that said, I led her from the dining room outside into the warm late summer breeze before she could ban that endearment from my vocabulary as well. Not that I wouldn't be able to find another suitable word from within the depths of my vast mind.

All was silent as we started across the brick path that led the way into the swirl of falling leaves that were stirred by the wind, a content silence that seemed to envelope us in its warmth, assuring me that the worst was now over and the best was yet to come.

But then the sight of a flaming red rose that had begun to wilt in the heat reminded me of the red hair of that Scottish killer Rina was so afraid of. The worst was not over, for Rina still lived in danger. And if Foxe had so easily found her on board my ship, how hard would it be for this Wilde to discover her whereabouts?

Rina's thoughts must have followed mine, for I could feel her body tense against mine, a tremble running through her. Her fingers tightened around my forearm, her muscles taut as she drew in a deep breath. She glanced at me, only one eye open as though she were trying not to relive the last day she'd felt air over her left eye. "Tell me I'm safe here."

The words came out choked with emotion, causing my heart to ache for her. I slid my arms around her waist and held her tightly against me, longing only to keep her safe.

Father, please… I was unsure what to say, what to think, but only to hope that He would not take her from me. Not now, not when I had just realized my feelings for her. Not when she had only just found her family, had found love and hope and forgiveness.

Not before she found Him.

I threaded my fingers through her hair, the feel of the silky tresses reminding me of the short time that I had spent with her, of how much more I longed to spend with her. "I won't let him get you. I promise you, Rina." If only I could be so sure.

A drop of warm liquid seeped into my shirt, and she pulled back an inch to reveal turquoise eyes glistening with moisture. Oh, but seeing her so vulnerable like this tore at me. She was supposed to be strong, needed to be strong. But in this moment, I had to be strong for her.

I wiped her tear away, brushing my thumb along the white line of her scar. He had cause her pain before; I could not allow him to again.

Another shiver ran through her as her hands slid up my chest to wind around my neck, pulling my mouth down to hers. Something sparked inside me as my lips touched hers, as I wished I could kiss away her pain just I had banished her tears.

But then Rina pressed herself against me, melting into my arms as her mouth melded to mine, turning the kiss from one of sorrow to one of hunger. Her fingers tangled in my hair, a moan escaping her lips that set me on fire.

I couldn't. I shouldn't. I wouldn't let that flame of desire overcome my control. I was better than that. Wasn't I?

I tugged away, but only an inch, leaning my forehead against hers. Her ragged breath mixed with mine, her tantalizing scent of oranges and cinnamon begging me not to pull back but to drown in her taste once again. "I love you, Rina." The words left my mouth before I could grant them passage, and the way Rina suddenly jerked from my arms made me wish I could take them back, no matter how true they were.

Instead of burning with tears, her eyes flamed with fury, her chest heaving in labored breaths. "You really are daft, Xavier Bennet." Her gaze searched mine, and it took everything within me not to drop down on my knee.

I had long ago shoved aside my earlier assumption of Xavier Bennet, but now I was beginning to agree with my first thought. He was daft. Silly, foolish, stupid, and daft. Very, very daft to think he could ever *love* me.

I didn't deserve love.

From anyone.

And especially not from Xavier Bennet.

Which was why he had to be teasing.

Yet by the sincerity glittering from within the depths of those dark black eyes, I knew he spoke the truth. A truth I didn't want to accept. I would hurt him. Again and again. Over and over. That was how I was. I could never be the woman he deserved, that he needed, that he wanted.

He was merely infatuated with me, surely. I was different than any other lady, any other woman. And in this moment, I was the vulnerable little girl that he could hold, that he could wrap in his arms and do the very thing Bennets did best. Comfort.

I didn't need to be comforted, did I? I didn't need a protector, a savior, a helper, or a friend. And I certainly didn't need the captor Xavier had turned out to be.

But I wanted him. I oh, so desperately wanted him with all my heart.

And I wanted someone to protect me, to save me from danger and help me in times of trouble. I wanted a shoulder to lean on, someone to talk to. I wanted someone to love me.

But I had Mother and Father to love me. Surely that was enough for someone as wicked as me. I didn't deserve even the love and forgiveness they had given me, and theirs was enough. Theirs was a gift I shouldn't have accepted. Xavier's love… That was a different story. I could never be good enough for a man like him, and I couldn't let him risk his heart on me.

I turned away, unable to watch the play of emotions on his handsome face. He would leave soon. Very soon, I hoped. And he would forget about me as I would forget about him. We would never see each other again. 'Twould be for the best. He would probably marry some beautiful *young* lady and have a wonderful family. He would be a great father and would teach his children about his God, and they would all grow up to be honorable men and women just like he was.

I would find a way back to the sea eventually. Probably sign up for some of that legal plundering or whatever they called it. Or else I would be confined to ladyship for the rest of my days, have to marry and provide an heir for the dukedom. And I would forget all about Xavier Bennet. In time.

Silence fell between us as I advanced a few paces, leaving Xavier behind me. I stepped into the shadows of an oak tree, wishing that the quiet all around could somehow sweep me away from my thoughts and into the swirl of orange and brown leaves that threatened to leave their branch home and flutter to the ground.

I shouldn't have kissed him just a second ago. Shouldn't have let myself get caught up in the moment, in the whirl of emotions that coursed through me. Perhaps if I hadn't allowed Xavier to have kissed me those two times back on the *Jessica*, if I hadn't warmed up to him, if I hadn't told him... Then maybe this, this ripping of my heart from my chest wouldn't be happening. Then maybe I could give my final farewell and never have to wonder what life would've been like if he hadn't left.

Where was the control that I had fought for so desperately? Where was my common sense? Where was the hatred for anything good and sweet that had taken over my heart when Uncle died?

Why did I suddenly want to feel things I had never felt before?

Was this how Elliot had felt when he had met Mary? Like nothing else mattered but being with her for the rest of his life? Perhaps that was why he had made such a rash decision, putting Mary's young life at risk just to sate the desire of his heart.

But I had more sensibility than to throw myself at Xavier's feet and beg him to marry me. And as I had said before, if he offered, I would refuse.

Perhaps.

"How are you and your mother getting along?"

I stiffened at the sound of Xavier's voice in my ear, at the feel of his warm breath on my neck. Odious man. I set my hand on the trunk of the oak tree and leaned away from the heat radiating from Xavier's body. "Quite well, I suppose."

Very, very well, actually. After the Duke of Mayshire had departed after dinner last night, Mother and I had spent the remainder of the night in the parlor just talking. All right, I had done the talking while Mother had listened. Listened as I had told her the truth behind all those pirating tales I had regaled our visitor with at dinner. Listened as I had poured out my feelings, my fears, my dreams.

There had been a few laughs during our conversation, and several tears had been shed, but I had enjoyed being with my mother. If all mothers were as mine was, then all the blessing a person needed was a mother.

"Good," was Xavier's reply. "And how about your father?"

Father. What a word, and what a title that I rejoiced in knowing belonged to Richard Winterbourne. "He's a pleasant fellow."

I could sense Xavier raise his eyebrow rather than see it. "Only pleasant?"

"Nice." How was I to put into words what I felt for my father?

"Anything else?"

"Kind." I paused for a moment, listening as a bird sang a morning song from its perch. "Thank you for bringing me to him. I suddenly cannot imagine my life without him." Or without Xavier.

A low chuckle met my ears, followed by the words, "I see my efforts were not without merit." Then the laughter faded, a sigh replacing the welcome sound. "Forgive me for my presumptuousness, my lady. I'm afraid my emotions got the best of me."

Ah, but he needed no forgiveness. What he needed was someone else to love him. Someone who was worthy of his love. Someone I could never be.

"You are not the only one with overcoming emotions, Captain Bennet. Now, your few meager minutes have come to an end. I must return to my castle." Pushing away from the trunk, I circled the tree before finding my feet back on the brick pathway and making my way towards the house.

Yet I could not help but miss the feel of his strong arm underneath my hand as my steps echoed hollow along the stones, my gazing falling upon a familiar crimson rose that dripped with the last of its life.

And I could not help but wonder why instead of him following me, the sound of carriage wheels and neighing horses trailed behind me like a dog nipping at my heels.

I forced my gaze up toward the front of the house, past the guardian trees and sheltering shrubs, to where a carriage pulled to a halt. Immediately, the door flung open and a woman all but jumped out. She stood there before the house, hands on her hips, as she called out, "Richard!" in a bellowing voice that threatened to shake the walls of the entire building.

Who was she to call Father by his Christian name? Family, perhaps? But surely someone would have made mention of a relative coming to visit today. Unless, of course, she wasn't family or was coming unannounced.

Then a man appeared at her side, along with a boy no more than twelve, who both sent the woman a withering glare that seemed to silence her.

Until Father came into view.

She took off then, running straight into Father's arms. He caught her in his embrace, his chuckling combining with her lilting laughter as he spun her around. Oh, what if Mother saw them!

I stepped out from behind a bush, determined to put an end to this nonsense. In a ladylike manner, mind you, for *someone* had confiscated my cutlass long ago. "Excuse me, Father, but I believe I have yet to meet our guests." I raised an eyebrow at my father as he placed the woman—who I now noted to be distinctively younger than Mother—onto the ground where she ought to have been.

The woman sent Father a knowing glance before turning her gaze upon me, her bright green eyes glittering like the sun. She could be not but a handful of years older than me, with an abundance of raven curls, fair skin, and very familiar facial features that brought me back to my earlier assumption that she had to be family.

Then she curtsied with perfect grace, causing me to roll my eyes as I stuck out my hand. It took her a moment of staring in bewilderment before she slipped her gloved hand into mine and shook it delicately. "Lady Thirwick, may I introduce myself as Lady Catherine Winterbourne Fortescue, your aunt."

For a split second, I merely looked at her, astounded at the sight. Goodness, but she looked like Uncle, from the black ringlets of hair that threatened to frizz, to the dimple in her right cheek that appeared as she smiled. And that grin, so like Julius's that it was uncanny.

Then the man—a tall, dark, and handsome man, so I noticed—slid up beside my aunt, his hand extended, a slip of white paper held out to me.

I looked from the man, who I figured had to be Catherine's husband, to Father, to the smile on his face that urged my fingers out. A tremble coursed through my blood, causing the fingers that grasped the paper to shake intensely. It could only be one thing…

The paper unfolded as if by its own accord, revealing words in a flourishing black script. The letters blurred in my sight, yet the largely printed word at the very bottom of the page was made perfectly clear.

"Parliament found your case quite interesting, your ladyship," Aunt Catherine's husband said, laughter in his voice. "I'm afraid you were more a cause of amusement rather than worry."

Tears clouded my vision, yet I could do nothing to keep them suppressed. Mother had joined the crowd now, along with the young boy, both wearing broad smiles that only added to my tears.

I had been pardoned.

It all seemed so surreal, as though I were only dreaming. I had to be, for this meant my life as a pirate had come to an end. And not once had I ever wished that to happen. But now… Now was different than every day of my past. And I hoped that my future could be just as sweet.

But was I even worthy of a future? I might have been saved from the noose, but nothing and no one could stop Wilde from getting me. As I had told Xavier, there was no hiding and certainly no running from my fate.

And as I had told myself over and over these last few weeks, I ought to savor what little life I had left.

Chapter 20

Cold fingers ran over the staircase railing, feeling of the smooth wood underneath my skin, so unlike the rough cedar that made up the ship that I had once called home. A home that I would lose forever if I did not figure out a way to return without breaking the law. I could always become a merchant, I supposed. But that vocation made so little money, and the *Rina* was a war ship, not a brig to cart around a few crates and barrels. I planned on looking into what they called privateering, which in reality was no different than pirating, only with the legal papers and sanction from the government.

One downside, privateering was reserved for wartime.

And as I stepped down the foyer staircase, my arm looped in Father's, I felt as though I were already charging onto the battlefield.

"Something on your mind?"

I turned my attention to the voice, to the quizzical look on my father's face. Dash it, but I shouldn't be so selfish as to leave so soon, when my parents had only just found me. But I was not meant for land, I knew, despite how much I found the solid ground likable. A stop in Port Royal or New York now and then was tolerable, but actually confining myself to this life was too much to ask of me. Especially when I was responsible for a hundred men and three little boys.

"Just thinking," I told Father as I took another tentative step down the stairs, creeping closer and closer to the lights and sounds and people. "Are you certain that you want to go through with this?"

He chuckled, patting the top of my head as though I were naught but a little girl. "You worry too much, dear."

"I have the worst social skills, terrible manners, and I simply cannot dance." Except at those late night "balls" my crew and I would host.

"Then dance with your uncle Dominic, and you'll be fine." He all but hopped down the last step, slid his arm out of mine, then pressed a kiss to my cheek. "Don't worry, Rina," he whispered in my ear before stepping away and wrapping an arm around the waist of the petite woman who sidled up beside her husband.

Father sent me a wink, leading Mother from the room and into the dining hall, where the clamor of the guests seeped into the foyer, tainting the quiet space with talking and laughter.

How was I to survive a dinner *and* a ball?

The entire day had proved itself to be an odd turn of events, from Xavier's declaration of love to Aunt Catherine's arrival. But what troubled me most of all was the grand gathering that Mother had insisted upon having all afternoon. Obviously, my parents had previously planned this, as Catherine and her family had arrived at the most opportune time, and Mother's family had already journeyed from

Colchester to London. Why they had not mentioned this to me until I was led up to my room for a change of attire, I did not know. But who was I to object to free food?

I heaved a sigh, turning away from the clang and clatter in the dining room, and started toward the opposite wall. Xavier was to escort me to dinner, though I was unsure as to why I needed someone to help me walk from one room to the other. Another one of those odd noble customs, I supposed.

But I most assuredly believed tardiness was not part of said custom.

Spinning around, I advanced to the door of the dining hall, tossing a glance over my shoulder to the top of the stairs, where a pair of black Hessian boots finally stepped into sight.

"Nervous?" his voice called out, drifting down the staircase to my ears.

I scoffed, returning to my position at the bottom of the steps. "I am never nervous."

"Then are you scared?" Xavier's voice was laced with an intimate teasing that set me on edge. His head was bent, his fingers fidgeting with his collar, though the grin on his lips was visible.

Father was right; I would be better off dancing with Uncle Dominic.

"Fear does not become a captain," I replied, unable to suppress a huff. I was not frightened nor nervous; I was furious.

Furious because I would never be a perfect lady. Furious because, no matter what, I could never be good enough for my parents. Furious because I would never be good enough for Xavier.

And certainly not for Xavier's God.

But then his head lifted, a rogue lock of blond hair falling over fathomless black eyes that raked over me intensely, until his gaze, dark and stormy with longing, met mine. "You look...beautiful." The word came out on a breath, light and airy and completely false.

I turned away, hardening my heart against the desire to run into his arms and beg him to never leave me. "I am not beautiful."

I was scarred, inside and out. I could never have the beauty that Mother did, that goodness of heart that seemed to make her face glow. I would always be bruised, broken, and battered.

"That's where you are wrong."

I started to object, to bring up that topic that had driven me into his arms on that early morning so many days ago. That I had sinned, had failed many a time. But I knew what he would say, and I wanted no part in that argument.

"I've seen you with your parents, Rina, how you treat them. I see the love you have for them. That's beautiful. How you gave up your hopes and dreams and beliefs just to give them back what they had lost. Yes, you're not perfect. You never will be. But you have a beautiful heart."

He was coming closer, the heat from his body seeming to engulf me in a forbidden warmth. And his hands were on my bare arms, his fingers running up and down my skin as though to soothe me. Instead his touch burned like fire, reminding me of every ship I had left to burn, of every man I had slayed.

Images of faces, of screams, invaded my mind in a way it never had before. Guilt seeped into me like a poison, contaminating my every cell.

Suddenly, I was on a ship, commanding my men like I always had. I surveyed the crates that marched up from the hold, calculating how much room the cargo would take up on my ship. Then a scream met my ears, a youthful cry that reminded me so much of Julius's last. I turned toward the sound, only to find one of my men holding a knife to the neck of a young, fair-haired boy. The boy's big blue eyes filled with tears, and his hand reached out as though to grab hold of me. But I stepped back, shoving my man aside to free the child.

He fell to his knees, breathless and afraid, words of thanks and promises of servitude spilling from his lips. He would do, I supposed. I always needed a younger one to step up once the older generation passed. Men did not live forever, after all. He was perhaps a bit scrawny, but I could toughen him up.

I bent down, jerking his head up to meet his gaze. But instead of barking out an order as I remembered doing and pushing the boy aside, the memory faded, and I was placing my hand on the boy's shoulder.

I ruffled his hair, smiling as I said, "Good, Sandes. I'm impressed."

Memories faded back into reality, and I was greeted by a blurred view of the wall. Billy, not but a young child with so much promise, had almost died at the hand of one of my men. And I would have condoned the action, had softness not filled my heart and Julius's face filled my mind.

I had no beautiful heart. I had only a fading memory of a child from long ago and an ounce of loyalty that tied me to my brother. Every child I saw was Julius, young and innocent and in danger. If I would save Julius, why oughtn't I save the other young, defenseless sons and brothers?

"Lying does not become you, Captain Bennet." I spat the words, starting away from the stairs.

Xavier caught me, threading his arm through mine. "Must you be so formal, Rina? We do know each other quite well now, after all."

"You do not know me at all." I tugged away from him and threw open the doors to the dining room, immediately finding Father's green eyes and bright smile, while a hush fell over the guests.

He motioned toward me, and every head turned my way. "My daughter, Lady Catherina Winterbourne, the Marchioness of Thirwick and the future duchess of Rothsford."

Applause flooded the room as all the men stood up from the table as though I deserved a standing ovation. But that was not what bothered me; it was that it had not once occurred to me that Father had no male heir. I would inherit the title. Not only the title, but both estates, the wealth, and half of my grandfather's shipping company.

Except I could not be a duchess, and in reality, Julius, being the son of the eldest of the Winterbourne brothers, ought to have been in line to inherit. That is, of course, if both he and his father had not been born illegitimate. Dash it.

I would inherit the dukedom and would eventually be expected to pass it on to my oldest child. But surely there was someone in the family tree who could take my place as heir, right?

My feet began to move, causing my attention to switch from my thoughts back to reality. Xavier had found my arm again and was dragging me toward the seat at my father's right. And then he was bowing as he pulled out my chair with a flourish.

I frowned at my captor, turned to Mother with a smile, then brought my attention to the crowd of people. A few I recognized: Aunt Catherine and her husband Dominic and their son Richard, the Duke of Mayshire and who appeared to be his wife, and all five of the beaming Bennets. Not to mention Kit Arlington, who I had happened upon once or twice in Port Royal. Others, bedecked in finery and pursuing me with curious glares that defied any sort of politeness, resembled the kings and queens from the paintings that hung in my cabin.

I cleared my throat, looking back to the father who gazed at me with a mix of love and admiration that caused a lump to appear once more in my throat. I tore my eyes away. "I am honored to be in your presence..." Wait. What was I to call all these people? I glanced at Cap'n Ben at the foot of the table and suddenly it came to me. "...mateys. It brings me great joy to see that I have become so popular among the English nobility."

A few chuckles sounded from somewhere in the crowd.

"And I thank you all for coming." My stomach rumbled, reminding me of how hungry I was. Nodding to my father, I returned to my chair and reached for my glass of wine, downing a gulp of the red liquid to loosen my tight nerves.

Which garnered me a quizzical look from the young woman who sat at my left side and a scolding glare from Mother.

Father, on the other hand, raised his glass as his smile broadened. "And I would like to propose a toast to Captain Xavier Bennet, the man who brought my daughter" — his gaze found his wife's—"*our* daughter back to us."

Glasses were lifted into the air, including young Richard's glass of water, the clinking sound echoing in my ears as though to seal my fate. But perhaps for once, I did not need to push against this current.

The first few courses of dinner resulted in a noisy hour, questions being tossed back and forth from the guests all around the table. Many I had answers for, but a few befuddled me. How was I to explain piracy to my twelve-year-old cousin or to the prim-and-proper lady at my side?

The Duke of Mayshire, who seemed to be in even greater spirits tonight than the last, lightened the darker moods of conversation by slipping in a sarcastic comment or amusing joke. His wife Sophia, a beautiful young woman with a soft laugh that flooded the room with joy, fulfilled my request by telling me of her two sons, while Jorie put in a few words about Bethany's own antics.

I was introduced to my grandparents, the Earl and Countess of Kinsley, whose arrival I had missed while changing for the event, as well as their son, my uncle James. It did strange things to my heart, meeting grandparents I had never known nor heard of.

And even stranger was wishing that Xavier wasn't sitting in between two gorgeous young ladies.

By the time dessert had arrived, my vision had began to blur and my head spin. Perhaps it was the twenty-some people crowding me or all six glasses of wine I had drunk. Either way, I was getting tired and the hour was late. But we had not even begun to dance yet, which was to be the most difficult part of the evening.

Obviously, my opinion was strictly my own, for Lady Chloe Wellington couldn't stop chattering on about how much fun the activity was from where she sat beside me. If only Mother had warned me beforehand, then I could've had someone teach me how. Unless, of course, everyone wanted their toes stepped on. In that case, I would happily comply.

Rubbing the back of my neck, I stabbed my itsy bitsy fork into an apple slice and attempted to take a bite of the tart flesh when the fruit fell from my fork and landed on the tablecloth. A dollop of white cream followed, and I quickly grabbed my napkin to clean up the mess. I was placing the apple in its rightful spot in my mouth when my gaze caught sight of Lady Chloe's dark black eyes glistening with arrogant amusement. Something in her gaze, in those thin blond eyebrows that arched upward, looked oddly familiar.

It wasn't until I turned my attention to Xavier that I realized it. The similarity in their features, from the midnight eyes to the mouth turned up in an amused smile, made me wonder if perhaps they were siblings. It was always possible, but Xavier had not once mentioned siblings outside of David and Jonathan.

Then again, there were quite a bit of things that he had neglected to mention.

Xavier caught sight of me, and the nervous expression on his face transitioned to his normal grin. He winked, causing my eyes to tear away, as involuntarily I reached for my glass. I raised it to my lips, catching sight of the scolding glower Mother wore. With a frown, I lowered the glass, ruby-red liquid sloshing out to stain the stark white tablecloth beneath it.

The next half hour dragged on, the seconds ticking away far too slowly for my taste. But finally everyone rose from their seats, ladies taking the offered arm of their escort, while I somehow managed to wrestle my way from my chair's grasp. Gripping the edge of the table, I steeled the muscles of my legs and returned my weight to my feet, hoping I wouldn't trip as I struggled to stand.

Although I was fortunate enough to have warded off a headache and had made it through dinner, that was as far as my fortune stretched. I knew I was drunk, likely staggering as I weaved through the crowd to where my father stood, and I did not expect to make it through the remainder of the evening. At least not without embarrassing myself and my parents.

Oh well.

Red was her color. I wasn't certain as to why, seeing as how red had always served to remind me of that one verse in Isaiah. But perhaps that was why, for the scarlet red that adorned her ladyship was a symbol of all her sins and all the blood on her hands. Yet just as the Lord said, her sins could be as white as snow.

If only she would believe that.

Something about the way she moved in her uncle's grasp, swaying and stepping with a carefree grace that seemed so unlike the stern captain who stood straight as a board with authority upon the deck of her ship, caused the faint glint in her eyes to become a twinkling star in the night sky, lighting up the room and making the slight grin her lips wore transform into a blooming smile.

Her skirt swished around her legs like waves against the hull of a ship as she turned, almost tripping over Lord Dominic's booted foot, her caramel curls bouncing around her. She really couldn't dance, I had to admit, but whenever the music picked up a faster tempo and Lord Dominic grabbed her hand, steps didn't matter.

And obviously I wasn't the only one who believed so, for every man present had risked their feet to have a chance to dance with a genuine pirate captain. Which surprised me, seeing as how my brothers Charles and David had both never been ones for dancing. Come to think of it, Charles Wellington had never been one for *anything* that required being around people.

The turn-out tonight was a good one, even if it consisted mostly of family. Well, my family, to be exact. Uncle Damian and Aunt Aria were here with four of their five children. Grandmother Susanna was present as well. And my father's two children, Chloe and Charles, had taken time out of their busy schedule to welcome home the Duke of Rothsford's long-lost daughter. In reality, Chloe had come only for the prospect of meeting some handsome young fellow, and Charles, I knew, was here just because it was a *duke* who had invited him. It would enhance his social status, I supposed, being one of the few who had been requested.

And who knew? Perhaps Chloe would indeed "find her man."

I chuckled to myself, turning my gaze onto my step-cousin Kit, who twirled my sister in his arms. Sometimes it bothered me, knowing the truth while my birth father's family never would. But at other times, I rejoiced in knowing that I did not have to prove myself to family that I wasn't familiar with. And I knew that if all of a sudden, a man stepped in, claiming to be the oldest son of the late Earl of Riveredge, it would resurrect a scandal from long ago and would cause quite a bit of strife between not only my brother and me, but between even my mother and Charles.

The song came to an end, finishing with a violin's high note. The couples bowed out and returned to the sides of their relatives and friends, laughing and conversing with not a care in the world.

I wanted so desperately to know how Rina was. If she was adjusting well. If she was enjoying herself. If she was still angry with me.

Very well, so I did feel a bit like a wounded swain, heartbroken that my love had been so carelessly tossed aside and my heart trampled. But I tried not to give it much thought. Now was not the time to drool over a woman, especially a woman who was experiencing such a change in her life.

"Daydreaming, are you?"

The familiar voice jolted me from my thoughts, and I looked to find a grinning-like-a-fool Christopher Arlington at my side. "Ah, yes. I find that there is much to dream about." I waggled my eyebrows and gave Kit a rakish smile.

Which he returned with a twinkle his dark turquoise eyes. "Her Royal Pirateness is quite the interesting lady, wouldn't you say?"

Blast that cousin of mine for reading my mind. "I would say. But 'tis not Lady Catherina who has captured your eye, is it?" I nodded toward Chloe, who was batting her long lashes at Jon and whispering something to Kit's half-sister Luisa.

Laughter erupted from Kit's mouth, drowning out the sound of everyone else. "You, my good man, are far too perceptive for your own good." But then he sobered, his gaze finding mine as a frown creased his face. "But, alas, the lady does not return my affections. In fact, she would rather I jump into the sea and drift off to some deserted island."

The mirth that tainted my thoughts faded. "Chloe said that?" Surely she had more breeding, more common sense. Kit could've carted her off and thrown her into the sea just for that. Actually, I was surprised he hadn't already. Anyone who'd met Kit Arlington would know that his, em, temper was not easily restrained.

My cousin nodded in reply, straightening his collar as he mumbled something under his breath that I was glad I couldn't hear.

"Talking about me?"

This time we both turned at the voice, stunned at the sight of Rothsford and his smile.

Kit bowed slightly towards the man, reminding me of our differences in station. Despite the fact that the duke and I were close friends, I was still the untitled son of a preacher, and Kit was a late lawyer's son who bore the title of his step-father.

But Rothsford merely grinned. "I will venture to say that you weren't talking about me. What a shame." He chuckled, wrapping a fatherly arm around my shoulders. "Tell me, Xavier, why have you not claimed a dance with my daughter yet? Afraid for your toes?"

Kit choked on his laughter from beside me, while I couldn't help it but to frown. How many times this evening had I wished I was the one holding Rina's hand and twirling her around the floor? Too many to count. But I did not know her, so she had told me, and I never danced with strangers. Besides, I wasn't much more graceful than her ladyship herself.

"Aye. My feet are in no condition to be stepped on," I replied with more than a little sarcasm. As I said the words, a flash of scarlet caught my eye. Rina was moving toward the orchestra with swaying steps, tripping once or twice over the hem of her skirt. Then she was leaning into the violinist's ear, obviously whispering something that made the elderly man smirk.

Rothsford elbowed me in the side, declaring, "She's up to something, Zay."

Chapter 21

The violinist turned to the rest of the orchestra and mouthed something before he positioned his bow over the strings of his instrument. Then the other three musicians began to play, picking up a fast tempo with a rhythm that formed a song I had never heard before in my life.

Yes, Rina was up to something.

And it was possible that my father was in on it, for he started clapping his hands to the beat and singing in his booming voice the lyrics to the song. Kit joined in from beside me, along with Uncle Damian and his son Caius, whose cheerful voices did nothing to drown out the sound of Rina's interesting, shall we say, singing.

Rothsford merely shrugged, moving to his wife across the room and twirling her onto the floor.

Father wrapped Mother in his arms and led her in a dance that I figured no preacher was allowed to participate in.

Now why did I suddenly feel left out?

Mother grabbed Jon and David's hands and dragged them into the middle of the room, her own voice stumbling over the words as something about a maid and a kiss was sung.

I was so immersed in the sight that I didn't notice Rina nearing me until her rough hand clasped mine. With the strength of an ox, she managed to uproot me from my hiding spot in the corner and pull me into the center of the ballroom as if I were a stump in need of removal.

But then she turned to face me, a smile a mile wide on her beautiful red lips, and her feet began to move in intricate steps that had my head spinning. And then she tugged on my hand and spun me around, and, with a laugh, I followed along with her, setting a hand on hers and skipping around in a circle like a drunken fool.

Or, in this case, a drunken pirate.

The music grew more intense, faster and faster, until no one could manage to sing the words. But still Catherina and I skipped, twirling under each other's arms until the world around us faded and the sights and sounds became no more. I could no longer control my laughter nor temper my smile, and when Rina began to sing again in her slurring voice, I found myself unable to keep from wishing that this night would never end.

But it soon did, much to my chagrin. The music came to a stop, the world seeming to suddenly appear out of the dark night air. And Rina bowed out, though the grin that twinkled deep in her bright emerald green eyes was not easily missed.

Then guests bid farewell, filing out of the room. A few, such as my brother and sister and grandmother, were unable to suppress their disgust over my Rina's wanton actions, but most left with smiles on their faces as they shook hands with Rothsford and kissed the duchess and lady goodnight.

I remained in the ballroom, watching the candles that illuminated the room flicker from their perch in the chandelier above and the candelabras mounted on the walls, dimming the room and casting an eerie shadow over the floor.

The once full room was now empty, making it seem as big as the ocean. And every tick of the clock was heard, echoing throughout the room with an intensity that belied the small gears that created the sound.

But then another sound was heard. Footsteps. Slow, wobbly footsteps.

Turning, I found Rina reentering the room with just as much grace as when she had exited it. None. Her hand felt along the surface of the wall, her fingers running over the raised embellishments. She stopped. And her hand began to shake. Then a tremor ran up her entire body.

I ran to her side, wrapping my arms around her small waist to catch her as she collapsed against me, no stronger than a fainting child.

"Are you all right?" I questioned, hoping, praying that she was fine, that she wasn't in pain or hurt. Perhaps she was just tired, or affected by the alcohol she'd consumed.

"I-I cannot see."

Oh. Of course. In a dark room with only one working eye, her sight wouldn't be at its best.

"And my head hurts."

A headache, I deduced, likely caused by overexertion. Fortunately no more head wounds.

"And my heart pains me."

Now *that* I had no explanation for.

I turned her in my arms to face me, searching her face. "How does it hurt?" *Please, let it not be a sharp pain*, I prayed, hoping against hope that she didn't suffer from the same ailment that had killed my mother's father seven years before.

"It's a hollow feeling. As though someone has cut a hole inside me," she replied with a sigh, seeming to wilt in my arms like a dying flower.

But then she jerked away, every muscle in her body tensing, as her piercing voice said to me, "What are you doing in here anyway? Oughtn't you have returned home with your family? You've no obligation to me nor my father." She paused in her interrogation, frowning. "Unless you are that determined to win my heart."

It was less a question and more a statement that suddenly made me feel stupid. Why was I still here?

And how had Rina abruptly sobered up?

I should've left days ago. I had completed this job, and the one that paid me still awaited my return. I had cargo to deliver before the season changed. And yet I remained in London. Not to enjoy the company of my family. Not to resolve any issue. Not for a birth or a death. Not even because I had broken my leg and had to return home as had happened four years ago, when the problem with Jorie and Jon arose.

Nay, I stayed because I wanted to savor every moment I had with Rina before I was forced to leave. But she already knew that.

I grasped her hands, keeping her from leaving as well. "The question is, why have you let me stay?"

There. Every flicker of emotion that had ever crossed her face appeared all at once: fear, peace, distress, sorrow, anger, joy, love, hope, loneliness...despair. Then the mask slipped on, covering up her raw feelings with a facade of indifference that shadowed the heart I longed to hold.

"I...uh..." she began, but she had no answer to give me. "Good night, Captain Bennet." And with that she spun around on her heel and left with room just as quickly as she had entered it.

There were those beautiful brown eyes I had sorely missed, smiling at me as they had so many times before, enveloping me in warmth. Father's gaze reached out to me with the softness of a caress. Oh, to be wrapped in his arms once again!

But for now I savored what I had left of him, glad that he had returned if only for a little while.

Then he reached out, and I felt his hand on mine, his large, calloused fingers around my small ones. And something cold and bulky was slipped onto my ring finger, easing on me like a cloud blanketed the sky...perfectly.

"It's yours, child," Father whispered, his voice tender yet filled with sorrow. "It always was." A tear fell from his eye, coursing down his cheek and splashing into the dark sea beneath us.

"Why do you cry, Father?" I asked, reaching out to brush away the water that filled his warm eyes. Oh, how it hurt my heart to see him sad! Whatever had him in such a state?

"Because, my dear one, I have lied. I have robbed you of love. And now I have brought this plague upon you." His voice was so quiet that I could hardly hear, yet the words rang out through my mind with an intensity that left me shaking.

My mind was muddled, uncertain of what he spoke. "What do you mean, Father?" I pleaded to know. But by the time the words left my mouth, the dark sea had covered my father, pulling him under, dragging him deeper, stealing him away from me and leaving me with naught but darkness.

"No!" I reached out, searching the depths for my father. This had happened before, I knew, as the feelings surging through me were not unknown. Feelings of loss, abandonment, anger...hatred.

But then a new face appeared before me, one with bright eyes as green as the grass that painted the lands I would see from a distance in a coat of emerald and jade. And a voice low and soft, with a richness that Father's rough voice did not have. He called out to me, "Child, come home. Come home to me. To the love that I have for you."

And I knew in my heart what I should do. I should follow him, this man with a gaze so loving and a voice so kind and a heart so open. And I knew that his home was mine. His blood was mine. His heart was tied to mine.

I held out my hand for him to take, for him to lead me home.

He did not take it.

But the darkness took him with a ferocity, devouring him with a growl. The darkness consumed him, not drowning him like the sea but engulfing him in flames of fire and claws of hate.

This time my cry was one not of just desperation, longing for the only love I had ever known, but one of despair, knowing that if he were gone, I would have no one left. "Father!" My voice trembled as the darkness came after me, its blazing eyes raking over me with hunger. Hunger for revenge. It came closer. And closer. And so close I could feel it slither over my skin, eating at my every cell and taking my every breath.

I was dying.

Slowly.

Painfully.

Just like my fathers before me.

All because of one sin. One act of injustice and disobedience.

But would I be with my father when I was gone? Or would I be alone, as I had been for so many years? Alone in my despair, in my fear, in my shame?

But wait.

It stopped. Suddenly I did not feel deprived. I felt whole. I felt safe. I felt loved and cherished and wanted. The pain drifted away on a cloud of Light that burst through the darkness and vanquished it with a shining sword.

I knew this feeling. This feeling of hope and healing. But in my memories, the feeling never lasted.

It would always fade. And guilt and pain would return.

But the feeling did not leave. It only grew stronger, more intense, more overwhelming. And I could not escape. Not even if I wanted to.

Then I heard a Voice. Not the voice of my father nor my uncle. Not the voice of darkness. Not even the voice of my lover.

Nay, this was a Voice so much different. So real and so pure and so...wonderful. One that whispered to me words I had never heard.

Then the Voice spoke in English, the language I knew well, and It said to me, "You are mine. And I can be yours if only you let me. Let me love you, Catherina. Let me be there for you. Let me wipe away your every tear and let me cleanse you of your every sin. You are mine. And I love you."

The words sunk into me, deeper and deeper until they melted into my soul. But how could it be true? How could I be loved and cleansed and free from this bondage?

I tore away from the Light, unable to see clearly, unable to hear correctly. "You cannot love me."

"That, Catherina, is where you are wrong."

"I am wretched!" I declared.

"You are mine."

"I am no one's!" But the truth my tone held, the conviction, wavered. It faltered and it failed and any thought I had proved false.

"Come home to me, my child."

"I can't."

Then the Light and the Voice were gone.

And I was in the dark of night, wrapped in a blanket of scarlet. I jerked up from where I laid sprawled out on my bed, sweat pouring from my face in huge salty drops, tossing the quilt around my legs to the ground. Blood pounded in my temples as a shudder shook my shoulders and a cold chill raced up my spine.

I could feel the presence of another person in the room, their strong arms wrapping around me. And, weary, I set my head on his shoulder and wound my arms around his waist, letting his soft voice soothe me as he rocked me back and forth, back and forth.

"Are you all right?" he murmured in my ear, his breath warm against my skin.

All I could do was mumble out a yes, relishing the feel of his fingers running through my hair and down my back.

"What happened?"

I stiffened at the question, yet I didn't dare pull away. Nay, I trusted him now. With my secrets. With my life. With my heart. How could I not trust him with my dreams and fears as well?

"I saw my fa—my uncle. H-he told me..." Choked with unbidden emotion, I knew I couldn't continue, could barely think without all the darkness and fear creeping back as it always would. So I merely sat there, hoping he understood what I could not put into words.

"You were yelling at someone."

He had heard me? But my words were present only in the dream. Surely I had not spoken aloud for all to hear. Then again, how else would he have known to come?

"You said you can't. What can't you do?" He wasn't pushing. Simply asking with complete gentleness, as though he knew it would lift a heavy yoke off my shoulders if I told.

"There was a Voice," I confessed, sounding even to myself as though I were out of my right mind. I likely was. "And It said to me, 'Come home.' I-I..." Tears burned my eyes, and I shoved them aside, swallowing back the lump in my throat. Reluctantly, I pulled away an inch, meeting Xavier's eyes. "I'm not what you or anyone else wants me to be. And I can never become that. I'm one of those sinners, condemned to, to..." I couldn't dare to say the word, for only thinking it made it seem all the more real.

All my life, I had never believed in a heaven or hell, in God or the devil. But now, all those things revealed themselves in a truth I could not shove aside and lock in a closet as I had all these years. I had seen the light of love that radiated from my parents, something that my hopeless uncle never had. And I knew somewhere deep in a crevice of my heart that there truly was a God who had wrapped Mother and Father and Xavier in His perfect love. And I knew that I did not deserve anything so grand and pure.

I deserved the hell that men cried out against as my blade slit their throat.

"'For God sent not his Son into the world to condemn the world; but that the world through him might be saved,'" Xavier quoted to me, the passage ringing familiar in my ears.

I had never understood what Mary Lynde had meant when she had told me that, lying pale on her deathbed. I still did not.

But by the serious expression on Xavier's face, he believed the words with every breath in his body. "Have you heard the story of Jesus?" he inquired.

I had heard the name before, I was sure. Probably when Mary had preached to me on those often occurrences. But this *story* I wasn't sure if I had heard. So I shook my head before returning it to his chest—his bare chest, come to think of it—letting down my every defense.

Xavier began his tale with the creation of the world, his words painting a picture of lush gardens, flowing rivers, and a very happy man and wife. Adam and Eve were their names, and they walked with God in their perfect home, untouched by sin and sickness, death and wrongdoing. It was heaven on earth, he said. Everything one would ever want.

But then Eve was deceived by the serpent, a devilish fiend who led her into doing the one thing she and her husband had been forbidden to do. She ate of the fruit of the tree of the knowledge of good and evil.

That one action ruined the universe forever. It allowed sin to enter the world.

His story was an interesting one, yet I still did not understand how this had anything to do with Jesus. Or with hope and love and forgiveness. In fact, it was a terrible tale of doom that caused a chill to slither up my spine.

Tugging my quilt up past my shoulders, I snuggled closer to Xavier, basking in the warmth that radiated from his body.

Then his story took a different turn. Many years had passed since that day in the Garden. People were committing crimes left and right, stealing and killing, lying and cheating. People no better than I was doing things no worse than I had.

Except for one man. This man was very special, the Savior the world had long awaited, whose virgin birth had been foretold centuries before. He taught the people how to be kind, how to love, how to forgive. He healed the sick, caused the lame to walk and the blind to see. And, most importantly, he loved even the worst of folks. The thieves and murderers and prostitutes. He forgave them and gave them a chance to live life the right way.

But not everyone liked this man, this Savior. He contradicted everything they knew, all that they had been taught. He even claimed to be the Son of God! So these men, religious teachers and priests, plotted to kill this perfect man.

They succeeded.

Jesus was tortured, mocked, hung upon a cross in the most gruesome of ways. But his death was not taken lightly. Even the earth mourned him. The noon sky darkened and a quake shook the earth. The veil in the temple was torn and the saints arose from their graves, breathing with new life.

He was buried in a tomb, laid to rest for eternity.

And yet three days later, the stone was rolled away, and the Christ departed from His grave and defeated death and hell with a shining sword! He was no longer dead.

"He was alive!" Xavier's impassioned exclamation shook the walls of my room even though he spoke no louder than a whisper.

The words touched someplace long neglected in my soul, the truth of the statement manifesting itself to me. And I knew, without the shadow of a doubt, that there was a God. Who had created the entire universe and brought life into this world. Who loved and forgave and redeemed.

But was I good enough for God?

I shoved aside the question, locking it away in a proverbial chest in the back of my mind. I would ponder it later. But now I would smile with the knowing that perhaps there was life beyond the grave, that there was a God out there.

"I believe, Xavier," I muttered against his chest, feeling as his muscles tensed and then relaxed as though some great burden had left him.

Then his arms around me tightened, and he held me to him with a mix of desperation and elation, whispering words of happiness as he trailed kisses from my forehead, along my scar, to my neck. His touch sent waves of fire coursing through my blood, and I could only join in with his rejoicing, unsure exactly why he seemed so ecstatic. I had merely changed my views from atheistic to believing. I was not, as they called it, saved quite yet, nor had I been dunked in the ocean or what have you.

But perhaps this had been his mission all along. To change my heart.

If only I could be certain that my heart was worth changing.

Oh, my fickle emotions!

I laughed at my mental declaration, returning to my position on my bed with a sigh. I laid my head on my pillow and soaked in the relief of knowing I was not alone.

Xavier, still sitting at my side, leaned over to press a warm, gentle kiss to my forehead before he swung himself over the side of bed, about to rise when I stopped him with a hand on his arm.

Impulsively, words I ought not to say and had never said before barged their way past my tongue and through my mouth. "Stay with me."

The question in Xavier's eyes was one I couldn't answer, but even though I knew not why I sought his comfort, I could not stop my heart from leaping when he returned to the bed and wrapped his arms around me, blanketing me in warmth.

All was silent except for our deep breathing, the beating of his heart becoming one with mine. Suddenly I felt more at home than I ever had before, safe in Xavier's arms, safe in my father's house, safe within a cocoon of love.

"I shall have to marry you after this," he mumbled, his sincere voice husky in my ear.

I chuckled softly, even as the prospect of spending the remainder of my life with this wonderful man caused a wistful smile to creep its way onto my mouth. "Father will not fancy the idea of you stealing me back so soon," I teased, trying to make light of such a weighty topic.

Hadn't I just this morning decided that I would not pledge my life, my heart to Xavier Collin Bennet? Had I not just chosen to avoid the very man whose hands I held, whose lips kissed the curve of my neck? I was not supposed to even *like* him! Oh, dash it! I could no longer control myself! I had gotten drunk earlier this evening, and though the memory was faint, I knew I had made a fool of myself during the ball. Now I toyed with the idea of actually marrying Xavier!

But perhaps this was my chance to start over. I could give up my life as a pirate, as I had already decided, and become Mrs. Xavier Bennet. We could sail together on his ship, maybe even have a child or two. It would be like a dream come true, a childhood fantasy brought to life, a long-lost wish…

Chapter 22

Sunlight streamed in from the window, casting the brightness of dawn upon the room, illuminating the red of the quilt tossed over the bed, adorning the beautiful sun-kissed face that laid on her pillow with the sparkles of day. The scar running down the length of her face appeared stark white, drawing a line through a thin, aristocratic caramel brown eyebrow that was positioned haughtily above long lashes that rested against a high freckled cheek. Those lashes fluttered up to reveal glassy eyes the color of the ocean at dawn.

She had slept peacefully all night long, no longer plagued by nightmares and memories, but instead breathing easily, the expression on her face serene and hopeful. She must have drifted off into the land of sweet dreams not long after her episode. And for that, I was grateful.

I was also grateful that she had finally let her guard down after changing her mind at least seventeen times in the past day. She had gone from wanting me to hating me, from dancing the night away to demanding I leave. Perhaps now I at last had the chance to prove to her how much she was loved, how much *I* loved her, and how she never needed to hide the emotions raging inside her.

She was still right, though, for Rothsford wouldn't like the idea of me "stealing" Rina away from him after only three days. But nothing had happened tonight, and as long as no one found out, our reputations—well, my reputation, as Her Royal Pirateness's was already ruined—would be safe. We could have a long courtship and marry once we felt the time was right.

That is, if Rina didn't change her mind again and go back to hating me.

But by the way she turned in her bed to face me, a sigh escaping her lips as she gripped my hand tighter, I knew this time was the last.

Once I had been certain she was asleep, I had slipped out of the bed and prepared to leave. Yet when she had moaned and her face tightened in anguish, I knew that I couldn't have left her. Sleep had eluded me all night already, so I'd merely gotten down onto my knees and stayed at her bedside, her hand in mine.

Her eyes opened momentarily, glancing around the room as though to ensure she was still there, before they closed again and she seemed to return to her slumber.

"Good morning, Captain," I leaned forward and whispered in her ear, loving the feel of her soft skin beneath my lips.

Rina stirred, her gaze meeting mine as she pushed herself up into a sitting position. Confusion tugged her brows together, anger flickering for a split second in her eyes before remembrance dawned in her expression. She stretched her arms above her head and yawned, reminding me of the first time I had stared into that bold silver eye and knew that none were safe in the presence of Rina Blackstone.

I was right.

"I figured you would've slipped out by now," she told me, the accusation I had come to expect from her absent.

"And leave you alone and cold? Absolutely not!" I feigned disgust at the idea, splaying a hand over my forehead as though I would faint.

Rina giggled at that, the sound girlish and cheerful and oh, so delightful. She flashed a beautiful smile at me, not one of playful seductiveness but one of childlike innocence that made my heart ache. Reaching out, she threaded her fingers through my hair, running her soft fingertips through the strands that fell over my shoulders.

A soft sigh left her lips, and I leaned in and claimed her mouth as mine, delighting in the way she fit against me perfectly, her arms slipping around my neck, her fingers tangling in my hair. This was home, and I never wanted to leave.

But I soon pulled away despite my every desire, leaving her with one last kiss on her forehead, and left the room.

I eased the door shut as quietly as possible, hoping that it was earlier in the morning than it seemed. But by the sound of heavy footsteps from behind me, I knew the rest of the world was awake as well. Turning around, I pasted on a look of nonchalance, praying that the man before me would not perceive the situation to be anything more than it truly was. The look on his face said my prayers were not to be answered.

Rothsford crossed his arms over his chest, titling his head to the side while he glowered at me as though I were a killer to be prosecuted. "Care to explain?"

Avoiding his eyes, I glanced at the door behind the duke, to the right where the empty hallway glared at me, then to the left where the staircase beckoned me. Then I looked my merciful judge right in the eye and said, "She had a nightmare."

He nodded in contemplation of my punishment, I supposed, then, with a glance over his own shoulder, leaned forward and whispered, "You'll have to marry her, you know." The look in his eyes was almost amused, and it took me a moment to realize that he actually fancied the idea of having me for a son-in-law.

Not that my opinion differed much.

"I truly pity this poor woman who's to be stuck with the likes of you for the rest of her life."

At the sound of the voice, sarcastic and flat, I spun around as Rothsford craned to see Rina leaning back against her bedroom doorframe, scratching the top of her head of tangled hair with a yawn. "Poor, poor girl indeed."

I merely frowned, wishing the two minutes of conversation between the duke and I had not been witnessed. At least, not by her. "You wound me, my lady," I said, unsure if the grin on her face was real or fake. I hoped it was real.

As though sensing the direction of my thought, Rina's smirk grew. "You will heal in time, my lord." But then that smile was bestowed upon Rothsford, and her ladyship pushed away from the doorframe to come to her father's side. "Surely you do not plan on foisting marriage upon me so soon?" Her tone was intended to sound disgusted, I could tell, yet instead came out on sigh that befitted the average young lady rather than Rina, who was, well, not average.

The duke returned his daughter's smile, although I found his less enchanting. He patted her head—which happened to be just a hair above his own—and pressed a quick kiss onto her cheek. "Of course not, my dear. I plan on keeping you for just a smidgen longer," he replied with a wink. "Now"—his tone took on a stern edge—"you two change and get ready to break your fast. You've already wasted half the day as it is." And with that, he descended down the stairs.

A frown creased Rina's face as she disappeared back into the room from whence she came, leaving me to wonder exactly what to do.

Perhaps it was time I returned home.

I wanted to curse myself for last night. I wanted to kick myself for actually toying with the idea of marriage. And I wanted to string myself up for noting Xavier's absence already—and missing him.

But the most I could do was pace across the room, much to Delphie's dismay, and watch the last bit of sunlight fade from my window, both berating and forgiving myself for my earlier actions. I would most assuredly have to conduct myself in a more ladylike fashion from now on. Especially seeing as how I *was* a lady.

Oh, dash me for being so wanton!

Very well, I could not genuinely be mad at myself, not when I had finally declared my raging emotions victorious. Fate, or perhaps God, had defeated me, and now I was at the mercy of I heart I had little to no experience with.

Ugh! How was I supposed to handle all this change? I had only just become accustomed to the idea of having parents, and now I had been thrust into a battle with my feelings for Xavier! Not to mention that fact that I had to find Elliot and my ship before Roger began a mutiny or Ellie fell off the ship or Billy got lost in the hold or...if Wilde found them rather than me.

I had come to the conclusion that as soon as I could, I would find the *Rina* and officially lower my flag. I could have my crew pardoned, and Elliot could return to Portsmouth and I could find Billy someplace to work and the rest of my crew could venture back to their birthplaces or take off on their own. Heaven only knew exactly what some of them would do.

But my mission of mercy had been put on hold, for now the threat of marriage hung above my head like a noose waiting to slip on and choke the life out of me. Very well, said threat was not that bad, but you get the point.

I knew with all my heart that I wanted to marry Xavier, even if the thought was actually quite ludicrous. And I knew deep in my spirit that if I did, I would never regret my decision. But I had already come to the conclusion just yesterday that if Xavier saddled himself with me, he would be sorely disappointed. He needed someone sweet and kind, so I had told myself over and over again.

Something within me disagreed. No matter what I believed he needed, I knew he wanted only me. What a way to fuel my pride!

I would have to talk to Mother about it. Surely she would know the answer to my problems. Should I marry a man that I don't deserve? Should I find the home and family I had deserted? Should I live out the remainder of my days in the way I ought to, or return to the life I had once known and still loved?

Should I believe in a God who I knew could never forgive nor love the likes of me?

That question had stuck in my mind all morning, noon, and evening. I could not deny the existence of God. I had seen His hand, *felt* His hand so prominently in my life. How else could this beautiful world have come to be? By some random bang? Nay, but by the breath of the Almighty, so Mary Lynde had called Him.

How else could I have found this family I had always dreamed of yet never known? Not on my own; not by my wishes. But by the hand of a God who knew my every dream and desire.

How else would I have received the love of such a wonderful man? Not by the swish of a fairy's wand or by the casting of a witch's spell, but by God.

Yet why would a God so perfect care so much about me as to give me a second chance at life? To give me love and hope and a family and a home?

"You were made in the perfect image of God."

The words Xavier had spoken to me what seemed so many days ago came back to my mind. God had made me, as He had all those other wretched criminals that His Son had died to save.

"God cared enough about you to send His only Son to die for you. If the King of kings can love someone that much, why shouldn't I?"

He loved me. Not with the conditional love of man that demanded something in return, not even with the wholehearted love of a mother, but with the overwhelming love of a king who would give it all for his people, of a creator who would give it all for his creation, of a father who would give it all for his child.

"Catherina dear, you might wear a hole in the rug if you don't cease such awful pacing."

At the voice, I glanced down at the red and cream colored rug that my thread-thin slippers could do positively no harm to, then up at the frowning yet beautiful face of my mother from where she stood in the doorway.

I could only watch in amazement as she glided into the room with such grace, shutting the door behind her without so much as a *click*, not a single hair on her head out of place. I wondered again how this woman could be my mother, this vibrant young woman whose eyes had not once lost their sparkle. She was so strong; not physically, but with an inner strength that I knew had gotten her through such a tough time losing me. And I was proud to call her my mother.

"Yes, Mother," I replied to her earlier scolding, stepping away from the rug.

"Now, Delphine, thank you ever so much for assisting Catherina into her nightclothes. And, I must say, you have worked wonders with her hair!" Mother clasped her hands even as she shooed the maid away, her blue eyes twinkling knowingly.

She was right, for my Medusa style of snake-hair had never looked better. Delphie had gotten all the tangles out, and after having washed my hair thrice since I had arrived, my caramel locks had taken on a beautiful sheen. Even now, I ran my fingers through the strands and smiled to myself. What Elliot would think—nay, what my entire crew would think if they saw me all dressed up like this!

Then again, 'twas probably best if I didn't know.

"Tell me, Mother," I began, suddenly curious, "why are you so kind to the servants? Most nobility I know treat their hired help like dogs."

Mother laughed. "And what nobility do you know?"

Um...none, unless Kit Arlington, whom I had met upon occasion in Port Royal, counted. "Never mind that. But I've heard the stories." Like from Dorian, who had once served in a baron's kitchen. Although I wouldn't blame his lordship from being hard on the man; he couldn't cook to save his life. And Stark, who had been an indentured servant during his youth.

"Catherina dear, your father and I believe that all men deserve to be treated like they are worth something, like they are loved by God. Because we all are. And if I treat you with respect and love, then why should I not treat my servants the same?"

My jaw dropped at the answer. Why, that was the most absurd thing I had ever heard before in my entire life! Not that didn't agree, mind you, for I held the same idea for the treatment of my crew. But what astounded me was that someone of such authority and high standing would actually possess the same opinion as me. If Captain Ben had said this, I wouldn't have been surprised. But coming from a duchess…

It was as though Xavier was speaking through my mother. Which was a thought that only proved my insanity.

"Mother, do you believe that God loves everyone?"

At first I expected her to laugh and say something along the lines of, "You daft goose, of course I do!" But instead, her eyes shone with sympathy as she laid a gentle hand on my shoulder, titling her head up to meet my gaze. "He loves you more than you know."

I shook her hand away, turning toward the mirror that reflected back at me not an image of a ruthless, irredeemable pirate but of a daughter loved by her Father and clothed in light. I looked away, unable to bear it.

"How can He?"

"Because, Catherina, you don't always have to be a pirate. You have a wonderful heart, and you have the chance to become something so much more than you could ever imagine. When you accept the call of the Holy Spirit—that's God's spirit—you are changed from the inside out. God sees you not as a criminal to be condemned, but as His child, clothed in Jesus's white robes."

Mother spoke the words with such conviction, the truth in her tone undeniable. As was the feeling that overcame me as my legs turned to mush and I lowered myself to my bed.

"How long will you run from me, child? What more must I do to make you realize, Catherina, that I love you?"

I glanced at Mother, even as I knew she had not spoken the words. It was the same Voice from my dream, its tone soft and gentle. Could it be true? Could God care enough about me to sacrifice His only Son, to chase after me even as I shoved Him away, to forgive my every wrongdoing?

"Why do you doubt me?"

Yes, why did I? Why could I not let go of this overwhelming need for control and let God love me?

"Help my unbelief, God. Help me see," I whispered to the Voice, my eyes welling with tears as I tore my gaze from the wood floor to my hands. They were red. Blood coated my fingers, my nails, the palms of my hands. 'Twas not my blood, but the blood of so many innocent men. Desperation clawed at my heart as guilt tore my cells apart, piece by piece. I rubbed my hands on my nightgown, wishing somehow that the blood would go away, that the shame would leave me.

But it wouldn't.

Oh, what had I done?

"God, please..." I couldn't speak, couldn't think. My head was pounding, my pulse galloping. The entire world was a blur. And my soul cried out, *Save me!*

And then the blood was gone.

A peace fell over me, like the blanket of light I had been wrapped in last night. But it didn't leave. And I didn't push it away. I welcomed it, letting it flood my heart and sew me back up, mending me and making me new.

Fingers brushed against my cheek, almost invisible, as though they were but a vapor in the air. The hand was rough and calloused, yet its touch was gentle.

"See how much I love you?" the Voice said, holding out the hand to reveal a gaping hole at the wrist, a wound that, though it had long since healed, spoke of continual pain.

I reached out to grasp the hand just as it disappeared into the air. My voice trembled along with my body as I replied, "Thank you."

Then this fuzzy world I lived in came slowly into view, and my nerves tightened at the feel of a hand on my shoulder. But I gladly leaned into my mother's arms and let her rock me, back and forth, back and forth, as though I were still a child.

Chapter 23

It must have been well into the night by the time I managed to untangle myself from my mother's arms. And it must have been two hours that we had sat there together, the world completely silent except for the beating of my heart.

My new heart.

The thought sent a jolt of joy through me as I savored the feel of this salvation of mine. Mary and Charlie would be so happy, if only they were present for me to tell them. But as Mary Lynde had said, we would now see each other in eternity, whatever she had meant by that.

But even as happiness bubbled up inside me, a thought hovered over me like a storm cloud. Uncle had never accepted the truth, and I now knew that he spent his time in hell, paying the consequences for his actions. If only he had believed…

Yet Julius still had the chance to believe, as did Billy and Elliot and so many others. What a thought that was. Oh, if only I could tell them all of this miracle I had experienced!

And Xavier, he would be so happy. And how I wanted to tell him, though now was not the time. Not when he was finally back in his own home, in his own bed, probably sleeping like a babe.

Lucky him.

"Something else is on your mind," Mother stated, breaking the silence while a smile crept onto her face.

"Mayhap." What would Mother think if I told her? After all, a woman like myself with such prestige could surely make a better match than a mere sailor. Even if Xavier's veins flowed with just as much noble blood as mine. Even if he was so much more than just a sailor. Even if, now that Father and perhaps a few servants knew, our reputations were ruined. Even if, at eight and twenty, I was an old maid. Not that I saw myself as one. Nay, I was as young as a baby chick in the spring. And just as spry.

"Perhaps having to do with a certain captain?" A pair of thin brown eyebrows rose above mischievous blue eyes.

"Is it that obvious?"

"It has been written all over your face since the day I met you. You love him."

I sighed. The words sounded so right, so true. And yet it seemed so odd admitting it to myself. I loved him. How could it be?

Oh, what did it matter? I was sure of my feelings and sure of his. And now I knew that no matter what came my way, God was in control and as long as He loved me, I would be all right. Even if I never get to sail again. Even if Xavier had changed his mind overnight. Even if I lost my parents for the second time.

He was with me, and that was all that mattered.

"So what are you going to do about it?"

I startled at the question, confused by what Mother said. "What am I supposed to do?" Surely in this world of nobility, the woman was not expected to propose. Not that I wouldn't put it past the vicious minxes of the aristocracy to at the very least attempt it.

"Well, you could always talk with your father. He would prefer to know when his daughter is madly in love."

I roll my eyes with a breathy laugh. "I wouldn't call it 'madly.'" Although it wasn't necessarily sanely, either.

"Aside from that, I think you have piece of even better news to share." Mother passed an arm around my waist as she dragged me off my bed and to my feet.

"I do believe thou art correct, dearest Mother," I agreed, leaning down to press a kiss the top of her head with a smile that I hoped appeared as joyous as it felt. And with that having been said, I crossed the room and swung open the door. But before my feet made it over the threshold, I glanced over my shoulder and said with mock severity, "Now get some sleep."

Father's study lay beyond the vast hallways of the Rothsford's London manor, the very last room on the top floor, hidden in a small corner past various twists and turns. I ran straight there in less than a minute. And with the enthusiasm of a child and the carelessness of a drunkard, I burst into the room and dashed into my father's arms.

Struggling to rise from his chair, Father wound his beefy arms tight around me, his deep laughter reverberating throughout the room. "And to what do I owe the pleasure of such an embrace?" he managed to say between laughs and tears and kisses to my forehead.

I clung to him with all my might, determined never to let go again. "I love you, Father." The words tumbled from my mouth as my eyes met his shimmering green, and the way his smile only grew and tears streamed down his face told me that not only did he feel the same, but that he knew why I was here.

"I love you too, Rina."

The feel of his daughter pressed against him, her head buried in his shoulder, her voice so tender as she spoke, brought a rushing tide of love over Richard that threatened to drown him. And he would gladly go under.

He nudged Rina's face up, overwhelmed by the sight of her green-blue eyes swirling with love and hope and joy. Tears streaked her face even as more welled up in her eyes, and he gently wiped them away with his thumb.

Thank you, Jesus, was all he knew to say.

Wrapping his arms tighter around her, Richard could only smile, rubbing circles on her back and relishing the feeling of having his only child home and in his arms. No longer was her embrace stiff, nor her smile forced. Nay, she gazed up at him with childlike wonder, snuggling close to him like she had when she was but a babe. Oh, how wonderful it was to have her here!

But then she pulled back, letting the arms that had slid around his neck fall down to her sides, the only thing connecting them now the rough hands that gripped his and the bright eyes that reached through the air and held his gaze.

"I believe, Father!" Her exclamation was but a breath, her smile like the sun breaking through the night sky. And yet the words shook him to the core. "An-and He..." Her words trailed off as though she didn't know what to say or how to say it. Then she rushed forward again, grasping his upper arms and shaking him as though to make him realize what great thing had happened to her. "He loves me! God loves me! And He's forgiven me and I'm His child now! And He's my Heavenly Father!"

She all but leapt off the ground and floated up into the air, for her happiness was so bright and lifting. And it was all Richard could do not to float away with her.

Something inside him warmed, his stomach turning flips as his heart stuck in his throat. "That's wonderful." He barely choked out the words. Oh, but it was more than wonderful! It was amazing!

Thank you, Lord! Thank you!

Rina leaned in and pressed a kiss to his cheek before hugging him yet again. "Thank you, Father. For showing me. And Mother too. If it weren't for you...I don't know where I'd be." She paused, chuckling softly, her head cocked to the side. "Well, I mean, I'd probably be on my ship, but...oh, you know!"

He did. He knew that God had answered his many prayers, and that everything would work out for the better. If only it hadn't taken twenty-eight years for this day to come.

"What will you do now?" The question was out before he could stop it. But he needed an answer. Now that she was unable to pirate, and not just because she had been pardoned, he didn't expect her to return to her ship. But he knew she wouldn't stay here forever. She wanted adventure; he could see it in her eyes. And she wanted a certain captain as well.

But Richard wasn't ready to release her quite yet. Nay, he wanted to hold onto her for the rest of her life, to teach her and raise her and just be near her. Except his Catherina was no longer a child, and he could not expect a woman who had lived under her own roof for so long to suddenly subject herself to his rule, shall we say.

Nor could he expect his question not to make the light in Rina's eyes dim. "Well, I suppose I shall head to bed."

"After that." Oh, but he really shouldn't push.

"I'll wake up." She was silent for a moment, her jaw working in contemplation. "I cannot be certain. I have many obligations, you see. And I've made many a promise."

That something warm inside him turned freezing cold. "Do you think of your mother and I as an obligation?"

Her head jerked up at that. "Nay! Of course not. I just...There's a baby."

No. No, no, no, no, no! He knew it! He just knew it. Even if Xavier had assured him that he knew of no children, Richard knew that Rina had...had... "Why didn't you tell me?" He had a grandchild. A little boy or girl. And she hadn't told him.

Oh, Lord.

"I didn't think it would matter much." Her tone bore no trace of guilt, as though she actually didn't think it mattered. But it did. So very much.

"Rina, it matters. It matters a good bit," he told her, unable to keep the edge out of his voice.

Her eyes sparked, not with tears or shame but with mirth. And then she laughed. "You think that I...oh, goodness! No, Father. It is not my child. My first mate, his wife died in childbirth. I'm raising his son. Darling little child. Ten and eight months of age. Brightest blue eyes you've ever seen. I'm the only mother he has, and I cannot expect Elliot to raise him on his own."

The blood seemed to drain from his head down to his toes, leaving Richard feeling hazy and yet relieved.

Even if the idea of having a grandchild was a pleasant one, he would rather it be a legitimate child. "You...It's not your child." Saying the words caused it to finally register in his mind, and he sucked in a breath.

"Yes. He is not mine. But I must care for him. And I cannot abandon my crew. It wouldn't be the right thing to do, and I've come to view them all as family." Rina reached for his hand again. "Tell me, Father, what do you suggest I do?"

What did he suggest? Richard almost scoffed. He suggested that Rina stay right here with him, that she marry and have a family and one day bear his title. But that was selfish, wasn't it?

"I suggest that you follow God's will for your life."

Her eyebrows scrunched together, making an adorable *v* in the middle of her forehead. "How do I know what His will is?"

"You read His Word and pray. He will lead you to where you need to be, you'll see." He squeezed her hand in assurance, but her confused expression did not disappear.

"I can't read."

"I can teach you."

"Nay. I mean, I cannot read. The letters blur before my eyes. I've tried before, trust me."

"Then I shall read to you." He tugged her back into his arms. "Don't worry, Rina. You'll know what to do."

The sun was just beginning to peek up from above the roofs of the buildings that lined the horizon, bathing the streets of London in golden light and illuminating the way towards the parsonage.

Last night brought about so much change. Welcome change, in fact. And I was bursting at the seams to tell someone—anyone. I had already run throughout the house shouting for all to hear of my good news after I had left Father's study, and now I was determined to tell the one man who deserved to know that I had accepted Jesus. Of course, I planned on telling Captain Bennet and Lady Jess and the rest of the family. But most of all, my heart was leaping at the prospect of seeing Xavier's face again. And he hadn't even been gone for a whole day!

So as soon as dawn had arrived, I had rushed to get dressed and to find Edmond, who was still playing the part of the skeptic. I doubted he would ever believe that I was *really* Lady Catherina. In all truth, I myself was still shocked at the turn of events. So much had happened in just more than a score of days, and the surprise had yet to wear off.

But at least the good man had only muttered a curse under his breath before driving me into town. I had experienced much worse.

Now we turned down a road, the carriage bumping over each cobblestone, threatening to send me flying through the roof. And heaven knew I felt light enough to fly as it was. Fortunately, I managed to remain seated, having to grip the edge of the bench seat and hold on for dear life to do so. This was why I sailed. The sea was ever so much smoother. Well, at least during good weather.

I peered out my foggy window, watching as houses and buildings rolled by at a leisurely pace. With a huff that would've garnered me a scolding from my mother, I turned from the window in my door to the one that granted me a view of my half-asleep driver and banged on the glass, jolting Edmond from his slumber.

"Faster!" I mouthed to him once he looked my way, feeling a surge of triumph when he urged the horses to a near gallop.

Even still, the minutes ticked by slowly, feeling to me more like hours before the carriage pulled to a halt in front of that familiar brick house. All was dark except for one window alight with golden flickers from a candle up at what appeared to be the top floor of the house. Xavier's room.

He was likely up reading, and by the smell of bacon and eggs that emanated from the house and filled the air I breathed in as I stepped out of the carriage, I knew Mrs. Bennet was preparing breakfast.

At the thought, my stomach gurgled, and I shoved back my rising hunger. Though Mother's cook Jewell was a much better cook than my Dorian, no meal I had ever tasted had been as good as Jessica Bennet's roasted beef and vegetables. How she had learned to cook so well, I would never know.

Inhaling deeply of the crisp morning air, I hurried to the door, raised my fist to knock, and watched as the door flung open to reveal a slightly disheveled Collin Bennet.

These people really needed a footman.

All thought fled my mind as I rushed into the captain's arms and squeezed him tightly. The older man stumbled backwards with a chuckle, one arm around my back as the other one pushed the door closed.

"Jess, look who I found!"

At the sound of her husband's booming voice, Jessica came darting out of the kitchen, face covered in flour, smile only adding to her beauty. "Oh, Rina! What a surprise!" Yet by the knowing in her voice, I knew she lied.

I released the captain, heat rising to my cheeks in a rush of embarrassment over my ridiculous display of emotion. Wait. Had I ever blushed before?

Before Jessica could wrap me in her arms as well, a flurry of red and green dashed down the stairs and found its place at my legs. Young Bethany clung to my side, her face buried in my thigh, a jolt of warmth coursing up my body at the touch. "Miss Wina, I so happy to see you!"

I bent down and playfully ruffled the girl's strawberry-blonde curls. "I'm happy to see you as well, Bethany."

Her mother soon appeared before me, a Bennet-sized grin on her youthful face. "I'm sorry, Lady Catherina," Jorie said, even though her eyes belied her words. She turned to her child. "Beth, please let go of our visitor."

Before Bethany could ease away and deprive me of the sweet feeling of having her near, I held up my hand. "Oh, she's fine." I slipped my arms around the child's waist and set her on my hip as I did with Ellie. Although I'd admit that this spirited little girl was much heavier.

"Now, I'm afraid I did not stop by to break my fast." I glanced toward the staircase, not wanting to make my announcement without him, yet unable to wait any longer. But the tall figure I sought could not be found. "I wanted to tell you all that, by the grace of God, I've been saved!"

Within mere seconds, everyone—Jessica, the captain, even David, who had appeared out of nowhere—was at my side, hugging me, kissing me, congratulating me. The joy that filled the room was overwhelming.

I had only just finished embracing Jorie when my gaze finally caught sight of the one man I wanted to see. Somehow, he had slipped down the stairs, I supposed, and now he stood, arms folded over his muscular chest, leaning against the doorframe of the kitchen. His eyes met mine, and something deep and abiding sparked to life in them, the light in his gaze matching the light in his grin as his lips stretched upward in a smile that threatened to make my knees buckle.

I let them. I placed Beth gently onto the floor, crossing the room on feet that felt as though they were walking on air. That air lifted me up and carried me to where Xavier stood, to where his arms awaited me, to where his smile welcomed me.

I all but leapt into his embrace, clinging to his neck as though he were my only lifeline as his arms slid around my waist and held me against him.

"Oh, Rina," he mumbled in my ear, softly, sweetly, burying his head in my shoulder.

Tears sprang to my eyes, and I could do nothing to keep them back. "Xavier, I love you."

Chapter 24

"I hereby baptize you in the name of the Father, of the Son, and of the Holy Spirit."

The words, so gentle and kind, so deep and wonderful, reverberated through my very being, surging through the blood that pounded in my veins, even as they faded, along with every other sound in the universe, out of existence. All was silent for what seemed an eternity, the beating of even my heart no more. It was as though I were dying, slowly, painlessly, every fiber of my being gone.

Then I was brought forth, and the breath was restored to my lungs. I inhaled the sweet, salty air of the sea, breathing in not just oxygen but new life. For I stood a new creature in Christ, a new person. And now everyone knew it.

Water dripped from my hair, splattering the ocean with glittering droplets of blue, rippling across the still sea. It was as though the very Spirit of God was here, calming the waves and shining the light of the sun, warming me when I ought to feel chilled by the breeze that swept through my hair and through the fabric of my simple white dress.

I brushed strands of hair and drops of water from my eyes, glancing first at the pillar of strength beside me, whose hand still rested gently on my shoulder. Reverend Collin Bennet found my gaze and sent me a soft smile that stilled the suddenly frantic beating of my heart. Then my eyes sought out the man I loved, my captor, my friend, my groom.

The very word warmed my soul. I was to be joined, heart, body, and soul, to this man. This kind, amazing, forgiving, loving man. And my head spun at the idea even as my hand gladly slipped into the one he offered.

It had been three days since I had shown up unbidden at his house. Three whole days. Yet they seemed to have passed like only moments. For now I stood in the Atlantic Ocean off the shore of Southend-on-Sea, surrounded by friends and family and peasants and nobility. Even the King of England was present, so they had told me, despite the fact a Baptist preacher was preforming the ceremony.

Mother and Captain Bennet—or ought I call him Father now as well?—had planned this event specially so that I could be baptized on my wedding day. A special license had been procured that allowed Xavier and I to marry so soon. And Father had given his blessing, so long as I came to visit every holiday, every birthday, every month. Every day, if he had his way. But I still had things to tend to and people to see and—I smiled at my husband-to-be—a man to sail away with.

Captain Bennet flipped open his Bible, reciting scriptures and starting on with the vows. But though I knew I ought to treasure the words he spoke, I barely heard them, for I was so immersed in the feelings that swirled about me. So the most I could do was mutter what I was supposed to, hoping the words came out correctly.

By the way Xavier squeezed my hand, his eyes alight with love, I was doing all right.

Silence fell upon the crowd as the captain turned to me and said, "Do you, Catherina, take this man to be your lawfully wedded husband?"

My mind and spirit pounded with the words, chanting, *I do, I do, I do.* But something didn't feel right. That silence had turned ominous, and suddenly the sound of boots clomping and metal clanking came into earshot.

A bright and gleaming cutlass was thrust between Xavier and me. "She doesn't."

The voice was so familiar that it made my heart ache. Mindless of the cutlass before me, I spun around and launched myself at the owner of the voice, shouting for joy as I breathed in the scent of tobacco and leather and gunpowder that I knew could only belong to Elliot.

A gasp then rang out from the crowd, so I tore myself away before motioning to my first mate. "Xavier, everyone, this is Elliot Fulton Sr, my first mate."

A collective sigh of relief replaced the gasp as Elliot bowed gallantly—and mockingly, to be truthful—towards the crowd.

I grabbed his hand and tugged him towards Xavier. "And this is my fiancé, Xavier Bennet."

Elliot shot me a look, one that all but yelled, *"Are you out of your mind?"*

With a nod to answer his unspoken inquiry, I continued, "And he will certainly make you pay for interrupting our wedding." This time I was the one glowering, directing a glare that caused most men to tremble at my oldest and dearest friend.

The cutlass appeared again, this time pointed right at Xavier's throat. He only lifted an eyebrow, courageous man of mine.

"He abducted you, Rina!" Elliot exclaimed, his booming voice shaking the once calm seas.

I cocked my head, hands on my hips. "You don't think I know that? A lot has happened while you've been gallivanting all over the ocean, selling my goods and drinking my rum. Now, I insist you refrain from bothering me any further. I have a man to marry." And with that said, I flicked my hand through the air, dismissing my first mate as though he were a slave.

Unfortunately, he remained planted in the soft sand before me.

And immediately, other figures came into view. Billy rushed at me, a stern expression on his young face as though he were prepared to save his captain from whatever evil oppressed me. Following him was Keaton, Charlie, Dorian, Stark, Kiah, Nate, Galiel, Terry, and many others of my crew.

I couldn't help it but grin. My crew was here for my wedding. Perfect timing, I'd say. Cupping my hands around my mouth, I shouted for all to hear, "Thank you all for joining me. This is my pirate crew. They will do you no harm. They mean only to join me as well for this special occasion." I looked towards my men. "Isn't that right, boys?"

A chorus of ayes rang out, although I noticed many men hesitated to respond. But I was captain, and I always got my way. Well, sort of.

I nodded towards Captain Ben, and he repeated his last question.

With a haughty look sent to Elliot, I replied, "I do."

"And do you, Xavier, take this woman to be your lawfully wedded wife?" The captain gazed upon his son as he asked the question with such love that it nearly made my heart burst. Not only had I gained in the last month a mother and father, I'd gained an uncle and a cousin, and now I received a whole other family, a father and mother, brothers and sister, even a darling little niece.

God had blessed me more than I could ever imagine or deserve.

"I do." Xavier's deep voice rumbled over the waves and over me, sending eddies of warmth up my spine.

Whatever was spoken was not heard as Xavier slid a simple gold band onto my finger and then I did the same. I could only stare at him, this man who had held me captive on his ship, and rejoice in knowing he held my heart.

"I now pronounce you husband and wife. You may kiss the bride."

I hadn't realized what my father-in-law said until my husband pulled me into his arms and claimed my mouth as his own. His kiss was passionate and filled with love, and I longed only to drown in his taste.

But all too soon, he pulled away, the glitter in his dark eyes reminding me of what was to come. He winked, his lips curved upward, and I slapped him on the arm as I returned his smile.

Thank you, Lord.

"Are you sure about this?"

I could only scoff. "Of course I am. I've already talked with Charles about this. Everything is in order. As soon as we return, we will be able to hoist the Union flag and set sail as privateers." Dismissing Keaton's obvious worry, I spun around on my bare heel and proceeded to the edge of my ship, leaning against the railing as I dragged in a deep breath and watched Xavier speak with Elliot along the shore.

But Keaton did not relent. "The crew won't like it, you know. And you shouldn't refer so familiarly to the king." The burly man came to stand beside me, arms folded over his chest. "They're pirates; not privateers. They will want to capture everything in sight."

I cocked my head, avoiding the niggling doubts of my decision that rang throughout my mind. "They? Are you not a pirate as well? Am I not? I am the captain, and *they* signed my articles. If they want employment, provisions, and a decent roof over their heads, they will consent. And aside from that, the king is my cousin. I may refer to him as whatever I so desire."

But he was right. My crew may treat me with loyalty as long as I let them plunder and revel and kill to their heart's content, but now that everything was changing, I could not rely on them to remain faithful. Mutinous desires were already lurking in the hearts of those such as Roger. Now that I had brought along a husband, a letter of marque, and new set of morals, discontent would rage even more so than before.

But as Father had said, God's will would be done in my life. And if that meant a mutiny or a crewless ship, then so be it.

"I will talk it over with them on the morrow. For now, I have things to attend to." Those things included getting my husband of exactly two hours off the sand and into my bed.

With a huff, I turned away from my quarter-master and ordered my men to prepare to sat sail. Leaving them to Keat, I then swung over the railing and started down the Jacob's ladder to where Xavier stood, immersed in some boring conversation with Elliot.

After the crowd of wedding guests had dispersed, I had discussed with Elliot, Keaton, Father, and Xavier my next plan of attack. Our original plan was to honeymoon—that was what it was called, right?—on the *Jessica*. I hadn't told Xavier about it, but I had hoped to run into my ship while we sailed. There was no need.

Now that the *Rina* was back with her captain, I wanted to go through with my other plan. The one that had taken a long three nights of praying and seeking God to figure out. I wanted to privateer. England always seemed to be at war with someone, whether it be Spain or France, and so I could easily obtain the permission to plunder belligerent ships during wartime. I had spoken with King Charles about it after the ceremony, and he had agreed. As long as I didn't overstep my bounds and plunder the ships of an ally or England itself. He had also mentioned to me the idea of hunting down other pirates and bringing them to justice.

Xavier and Elliot, who had become fast friends within just moments—after Xavier apologized for stealing his captain, of course—were fine with the prospect of privateering. In fact, Xavier's eyes had sparked with an excitement that I had never seen in his gaze before. I knew he had some pirate in him, after all.

Logical Keaton, on the other hand, wasn't so agreeable. In fact, he was all but dead set against it. I knew that dear Keat had a bit of an aversion toward water and pirating in general, but he had stayed with me this long, and I was determined not to let one small change of plans get in the way of our friendship nor my mission.

Besides, the man was a crucial part of my crew. He couldn't give up on me now.

Nor could any other man in my crew.

Father wasn't so happy about it either. He wanted me in London with him. He wanted me to bear his title one day. But I couldn't. I couldn't confine myself to a life on land. So I'd said that as long as I was welcome at his house at anytime, he was welcome on board my ship. In fact, I was toying with the idea of spending Christmas with both mine and Xavier's families on the *Rina*. Perhaps not the most mother-friendly of ideas, but as long as Mother was the first to meet any children I had, I knew she would be just fine with whatever I decided.

"Permission to come aboard, Captain?" Xavier shouted up at me, hand shielding his eyes from the sun.

I merely stared at him for a moment, admiring the man I now called my husband. He looked so handsome there, his hair flapping around his face like sails in the wind, his face adorned with his broad grin. He was still wet up to his knees, and a few drops of water and sweat glistened on his forehead.

How did I ever manage to steal the heart of such a man?

"Permission granted, Captain," I called back, swinging down the last rope steps of the ladder and placing my feet on the hot sand.

We were now the only ones here, as everyone else had headed home. The wedding had been a short one, and though Mother had wanted a grand celebration with a feast and ball afterwards, my idea of being baptized during the ceremony had easily deterred her from that plan. Instead, we had a huge dinner beforehand some few hours after noon, and allowed all the guests to return home earlier in the evening rather than staying up late. Besides, I had things to do.

I darted across the blazing sand of the seashore and reached for my husband's hand, pulling him toward me. "Come now, husband. My patience is running out." As was the sunlight. The sun had already begun to set, casting hues of pink and orange over the ocean. Night was upon us, and not only was I dying to get out of my itchy wet gown, I was more than ready to spend the night with my husband.

Xavier followed as I tugged him toward the ship, his eyes trained on me while I couldn't help but toss Elliot a roguish grin over my shoulder.

He replied with a waggle of his eyebrows, his murky eyes the color of a forest glinting mischievously.

Just as I set my foot onto the first rope, Xavier slid an arm around my waist and threw me over his shoulder, climbing to the deck of the ship two steps at a time.

I threaded my fingers through the hair running down his back, relishing the feeling of being in his arms. "I love you, my dear, daft, devilish knave."

Xavier chuckled. "And I love you, my darling, ruthless, rascally lady pirate."

Epilogue

Atlantic Ocean
Early February 1684

The chilly winter's breeze whistled through my sails, counteracting the heat that radiated from the noon sun that hung high up in cloudless sky. I dragged in a deep breath of the sweet scent of salt, lime, and just a lingering hint of rum from last night's revelry, letting my lungs fill with the taste of home.

A hand rested against my stomach, where I could almost feel my child's tiny little feet kicking against its confines, begging to be released. "Not yet, dear one." I stifled a sigh, imagining what it would be like to hold my son or daughter in my arms and gaze upon their precious face. If the feeling of cradling newborn Ellie had been so glorious, I could only guess at the amazement of holding my own child.

I tore my gaze from my swelling belly and looked out upon the horizon. The fog of morning had finally cleared, granting me view of the faint outline of the Spanish colony of Cuba. We were almost to our destination of Port Royal, where I would sell my captured goods and deposit my prisoners onto land.

Hopefully, my good friend and cousin Kit Arlington would have some information for me concerning the whereabouts of Timothy Wilde. That, I would admit, was what had my hopes up considerably. I needed to find Julius. I was done waiting around for Wilde to find me.

But one thing held me back from sailing straight to wherever Wilde was. My baby. I could not, would not put my unborn child at such risk.

"A sail!"

The cry rang out from the crow's nest, and I immediately grabbed my spyglass from my belt and held it up to my right eye, gazing upon the vast ocean, where the faint outline of a sail caught my eye. Focusing in on the ship, I searched for a familiar color. No orange or red of Spain. No blue, red, or white of France nor England. In fact, all I saw was black. Dark black and the familiar slash of white that made up a figure of a very rogue maiden.

Wilde.

He was here. And he was coming after me.